GEOMANCER

◆◇◆◇◆◇◆◇◆

DON CALLANDER

ACE BOOKS, NEW YORK

This book is an Ace original edition,
and has never been previously published.

GEOMANCER

An Ace Book / published by arrangement with
the author

PRINTING HISTORY
Ace edition / January 1994

ISBN: 0-441-28036-6

ACE®
Ace Books are published by The Berkley Publishing Group,
200 Madison Avenue, New York, New York 10016.
ACE and the "A" design
are trademarks belonging to Charter Communications, Inc.

PRINTED IN THE UNITED STATES OF AMERICA

10 9 8 7 6 5 4 3 2 1

The Magical Mancer
Novels Of
DON CALLANDER

The adventures begin when a young man answers a strange advertisement: APPRENTICE WANTED to learn the MYSTERIES and SECRETS of WIZARDRY in the Discipline of FIRE . . .

PYROMANCER

"THE SORCERER'S ANIMATED KITCHEN IS A DELIGHT, AS IS HIS BRASSY BRONZE OWL . . . THERE ARE NICE ORIGINAL TOUCHES HERE."   —PIERS ANTHONY

Then the young Pyromancer meets his match—a beautiful and beguiling apprentice learning the Mysteries of WATER . . .

AQUAMANCER

"GOOD SENSE OF HUMOR!"   —Publishers Weekly

Now, the Pyromancer and Aquamancer try to free a tribe of men enslaved in stone by a treacherous Master of the EARTH . . .

GEOMANCER

THE MANCER NOVELS ARE "DELIGHTFUL . . . FUN TO READ!"   —South Florida SF Society

Ace Books by Don Callander

PYROMANCER
AQUAMANCER
GEOMANCER

This book is dedicated, with love and endless delight and not a little pride, to my very good friend and youngest son, Alan Brian Callander. Alan is my very own computer expert. He's given me a world of good, solid help and advice on which buttons to push and how to find things when I've lost them. I can truthfully say none of my books would have turned out *nearly* so well without his help, patience and encouragement! (I'll be very surprised if a copy of *Geomancer* doesn't appear, after publication, in Bender Library at American University in Washington, D.C.)

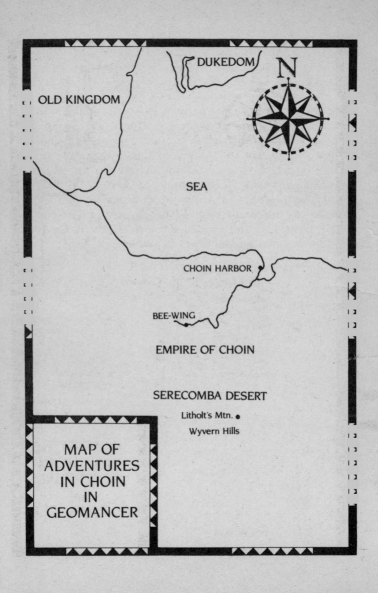

MAP OF
ADVENTURES
IN CHOIN
IN
GEOMANCER

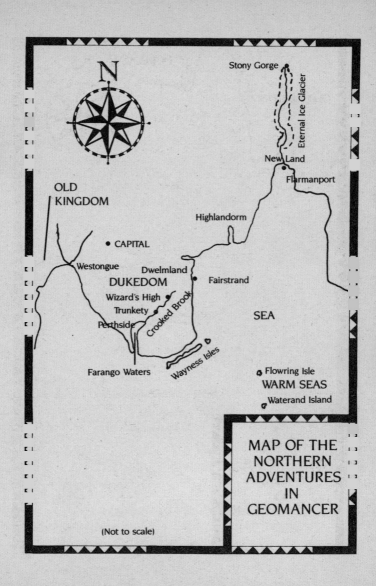

N

Stony Gorge

Eternal Ice Glacier

New Land

Flarmanport

OLD
KINGDOM

Highlandorm

• CAPITAL

Westongue

Dwelmland

Fairstrand

DUKEDOM

Wizard's High

Trunkety

Crooked Brook

SEA

Perthside

Farango Waters

Wayness Isles

Flowring Isle

WARM SEAS

Waterand Island

MAP OF THE
NORTHERN
ADVENTURES
IN
GEOMANCER

(Not to scale)

GEOMANCER

Introduction

The Story Up to Now

DOUGLAS Brightglade, the son of a shipwright of Dukedom lost at Sea, came to Wizard's High, a magical cottage under a tall hill, in Valley of Dukedom in the days when Frigeon the Ice King strove to enthrall World. Once there, he applied for the position of Apprentice to the Master Pyromancer, a Fire Wizard, Flarman Flowerstalk.

For a number of years Douglas's education proceeded as he learned the rudiments of wizardry in general and pyromancy in particular. In due time he joined Flarman and the Pyromancer's oldest friend, Augurian the Aquamancer, in an attempt to stop Frigeon's wicked conquests.

Cast away on a Warm Seas island while carrying a mysterious Grey Pearl to Augurian, Douglas met and fell in love with Myrn Manstar, a pearl fisher's daughter. When Myrn was carried off by the usurping Duke Eunicet of Dukedom, Douglas went to her rescue, with the help of a Great Sea Tortoise named Oval. They managed to capture the Duke and his crew and set Myrn free.

Under cover of the Battle of Sea against Frigeon's hordes of monsters, ghouls, banshees, and evil goblins, Flarman and Douglas entered Frigeon's Ice Palace and destroyed the Grey Pearl, in which the Ice King had locked his conscience. Frigeon defeated, work to restore peace and well-being began at a Grand Homecoming Party at Wizards' High.

In the second book of Douglas's and Myrn's adventures, Douglas set off alone on a Journey, necessary to earn promotion to Mastery, to investigate a Coven of Witches in Old Kingdom.

Assisted by a newfound friend, Marbleheart Sea Otter, Douglas tracked down the wicked Witch Queen Emaldar on her mountain. Nearly killed by an eruption of the volcano, Douglas was rescued at the last moment by Myrn, now an Apprentice Aquamancer, who had followed him to Old Kingdom.

Emaldar was destroyed by her own selfishness and distrust in the awful eruption. Douglas and Myrn managed to save her victims and slaves and set them to restoring their land, which the witch had enchanted.

Planning to marry in December, the young couple returned with the Otter, now Douglas's Familiar, to Wizards' High to prepare for the Journeyman's Examination for Advancement to full Wizardry.

As a break from studying, Douglas went to visit Serenit, the former Frigeon, now First Citizen of New Land. Here the story continues. . . .

Chapter One

Preparations

BRONZE Owl, perched on the courtyard well curbing, nodded with satisfaction and a shrill screech of metal on metal.

He waved aside ornate Ostrich-Plume Pen, which had been busily writing to his dictation all morning, and beckoned to a pot of fine sand on the wide, flat well curbing.

The wedding guest list was completed.

The bowlegged clay Pot hopped cheerfully forward on its three stubby feet and broadcast fine yellow grains over the last page, being very careful not to smudge the flourishes and serifs of Plume Pen's swirled and curlicued calligraphy.

Bronze Owl hummed to himself for as long as it took a bluebird to loop lazily from the byre door to the meadow gate and back, carrying a kernel of fall wheat to her summer brood of chicks in her nesting box above the Wizards' workshop door. He then picked up the last page and poured the sand back into the Pot. He fanned the page three more times to be certain it was dry and, gathering up the thick sheaf of parchment, flew with a clatter of brazen wing-feathers to the open window of the Wizard's study on the second-floor front of the cottage.

Flarman Flowerstalk, sometimes known as Firemaster, was nodding over his own high stack of papers, his hand so relaxed in sleep that even businesslike Crow-Quill Pen had fluttered to the floor.

"Wake up! Awaken, useless old firebreather!" cried Owl fondly. "This is no way to perform your important magical duties!"

The Wizard of Wizards' High—one of the two such Wizards, he being the elder—jerked awake, blinked his eyes twice, and twisted about to face the bird in a whirl of stars, moons, comets, and other mystic symbols appliquéd on his second best wizard's gown.

"Ha! Huh?" he muttered, rubbing his chin, forehead, and ears vigorously. "Resting the old eyes, old friend."

He rose and stretched his arms above his silver-fringed bald head and waggled his snowy beard, working out kinks and creaks.

In his mind he heard echoes of Bronze Owl's words.

"Useless? Old! Who says I'm useless? Why, I'm not more than three centuries! Or is it four? Young by wizardly standards, even you must admit."

"Young is as young does," said Owl, shaking a claw significantly. "I've finished the guest list. You may want to cut it back. It runs forty pages, closely written!"

"Forty . . . !" cried Flarman, fully awake at last. "There must be close on a thousand names!"

"I thought it best to include *everyone* and let you and Douglas and Myrn cut it down to size," Owl explained.

The Wizard took the hefty list and began to read, pausing to draw a line through a name here and there, muttering his reasons as he went along. Bronze Owl listened carefully but said little.

"Hmm! Hmm?" said Flarman, scratching his nose with Crow-Quill Pen. "Asrai should be invited, of course, but can it come?"

"The Phosphorescence cannot exist in fresh water or in light of day, I agree," replied the Owl, finding a perch on the tall back of the Wizard's wing chair. "But it should receive an invitation out of courtesy, don't you think? It saved Douglas's life at least twice that I know of."

"Of course! Oh, yes! I presume a great many of these people will fail to show, for a variety of reasons."

"It's always that way at weddings," the doorknocker predicted confidently. "But you must ask them, anyway."

"And hope they don't all show up, I suppose. What would we do with a thousand guests? I shudder to think . . ."

"Marget of Faerie and her Consort and their newborn son alone will bring a couple dozen courtiers, I imagine," Bronze Owl mused. "The Becketts of Fairstrand number close to fifty."

"Bigbelly! You've put him down?" cried Flarman. "He's but a rough, uncultured sailor! He wouldn't know what to do at a grand wedding—except eat and drink himself silly!"

"That could apply to a lot of them," Owl laughed aloud. "Say, do we agree or not? Ask 'em all and hope some of them are too busy to attend?"

Flarman Flowerstalk grumbled agreement and returned to the list.

"Here's a problem now. Cerfew the Great White Gull? His family is very large and very close-knit."

Bronze Owl shrugged his wings with a clash of metal feathers. "A person receiving an invitation to a wedding must know it is he alone who is invited, not his entire flock!"

"We'll hope so," sighed the Wizard. "Actually, housing and feeding the Faeries will be no problem. They can come and go as they please, as does Deka the Wraith—between dimensions, so to speak. Bryarmote and his bride and his mother Finesgold, however, must be housed here at the High, of course. Bryarmote built the High, you'll recall."

"I was here," reminded Owl, nodding several times.

A great deal had happened since then, but few times, good or bad, equaled the excitement and satisfaction the Fire Wizard and his household had experienced while building the cottage under the hill called Wizard's High . . . as it was called in those days.

But then one morning a lad of fourteen, small for his age, tousle-haired and a bit ragged looking, had come to the front door, seeking the post of Apprentice to the Fire Wizard.

Flarman, preoccupied by the rise to power of the wicked Frigeon the Ice King, had almost turned him away.

Douglas Brightglade got the job, however, and the history of World would have been quite different if he hadn't, Bronze Owl knew. Together the Wizard and his Apprentice had marshaled the Forces of Light against the Ice King. They discovered the secret of Frigeon's invincibility and conquered him before he could plunge World into an arctic nightmare that would have lasted eons.

"All these sailors and warriors who helped us in the Battle of Sea," Flarman was saying. "Yes, I suppose we'll have to invite them, although I admit I don't know many of these names."

"They're all listed in the ships' logs and records," Owl assured him.

After the great sea fight and the destruction of Frigeon's Grey Pearl, things might have settled down for the Wizard and his Journeyman, but word came from afar that a Black Witch named Emaldar had formed a Coven of Witches with plans for conquering and enchanting the poor, scattered peoples of Old Kingdom, in the west, beyond the Broad.

Douglas had gone off to check the witches' ambitions and, helped by his pretty and gritty fiancée, Myrn Manstar of Flowring Isle, an Aquamancer's Apprentice herself, had seen the Coven and Emaldar utterly destroyed in a terrible volcanic eruption.

"Who in World are Delond and Antia?" inquired Flarman, keeping his place on the list with a stubby forefinger.

"You met them briefly on your return from Pfantas," said the metal bird. "Delond is the Mayor of Summer Palace and Antia is his wife, I believe."

"Ah, yes, now I remember," murmured Flarman. "Nice people!"

"There are a number of people from Pfantas on the list, too, but I doubt many will actually come," Owl went on. "They're very busy setting things aright since the dissolution of the Coven."

In a very few days, at the Autumnal Equinox, Douglas would be examined by a panel of Master Wizards consisting of Flarman, Augurian the Water Adept, and the elderly Choinese Magician, Wong Tscha San. If Douglas passed the orals, and his journeying was deemed sufficient (*No doubt about that*, thought the Owl), the young man would be elevated to full Mastery, a Fire Wizard like Flarman, his teacher and close friend.

Three months later the whole World, it seemed, would descend on Dukedom's Valley and on Wizards' High (as it was now called) for the wedding of Douglas and Myrn. The invitations were ready to be sent out.

"What do ye hear from Douglas?" asked Flarman, looking up from the long list. "Did I miss his latest message?"

"No," responded Bronze Owl, preparing to depart for the nail on the double front door of the cottage, his post as Doorknocker and official greeter. "He sent word yesterday that he'd go with Serenit to the face of the glacier today. Serenit had something strange to show him that has been uncovered by the melting ice."

"I recall," said the Wizard. A worried frown creased his brow for a moment. "Well, let me know when he checks in, won't you? He should be back here at his books. I should have gone to check on Serenit myself."

"You are quite overwhelmed with disenchanting all those people Serenit put under spell when he was Frigeon."

"Yes, and I must get back to it quickly. Here, send all these invitations as quickly as possible. The Wraith can do it faster than anyone, I suppose, and with less fuss. We can only hope that our honored guests won't eat all Valley out of houses, homes, barns, bins, cribs, and silos, and the High, too!"

Journeyman Pyromancer Douglas Brightglade followed Serenit, the reformed Ice King, up a steep, rocky path winding between enormous, round-shouldered boulders. Trotting behind them came the Sea Otter, Marbleheart, Douglas's Familiar.

Traveling afoot, especially on uneven roads, was hardly Marbleheart's favorite exercise but he didn't complain. He loved, most of all, an adventure.

From all around them came the rushing, gushing, gurgling, and tinkling of water dashing over stones and minor falls, hidden in cracks and crevices or dashing across smooth, flat slabs of dark blue gabro granite. Where their way crossed an icy streamlet or skirted a shallow pool of meltwater, the Otter paused a moment to splash and dabble. Cold or not, water was his preferred element.

The chill breath of the ice field ahead of and above them whistled down the twisting pathway to pluck at the men's heavy, fur-lined cloaks and threaten to whip away their woolen caps.

"Not much farther, young Douglas," Serenit assured him as they stopped to catch their breaths in the lee of a curved, ice-carved outcrop.

"How far has Eternal Ice retreated since . . . since Flarman and I came to Ice Palace?"

Serenit was unbothered by the Journeyman's oblique reference to his downfall. Flarman and Douglas had burrowed into the cellar of his Ice Palace from below and destroyed the Great Grey Pearl in which Serenit, then known as Frigeon, had locked his human conscience, his sense of right and wrong.

The resulting catastrophe destroyed the Ice King's fortress on the ice—and the vast glacier on which it had been built, as well. The glacier had been retreating to the north ever since.

Since his conscience had been restored, Frigeon changed dramatically—he'd even taken a new name. He'd striven and worked and suffered and struggled to make restitution for his evil doings, reclaiming the rock-strewn valley the glacier left behind.

In less than two years Serenit and his friend and former steward, Clangeon, had begun attracting Men to settle on the empty, harsh land. They'd managed to find markets in the south for the excess glacier ice, discovering ingenious ways to preserve it as it was carried by the merchant ships of Wayness and Westongue to distant ports. The frozen cargoes brought high prices in places where ice had been virtually unknown before.

Now the southern margin of New Land, as Serenit called his empty wilderness, was beginning to show new greenery, rapidly growing spruce, cedar, fir, and pine forests, careful-ly tended by the earliest of the settlers against a day when they would cut lumber and saw timbers for the ships that increasingly plied a newly peaceful Sea.

It was a hard life, with backbreaking labor and only small rewards, as yet.

"We're eighteen miles from the coast, from Flarmanport," Serenit answered the Journeyman's question. "The ice retreated twelve miles in the first few months after the destruction of Ice Palace. Slowed considerably since then, but still retreated five or more miles last year."

"The ground beneath is still frozen, then?" asked Marbleheart. "It's that hard, I see."

"Here it's still frozen. The warm winds Augurian sends from Warm Sea have melted and dried the coast. Our trees are growing as fast as the ice departs."

He was proud of what he and his few men—and a few women, now, also—had accomplished. It showed in his eyes and step and sounded in his deep voice. He was no longer the proud, bitterly cold, wickedly arrogant Air Adept who had locked away his humanity.

He was still imposingly tall, still had a ringing voice when he wanted to be heard. But his coloring, pale and aes-thetic in his days of power, was more the warm gray of the tough moss on the north sides of his young evergreens.

Despite Frigeon's past, Douglas liked the new Serenit. He was modest, intelligent, witty, determined but kind, generous and thoughtful. He accomplished things but didn't brag about them, as Frigeon would have.

"Twelve children were born in Flarmanport this year!" Serenit said, stepping out on the path once more. "I wish one or two had been mine! But I fail, yet, to find a lady who will marry such as I. Who blames them? You'll marry soon, I know, Douglas. Do you understand my desire to share my life with a special helpmeet—and sire children to make this thawing earth fruitful?''

Douglas nodded a bit wistfully, thinking of Myrn. She was far away to the south on Waterand Isle. Realizing that the First Citizen of New Land—all the title Serenit would allow himself—couldn't hear him nod, he answered aloud.

"I've thought of marriage and decided it is many things. The comfort and the love of a good wife? Children are part of it, of course, and I know I'll love them when they come. If I can be as happy as some husbands I know, I'll be a much better Man and Wizard than otherwise."

Serenit turned his head to grin at his former enemy.

"Yet your Master, good old Flarman Flowerstalk, has never married. Nor the Water Adept, Augurian. Nor did I when I was a Master Aeromancer myself. Marriage and wizardry seem to conflict, for some of us."

"Myrn *is* Apprentice Aquamancer. It probably doesn't make any difference, however," said Douglas, returning the warm grin. "I wanted to marry her when she was just a pearl fisher's daughter."

"The Lady Myrn seems to me to be an ideal candidate for wife and companion, from what I've heard of her. You're a fortunate man, Douglas Brightglade!"

Douglas saved his breath for a particularly steep scramble beside a misty spate of icy waterfall. At the top they paused while the Otter inspected the cascade and its pool as a possible water slide.

"There's the Face," said the First Citizen, pointing ahead.

"I'm glad you found me warm clothing," shivered Douglas. "Do you mind if I set a Warming Spell about us? Even this fur-lined jerkin leaks cold air down my back."

"Not at all," cried Serenit. "I wish I could do it for myself. The few times I regret losing my ability to spell, it's almost always in small matters like keeping warm."

The Journeyman made a small gesture and spoke a quiet word. Warmth flowed about them at once. They stood together surveying the Face—a towering, jagged, 200-foot cliff of clear, greenish ice topped with a gray mixture of dust and snow. At its foot lay great mounds of loose pebbles, ground-up stone torn from the mountains on either side of its broad glacial valley in both advance and retreat.

The view was awe inspiring, to say the least. Between them and the foot of the Face was a wide area of pulverized rock, polished pea-sized gravel that crunched pleasantly underfoot as they marched across it.

The sun was high overhead. Its rays provided some warmth, but the Journeyman's simple warming spell made them both feel more comfortable. The Otter was accustomed to cold, having been born in the Northlands on the salt Sea bay called the Briney.

In half an hour they'd crossed the rolling moraines and came to where the melting glacier gushed forth hundreds of streams of clear water from pores and channels both in the Face itself and underneath its foot, forming a crescent-shaped lake of wintry blue.

"Look sharp now," cautioned the former Ice King. "That formation seems . . ."

Before he could finish, a great pinnacle of green ice clinging to the Face shuddered, cracked like a cannon shot, screeched like a living thing, and collapsed into the lake, raising a cloud of mist, fine bits of stone, and ice.

When the cold cloud reached them they turned their backs to the gust, protecting their eyes with their mittened hands.

"Happens several times a day," Serenit commented, undaunted by the violence of the ice fall. "The Face is a dangerous place to walk without extreme care."

He led Douglas and Marbleheart off to one side, skirting the shallow lake between them and the foot of the glacier wall. They rounded a house-sized chunk of ice recently calved from the Face, and stopped on the shore of the lake.

"There it is, whatever *it* is," said Serenit, pointing across the again-calm water. "What do you make of it, I wonder?"

In the center of the lake rose a column of dark blue granite thrice as tall as a man. At first it seemed no more than that—a thin tower of smoothly polished stone. Looking more closely, Douglas realized that it was in the shape of an enormous man.

It had a warrior's broad shoulders and narrow waist, sturdy legs set slightly apart for firm balance on the gravel of the lake bed. Its up-tilted face was mostly hidden by a heavy helmet and slitted visor. From the peak of the helm flowed a stone plume that all but fluttered in the sharp wind off the ice field behind.

The statue wore a knee-length kilt, and its legs were encased in stone jambeaux and its torso in chain mail. A short sword, of a fashion so ancient that Douglas had only seen it in the very oldest of Flarman's books, hung from a wide belt.

The subject was a Man, or rather, a Warrior. A personage of stature and dignity, with an aura of defiance and tragedy.

It faced away from the wall of ice behind it, and the figure's eyes seemed to stare at the Journeyman, the Familiar, and the First Citizen on the shore.

A thousand miles due south of New Land at the same moment, a dark-haired lass in a red swimsuit popped out of Sea's depths, blew a gust of pent-up breath like a porpoise, and grasped the side of a small sailboat.

In the boat a graying, older man with the lined and weathered face of someone who spent all his days on salt water, reached over the gunwale to help Myrn Manstar over the side and into the boat.

"No luck?" the man asked.

Myrn picked up a rough towel and briskly dried her hair and her arms and hands as she answered.

"Oh, there's plenty of blue coral, Papa."

"Then why . . . ?" Myrn's father began to ask.

"I met one of our friends, the Horniads," Myrn explained quickly.

"They're supposed to be sound asleep all this year," Nick Manstar objected. "Or so say you and your intended Wizard. I never speak to Sea Worms, if I can help it."

"Oh, Papa!" cried Myrn in exasperation. "I've told you and told you, the Horniads are friendly and harmless. And they've been very, very helpful to us finding pearls and blue coral, you know."

"Noted and agreed upon," said her father with a rueful chuckle. "It's just that I feel the Worms would rather be left alone, and we Flowringers would prefer to be left alone, too, except on pearl business."

Myrn pulled a loose cotton dress over her bathing suit and fluffed her hair with a second towel, softly uttering a Drying Spell as she did so. Her hair became dry and shiny almost at once with no traces of residual salt.

"This Horniad told me worrisome news," the Apprentice Aquamancer said seriously. "I must return to Waterand Isle at once."

Nick didn't protest. Gathering up the proper halyards in his strong hands, he set the jibs'l and then the mains'l, sending his boat skimming toward the distant smudge of smoke and purple hills marking Flowring Isle.

"You care to say what it was, Daughter?" inquired Nick.

"He . . . it . . . didn't have any details. Sea creatures have several ways of sending information swiftly through the deeps but this Horniad had only heard rumors of serious events, somewhere in the Northlands."

"Could it be King Frigeon, again?"

Myrn shook her midnight-dark head.

"No, not Serenit. Douglas is convinced his alteration is sincere and permanent. Beside, Sea creatures are constantly watching Serenit as part of their agreement with us. No, the Sea Worm would have said if it involved the Ice King come back to plague us."

It took but a few minutes after they had reached shore for Myrn to say good-bye to her mother and brothers and her many friends on her home island.

"If ye must leave, ye must," Tomasina Manstar said, heaving a mother's deep sigh. "Will ye wait on nightfall, this time? Perhaps you'd better, for me to fix supper."

"I should use my pretty Feather Pin that Finesgold gave me," said Myrn hesitantly, digging the magic talisman out of her pocket and pinning it to her shoulder. "Although I'd rather travel Sea-bottom with Cold Fire. Flying over Sea is more than a little boring and very windy, unless you find some birds to talk to, or a ship or two."

"Ye say the Worm said it was urgent trouble," Nick reminded her. She couldn't call Asrai until full dark—five or six hours yet.

"You're right, Papa!" cried Myrn. "I can be home—at Waterand—before nightfall. Augurian needs to know this message, soonest. Yes, I'll go by way of the Pin."

Suiting her actions to her words, the young lady Apprentice kissed her folks once again, whispered, *Cumulo Nimbus!* . . . and shot into the clear, tropical island sky, heading south and a bit west for Waterand.

Pushing the Feather's considerable speed as much as she dared, Myrn arrived over the Palace of Augurian in just over three hours. Circling the highest tower, she landed like a bird on a balcony outside Augurian's tower-top laboratory and knocked on the casement before she entered.

"Back so soon?" asked the Water Adept, raising his eyes from an elaborate microscope under which he had been studying a bit of green metal in a glass dish. "I thought you'd be gone until Monday, at least."

"Master," Myrn gasped, flushed by the speed of her flight, "I heard word of danger, up north."

The Water Adept straightened from his instrument and laid aside his work apron as she told him the Horniad's cryptic message.

"I've heard no such rumor or rumbling," the Water Adept said.

He walked to a huge and well-worn tome chained to a marble stand under the westernmost of his tower windows, where the evening light was strongest, and began thumbing through it thoughtfully.

Myrn used the interval to straighten her clothes and comb the snarls out of her hair. She said nothing until he finished reading.

"Well, there's some small hint of . . . something unspecified," Augurian sighed at last, closing the heavy book. "Maybe Flarman has heard more of it from his vantage point. Call Deka, will you, lass? I'll look into the Crystal Pool. There may be news there."

It took Myrn a minute or less to summon the Wraith Messenger, first drawing the room's heavy drapes against the brilliant setting sun. Deka was hard to make out in strong light. By the time the interdimensional creature blinked into view, Myrn had lighted three candles and ordered a servant to bring a pitcher of lemonade—*misctywine,* a favorite food of the swift astral being—to the tower.

Deka shimmered in the candlelight, a rather thin, translucent femaleish figure with huge gray eyes and clouds of palest silvery hair. She was dressed in a pink-and-beige gown of a diaphanous material that floated about her restlessly on unseen, unfelt currents of air.

"Greeting, Myrn of Flowring Isle, beloved of Douglas Brightglade, my friend!" she said to Myrn with a solemn bow. As Augurian returned from an adjacent room she greeted him by name and several titles as well.

"Can you carry a message in haste to Wizards' High?" asked the Water Adept.

"In a twinkling," replied the Wraith, for whom no distance was too great. "What shall I say to Flarman Flowerstalk? Douglas himself is not at the High just now. I carried messages from him to Flarman yesterday. He and the Otter are with Serenit in New Land."

"Yes, I think we need to tell Flarman this news first," said Augurian. He dictated a short message about the Horniad's rumor and the hints he had seen in the *Book of Current Events* and in his Crystal Pool. Deka would deliver his words from memory, just as spoken. She would even reproduce Augurian's inflections and accents.

"Return with Flarman's answer, if it's not too long in coming," requested the Water Adept. "I know you are busy."

"Never too busy to serve friends," said Deka. She winked solemnly at Myrn. "I've just delivered hundreds upon hundreds of invitations to your nuptial feast, a total thirteen hundred and seventy-three persons all over World—and a few without!"

"Good gracious!" cried Myrn. "So many!"

"Perhaps they won't all come," said Deka, daintily finishing a second glass of lemonade and preparing to depart. "But think of the presents you'll get!"

She nodded politely to the Water Adept and went out— like a snuffed candle.

Chapter Two

Under Eternal Ice

"WHO'S the big guy?" wondered the Otter. "Long drink of water, at any rate!"

"Remarkably lifelike," was Serenit's comment. "Every muscle chiseled in its proper place. Remarkable! You see why I wanted you to see it, Douglas."

"Yes, it's most strange," Douglas murmured. "Yet . . . I feel something about it. Let me see . . ."

He seemed to be ticking items off on his fingers, one-two-three, but silently, when there was a great *bong!*, as of an enormous brass gong struck a single blow very close by.

"What the mackerel was that!" yelped Marbleheart, jumping straight up in the air.

"No idea!" replied Serenit. He added in a musing tone, "It's high noon, as you can see from the lack of shadows."

Douglas shaded his eyes against the glare of the sunlight reflecting from the Face and the still tarn waters, but he saw nothing unusual.

At first.

Three breaths after the ringing, they heard a loud, sharp crack and a low rumble, much like the calving of an iceberg from the glacier they'd heard a few minutes before, but nearer.

"The statue's moving!" shouted the Otter. "Did you do that, Master?"

"No," replied the Journeyman Wizard. "No, not at all!"

Before they could move or speak further the stone figure in the lake stepped directly toward them, dashing the water into a diamond-bright spray. Serenit and Douglas stood their ground as might be expected of a Wizard and an ex-Wizard, but the Otter ducked behind a smoothly rounded stone half-embedded in the beach gravel.

Douglas called hurriedly after the Otter, "Send for Flarman!"

The granite giant reached shore in four strides and, with a sound, like two smooth stones rubbed together, he bent forward to examine them.

"Ah, there you are, at last!" he said in a pleasantly hollow-ringing voice. "Come along! The Chief is waiting for you."

He grasped Douglas's waist in one hand and the former Ice King by the wrist in the other and, turning abruptly on his heel, waded back into the lake. In a moment the three disappeared beneath the disturbed surface.

Marbleheart, rushing to the lake's shore, could see them moving steadily away under the water, receding farther and farther toward the foot of the Face. A huge shard of ice cracked sharply, calved, and slipped with a great roar into the lake.

Marbleheart dashed to higher ground to avoid the ten-foot wave thrown up by the plunging berg. When he turned to look, the statue, the Journeyman, and the First Citizen had completely disappeared.

The lake waters surged back and forth, slowly calming again.

"By Remmit!" the Sea Otter swore to himself. "Kidnapped by a statue! Run for Flarman—or try to follow them?"

He plumped himself down on a flat stone and considered. It would take him two or three *weeks* to reach Wizards' High, all conditions being ideal. Warning the Fire Wizard of what had happened was most important—indeed, it was what Douglas had ordered him to do.

But wait that long? It might be days and days too late!

Still, the giant statue hadn't seemed particularly menacing. In fact, it had seemed to be expecting them. Yet, if Serenit was correct, this spot had been buried under a thousand feet of glacier ice for tens of thousands of years.

No doubt about it, it's Magic. Marbleheart murmured to himself. And Magic needed more than a novice Familiar. *What would Black Flame do in such a case? I wonder.*

Black Flame, Flarman's dignified, experienced tomcat Familiar, had become the Otter's mentor, teaching him the lore and precepts of Familiarity since Marbleheart's arrival at Wizards' High.

"Never leave your Master's side," the cat said in the Otter's mind's ear. "A Familiar's place is beside his Wizard, no matter what!"

"Damme!" cried the Sea Otter, who had learned the language of sailors long before he'd met Douglas. "What's to do?"

He looked around for inspiration and noticed a flock of white birds circling the head of the glacier, slowly and lazily, enjoying the updrafts caused when the warm southern wind struck the Face.

"Gulls? Yes, gulls! Hey, you guys! Ahoy! Ahoy!"

His words echoed from the Face and rebounded from the walls of the valley on either side. The birds paid no attention.

Drawing on his growing arsenal of useful little spells taught him by Douglas, Marbleheart gathered a double armful of dried grasses into a pile and set it afire with a certain gesture and a word.

A thick column of yellow smoke rose straight into the air until it was snatched quite away by the steady south wind.

The Sea Otter waved his forepaws and shouted "Ahoy!" again and again. At last one of the gulls dropped below the edge of the Face and lazily swooped to circle about the column of smoke, cocking its head to study the ground and the creature waving at him, below.

"Come down!" shouted the Otter. "You mangy, moulting fish thief! Pay attention!"

But the gull swung away and returned to its flock over the glacier. Marbleheart flung himself beside the dying grass fire in disgust.

"I suppose I could find someone down at New Land to carry the message for me," he said to himself aloud. "That Clangeon's a decent sort, I think. That'd take only a couple of days."

He had decided on this course when a shadow crossed overhead. Squinting up into the sun, Marbleheart saw three great white gulls flying there, looking down at him.

"It's a Sea Otter, only," one croaked derisively. "Fish stealers, they are. Let's go catch some nice, oily sardines in the fjord."

"He called to us, however," a larger, whiter gull reminded him. "Let's at least see what he wants."

"Wants to wring our necks, probably, and make supper of us," said the first, but he followed his leader down to land beside the ashes of the fire. They stood at stiff-legged attention, their heads cocked to the side, regarding the stranger with one wary, beady eye and then, turning their heads in unison, the other eye.

"You called us?" asked one.

"I need your help, really," said Marbleheart, "and I am not going to wring anybody's neck—least not anyone in this gathering, gulls dear!"

"Well, he's polite enough, anyway," said the sour-looking gull. "Who are you, Sea Otter? And who built a fire in this Man-forsaken place?"

"I did. I am Marbleheart Sea Otter of the Briney, far west of here. I am the Familiar of the Wizard Douglas Brightglade of Wizards' High. You may have heard of him, if not of me."

The gulls exchanged glances among themselves. Marbleheart felt he had said enough, so kept silent.

"I've heard of the Fire Wizard Brightglade of Farango Waters," said the largest of the three birds. "We all have heard of his exploits. How are we to know you are what you say?"

"I am his Familiar. I know Magic. I created the fire," the Otter pointed out, drawing himself up to stand tall on his hind legs.

"Not so very familiar, it seems to me," sneered the second gull. "Never heard of any Marbleheart Sea Otter, and I used to spend my summers on Briney."

"Well, I was just a kit when I left *the* Briney," argued Marbleheart earnestly. "I lived on the Farango Waters for a while, then crossed the Broad to the coast of Old Kingdom. That's where I met the Wizard Douglas."

"I believe you," said the largest gull. "I am Aurora and I am Wing Commander of the World-famous Blizzard Flight. What do you here, Otter Marbleheart?"

Marbleheart described Douglas's visit to New Land and his disappearance into the glacial lake, only moments before.

"Yes, I noticed the Man-like statue," observed the third gull, speaking for the first time. "It *has* disappeared, hasn't it? May have had something to do with the loud chime we heard."

"Magic, then!" cried the second gull, backing off quickly. "Clear out of here, I say, Aurora! Magic is nothing to mess around with, even for a Wing Commander!"

"It's gone now," observed Aurora calmly. "Keep cool, Codsnapper! The Otter has a claim to our assistance. Brightglade is the pupil of the Wizard Flarman Flowerstalk, and Flowerstalk has long since won gratitude and service of all Sea gulls, as you'll recall once you stop nattering."

Codsnapper shook his head angrily but accepted the rebuke in silence.

"What can we do for you, Familiar?" the Wing Commander asked.

"Merely take a message to Flarman Flowerstalk at his home in Valley. He must learn of this magical disappearance as quickly as possible. I can think of no faster means than gull-wing."

The flattery soothed even Codsnapper, and in a few
minutes the gulls flew off to rejoin their Wing, watching
from high above. After circling for a few more seconds, the
entire Wing suddenly wheeled and streaked south by west,
following their leader.

"I only hope they don't get distracted," Marbleheart muttered gloomily to himself. "Gulls can be so flighty!"

Marbleheart trotted down to the edge of the tarn, now
completely still, reflecting the sky and the Face as if it had
never been disturbed.

He slid smoothly into the bitterly cold water and began to
swim toward the far side, the direction the giant had carried
Douglas and Serenit.

When he reached the spot where the statue had disappeared beneath the foot of the glacier, Marbleheart took
several deep breaths and dived, swimming steeply, strongly,
and swiftly into the depths.

The glacial lake was much deeper here than he had
expected. Shortly he was swimming under the Face into
utter blackness.

The longest most Otters care to swim underwater is five
or six minutes. Marbleheart had long ago trained himself to
stay under, swimming fast, for as much as ten, a remarkably
long time even for otters. Even so, by the time he saw dim
light ahead his lungs were beginning to burn for air and his
head to pound painfully.

He swam toward the light, knowing he was beyond the
point of no return if the light didn't mean air, also. He was
deadly determined to follow his young Journeyman.

The spot of light proved to be a collapsed dome of ice
under the belly of the glacier itself, allowing a dim light and
a trickle of air to reach the surface of the water. Marbleheart
gasped great painful gulps of frigid air, paddling slowly
about the circular pocket, surrounded by smoothly translucent green ice.

Even here the situation was unstable. Any sounds louder
than his breathing and paddling brought slivers of ice crash-

ing down about his head. Marbleheart waited until his heart slowed, drew a dozen deep lungfuls of air, held the last, and dived again.

Now the bottom of the ice was only a few feet above the lake bottom and getting closer. Was the bottom coming up—or was the weight of the ice bearing it down? He couldn't decide.

Thrice more he found air in pockets and cracks in the ice above, managing to avoid drowning only by the narrowest of margins. He knew instinctively he was traveling in a straight line away from his entry point—you can't lose a Sea Otter that easily—and he estimated he had swum between four and five miles before he came to a much larger air pocket and crawled up on a beach of polished stones over which flowed a shallow stream of chill meltwater.

"Have to walk from here, I guess," he muttered aloud. His voice echoed down long, empty corridors, tall cracks in the ice.

While in most places the retreating ice rested solidly on the floor of its valley, there were vertical fissures wide enough to allow him to continue on—more to the sides of the ice river than in the center, he found. All the cracks ran parallel to the glacier's course.

From every side he heard constant sounds of rushing water, of groaning and snapping ice, and the ages-slow grinding of ice on stone and stone on stone. Where once the glacier had flowed toward Sea, inexorably and very, very slowly, now its course was reversed. It was creeping back to the everlasting ice fields far to the north.

Was that where the statue had taken Douglas? Only one way to find out!

By the time night crept into the cracks and passages about him, the Otter had settled his most common necessities. There were numerous pools, ponds, lakes, and streams under the glacier, teeming with water-life from tiny freshwater shrimps to thirty-pound tunas and ten-pound codfish descended from those trapped by the shifting ice ages before.

He took advantage of the last of day's meager light to shag a small cod. He took it to a fairly dry rock shelf, several inches above the stream.

He'd forgotten how good fresh-caught, raw fish could be. The cod was excellent.

Comes from living with Wizards and such creatures, he thought.

He finished off the fish down to the last scale and fin and curled himself into a heat-conserving ball, unmindful of the frigid air, water, and ice all about his sanctuary.

Before he slept he spared a thought for the gulls, wishing them good speed on their mission.

I could surely use a Wizard of some sort right now!

Chapter Three

A Wizard Whisked Away

"THAT double-dratted, rat-nosed, crab-backward, rancid-rotten, trouble-brewing prestidigitator!" Flarman said in a conversational tone more startling than any rant or rave.

He threw down his black Crow-Quill Pen, pushed the ivory-beaded Abacus away from his ample tummy, and puffed his cheeks until he looked like an angry Santa.

"Speaking of yourself?" inquired Bronze Owl mildly. "Or some other Wizard?"

"No, I'm but complimenting the craftsmanship of the late Ice King. What a loss his mind was to decent Wizardry! I've never seen a more devious, complicated, intertwined, cacophonous set of incantations than these he used to spell innocent, peaceful burghers and countryfolk!"

"Even with all the help Serenit-that-was-Frigeon can give you?" asked Owl. He was busy tallying the Valley-folk's first responses to the wedding invitations, a tedious task at best.

"Even *with* his willing help, yes! Serenit can't unravel his own purposes in some of these cases. Oh, my aching head! Oh, my aching fingers!"

"Take a break, old Fire-eater. You've been at it since before breakfast without pause," advised Bronze Owl, pushing his own letters and lists aside. "If I were of human flesh instead of good, solid, honest, sand-cast bronze, I'd have a cup of tea and some of Blue Kettle's lovely sticky currant buns as a sure cure."

"You are, without a doubt, the best adviser a Wizard ever had! These poor citizens of . . . Filabeggery, wherever that is . . . will have to wait a few minutes more while I tackle some current events. Currently I am dying of thirst and lack of sugar!"

So saying, the Wizard clapped his hands and called toward the stairway: "Ho, Blue! Ho, favorite housekeeper and cook! O estimable reviver and resuscitator of harassed Wizards!"

From below stairs rose a questioning whistle of steam.

"A pot of that really excellent Choin tea Master Wong brought us, if you please. And ask the Choinese gentleman to join me. Good tea should be drunk in good company."

From the kitchen came a clatter and a rattling as porcelain Teacups and Saucers rushed to arrange themselves on a silver Tea Tray, and Oven popped wide, allowing a savory cloud of cinnamon steam to precede Tea Cart up the kitchen stairs to the Wizard's study.

Blue Teakettle herself did the honors, pouring the green tea and offering sugar from silver Caster and cream just that morning separated from the milk of the cows in the hay-sweet byre.

"Where's Wong, I wonder?" asked Flarman. "It's not like him to miss midmorning tiffin."

Blue Teakettle pointed her spout out the window facing toward the east.

"Oh, off on another of his long rambles, eh?" Flarman said with a chuckle. "He says it's difficult to walk at home. The Imperial Police are always trailing him and spoiling his pleasure."

"He's also struggling with Question Number Twelve on the Master Pyromancer's Examination," his bronze adviser reminded.

"Well, Old Twelve's a real poser, no doubt about that. I wish I'd paid more attention to that branch of Wizardry myself. Fire always appealed to me more than rocks, stones, sand, silt, and dirt. I've forgotten most of what I learned about Geomancy as Apprentice and Journeyman myself."

"Understandable," observed Owl.

"Maybe and maybe not. I feel I'm letting Douglas down by not knowing more. It could cost him his Mastery, if its weight is enough to bend the curve."

He sipped his tea, already in a better mood than when he had thrown down Pen. Owl chatted on about the early responses to the invitations delivered early that morning by Priceless, their closest neighbor, who was ever willing to saddle his ancient gray mare and visit the rest of Valley.

"Bryarmote and Crystal will be here early, of course. Bryarmote has some ideas for additions to Wizards' High. Princess Crystal says he has been filling their cavern apartments with blueprints, sketches, and intricate little models for weeks."

"What does my cottage need with additions?" cried Flarman. "It's perfect as it is."

"Nearly correct," replied Owl, "but remember that after the wedding there'll be more people living here than ever."

"Myrn? She's no trouble. Takes very little space. Nor does Marbleheart, who spends his bits of spare time in Crooked Brook. Oh, well, maybe a dressing room and bath added to Douglas's room. Can't expect a lady to bathe at the well, I suppose. And maybe a sewing room . . . and space in the Workshop. Maybe *those* additions, I say. Not too much more."

Owl laughed aloud. "I'm only made of base metal but even I know one common consequence of marriage is children. How about adding a nursery and a schoolroom, and a play yard with a swing and sandbox—just in case?"

"Well . . . you're right, of course. But you know our good Dwarf. He'll go completely overboard, if I let him. He loves to build in stone and brick. He blasted out my Workshop last time I let him expand, and I still haven't found where all those passages go, deep under the High!"

Owl launched into a description of Bryarmote's Hall under the mountains almost a week's travel on horseback or afoot to the northeast. Shortly he stopped, for Flarman's attention was not on his chattering. He was peering intently into the bottom of his empty teacup.

"What is it, Magister?" asked Bronze Owl.

Even Blue Teakettle stopped her cheerful bubbling to turn and stare at the distracted Wizard.

"I see . . . some sort of . . . *trouble*!" Flarman said softly. "In the tea leaves! It's been a terribly long time since I saw *that* face . . ."

Without further word the Fire Wizard rose, snatched up his best cloak and conical Wizard's hat, and strode from the room. He plunged down the curved stairs at a quick trot, a most determined but distant look on his face.

"Care to tell us what you saw in the leaves?" called Owl, fluttering noisily to the rail at the top of the stairs. Below stairs there was no answering sound. Not even the click of a closing door latch.

At the kitchen-yard door, Owl met the elderly Magician of Choin, Wong Tscha San, back from his long morning stroll.

"Did you see Flarman just now?" asked the bird.

"No, not since breakfast," replied Wong. "Why? Is there something wrong?"

Owl told what had just happened in the study. A search of the house, the byre, the Workshop, and the gardens and lawns down as far as Crooked Brook uncovered no sign of Wizard anywhere about.

"If what he saw in his teacup sent him off, perhaps we should start by looking there," suggested Wong.

The bird and the Magician, followed by a worried Black Flame and a distractedly puffing Blue Teakettle, climbed the stairs and entered Flarman's study once more.

"Let me see the cup, please," said Wong.

He studied the soggy green-black dregs for a long time before putting the cup carefully down and covering it with its saucer, inverted.

"Reading tea leaves is something of a specialized art, of course, although I've often done it for amusement. Here, however"—he gestured to the cup with a graceful hand—

"if there is anything here to read, I quite miss it. Augurian or Myrn could undoubtedly do better. Reading tea leaves *is* in an Aquamancer's line of work. Leave the cup untouched, please, Blue Teakettle, so they can study it when we send for them."

Owl's sharp eye caught a shimmering movement in the far corner of the study among the stuffed lizards and the strange pink eggs under crystal domes.

Deka the Wraith had arrived.

"I'll pull the drapes," Owl said at once. "There, little mist lady! Welcome again!"

"I bring an urgent message to the Wizard Flowerstalk from the Water Adept," announced Deka with a tiny smile and a curtsy toward the Choinese Mage.

"Flarman has just departed and we don't know where he's gone, Starbeing," said Wong, returning her bow. "Can your message be delivered to any other here?"

"To you, Magician, or to Bronze Owl, an old and trusted friend, certainly," Deka declared, floating closer. "Listen, then, to the words of Augurian."

When she had finished Deka accepted a half cup of cooled tea from Teakettle, and perched daintily on the edge of Flarman's worn leather couch, waiting for a reply.

"Not much to go on, really," observed the metal bird. "Some sort of warning of trouble in the north? Surely Augurian and surely Myrn sense more to what they report than just that."

"I suspect they are concerned that young Douglas is in New Land and just now out of touch. Mistress Myrn, at least, would make an intuitive connection," observed Wong.

"And Flarman mentioned 'trouble' when he read the leaves—just before he dashed off. The connection becomes stronger. What else would cause Flarman to dash off without saying anything to anyone about his destination?"

"Precisely," agreed Wong thoughtfully. "You must return to Waterand, Child of the Stars, and tell the Water Adept what you've heard here and what has happened. We will need his experience and craft to look into this. Tell Master Augurian I will bend my own poor craft to discovering where the Wizard has gone, and how fares his Journeyman."

"At once!" replied Deka, sliding gravely off the couch. "If I knew where either Flarman or Douglas were, I would go to them myself. But for some unknown reason, their whereabouts are hidden from me. Most strange and certainly magical! Serenit was to show Douglas something he termed quite unusual in the north, where Eternal Ice melts away, day by day."

"In the north," repeated Wong. "Go, then! We will look further than tea leaves can show."

The Wraith nodded solemnly and abruptly . . . was no longer there.

Wong retired to his room, where he spread a red-and-gold carpet on the floor and sat upon it, cross-legged, with his hands folded in his lap and his eyes closed. Everyone in the cottage that night and the next day walked or slid or rolled with extreme care and spoke in softest whispers, so as not to distract his meditation.

It was so quiet that next afternoon that Bronze Owl heard the cries of a flock of gulls long before his sharp eyes could make them out in the darkening air over the Far Ridges. Gulls often passed over Wizards' High, and he thought no more of it until there came a sharp rap on the front door.

Owl went to answer and found a large, snowy white gull with a golden beak standing on the stoop, gazing about with great curiosity.

"Yes, ma'am?" asked Owl, for he recognized a ladybird of quality when he saw one.

"I am Aurora, Wing Commander of the Blizzard Flight of the Great White Gulls of Sea," she announced proudly. "I carry a message for the Wizard Flarman Flowerstalk."

"Wonderful! Come in, Wing Commander. Blizzard Flight is well known here in Valley. Unfortunately, the Wizard is not in just now."

"The message is most urgent," said Aurora, with a worried frown. "To whom or where should I deliver it, so that he will receive it as soon as possible?"

Owl considered sending for Wong Tscha San, but the Choinese magician was still entranced. Better not to disturb that important work.

"You can safely leave the message with me," he told the gull leader. "I am Flarman's adviser and assistant. My name is Bronze Owl."

Aurora bowed deeply at the introduction. Bronze Owl was as famous among birds as Flarman was among Men and Dwarfs. She at once repeated Marbleheart's words as exactly as she could remember them.

"And the great stone thing took the Journeyman and the First Citizen and carried them right into the tarn and under the glacier itself," she concluded. "The Sea Otter asks for assistance. I believe he intended to follow them, if he could, to see where the men were taken."

Owl thanked the Wing Commander profusely and offered her and her followers what food they might like from the High's larder, also recommending the quality of trout who lived in Crooked Brook. Aurora thanked him in return and went off to see to her flock—and the trout.

"This gets more and more weird," Owl said to Black Flame. "First Flarman and now Douglas! I must send word to Myrn and Augurian!"

Augurian that afternoon spent an intense session with several magical instruments and appliances, spells and enchantments, becoming more and more frustrated as the time flew by.

Myrn assisted him silently, handing him books, reading to him from charts and scales and making adjustments to equipment as he required.

At the fall of the short tropical dusk of Waterand the Water Adept sank wearily to a stool and shook his head.

"All I can discover is that *something* is blocking my farvision on every useful level of magic as regards this danger.

Or perhaps it really doesn't exist. No, the Horniads would never falsify such a rumor. It's like a stone wall between us and the Far Northlands."

"Neither natural nor usual, would you say?" the Apprentice asked, sinking down on the cushioned window seat, elbows on knees and looking as discouraged and upset as her Master felt.

"Not at all! We should be able to see at least the *shape* of what blocks our view, its size, its density. Nothing! The power behind it is both very great—and very, very old. Old as the hills!"

The sky about the westering sun flashed brilliant green just as the sun dipped below the horizon. Deka arrived, sharp and clear in the dim light.

"I have come from Wizards' High," she told them without her usual greetings.

"From Flarman?" asked Augurian eagerly.

"No, Aquamancer! Flarman is suddenly gone, his whereabouts unknown. He read tea leaves and simply rushed off without saying where he was bound. And Bronze Owl relays word, arrived by a Great White Gull from the Northland. Will you hear it?"

"Of course," replied Augurian and Myrn, together.

The Wraith repeated Marbleheart's message and Wong's addendum. After that the tower laboratory was completely still.

"Douglas captured by a stone giant?" Myrn cried. "There's our connection with the Horniad's vague warning! The danger the Sea creatures spoke of must surely have been the living statue of stone in the glacier."

Said Augurian, "I've learned to trust your intuitions, dear Apprentice. I agree that is my feeling, also."

"We must go at once, before the trail gets too cold to follow," said Myrn firmly. "Marbleheart is a resourceful creature, but he's just begun his Familiarity. He'll need help!"

Augurian nodded his head, but said, "I will be of more use here. I believe in time I can break down the wall of stony silence and see what lies beyond. We'll need to know what has caused this blockage, sooner or later. You must go alone . . . better yet, stop at Wizards' High and take Wong with you. He's older than the hills himself, and his magic is strong."

Myrn admitted to herself that the Water Adept was right. The Choinese gentleman, if he agreed to accompany her, could be most helpful. He had tremendous reserves of magic lore and a special way of looking at things that told him secrets others, even Augurian, might not see.

"I'm on my way!" she declared. "I'll keep in touch, if I can punch through this awful screening."

Augurian turned back to his complicated apparatuses and magical searching-spells. He waved at Myrn as she paused a moment at the door.

"You sense this spell-screen, do you?" he inquired of the Wraith. "If so, stay awhile and consult with me if you will, please."

Deka nodded brightly and perched daintily on the Water Adept's workbench.

"The flight to the High will take me five or six hours," Myrn said to herself. "I'd better get something to eat before I leave. I can sleep when I get there."

She headed for her apartments to throw together her traveling kit and ordered a light supper brought to her there. She ordered one sent to the tower for the Water Wizard, also, knowing he wouldn't think to eat unless the food was right there as he worked.

"Someone must go to aid the Otter," Wong decided. "He is capable of most things required from a Familiar, but . . ."

"Yes, there is strong magic in this, I'm afraid," Owl agreed.

"We'll await the Water Adept's response, however. It will be brought by his Apprentice, I'm sure, knowing the Lady Myrn as I do."

The metal bird consoled Black Flame, Flarman's own Familiar. He had never seen him so upset before.

"Sorry, old boy," he said to the tom. "I know you feel you should be with Flarman, but perhaps you can help Lady Myrn instead. Be patient."

Black Flame cocked his head to one side, sat on his haunches, and seemed to say, *Well, after all, patience is one quality we cats have in abundance.*

Chapter Four

Stony Gorge

BY midmorning of the third day since diving into the glacial lake Marbleheart was forced to climb out of what remained of the under-glacier stream and trot upon the surface of the ice. The corridors within the ice had become mere cracks and the cracks had become narrow scratches, only. It had grown ever colder, and very little water remained unfrozen on the surface.

The Sea Otter was well suited for this journey. His thick fur kept him warm, and his padded feet gave him good traction on the slippery ice. In truth, it should have been considerably colder, he thought as he *gallumped* along. Even this far from Warm Sea the southerly wind sent north by Augurian tempered the arctic air, where the late-summer sun touched it.

On either side the bare, blue mountains closed in, pinching off the glacier's valley at its head.

Before long, I'll lose the glacier altogether, he thought. *And the water, too, I suppose?*

Now he often trod on bare rock instead of slushy ice. He studied a series of fresh scratches in the blue gabro underfoot. Marbleheart decided that they were made by the stone man as he walked, dragging his feet slightly with each step. Ice-polished pebbles had split into jagged pieces, sharp-edged, where the statue crunched them under his ponderous feet.

The trail led between shoulders of barren cliffs rising

33

fifty times the height of a man. The path was paved with black ice here, sheltered as it was from the sun and the south wind. Marbleheart skated along blithely, making good time.

The ice stream ahead of him tumbled down a six-foot frozen fall. He stopped to rest and look about.

"Strange smell!" he sniffed. "Something like that volcano, Blueye, over to Old Kay. Sulfurous, Douglas termed it."

He scrambled to the top of the fall and stopped before a tall, black iron gate that closed off the way.

It stood at least fifty feet high and forty feet from side to side. The frozen headwaters of Eternal Ice flowed from under the gate.

"Arrrgh!" the Otter groaned. "How to get inside?"

The leaves of the gate met closely in the middle and were anchored flush with the vertical cliff sides, leaving no space at all for a six-foot Otter to wriggle through. The bottom of the gate rested on the ice. The thought of climbing over the top made the Otter dizzy.

Far above his furry head he spied a single keyhole. He thought, *If I can climb that high, I can perhaps squeeze in through the keyhole.*

"And soon!" he said aloud. "Before someone comes along and opens the gate."

If they were swung open, the leaves would crush him against the side walls—and even if he escaped that, there was absolutely no place to hide for a mile downstream.

"Us Otters are pretty good climbers," Marbleheart assured himself, although he remembered with a shudder the canyon walls along upper Bloody Brook. At least there there had been ledges and clefts to use as claw-holds. But he and Douglas had met the Falls Pixies, who had shown them a better way past the falls.

"No Pixies here!" he exclaimed, although he spent several minutes looking about for signs of little people or any sort of fairy, birds, or even an insect who might help.

"So, I'll do it for myself," he declared stoutly, and

began to climb. Fortunately the ornate scrollwork decorations some ancient Dwarf blacksmith had hammered and welded to the sheet iron surface of the gate provided ample claw-holds.

The going became easier as he climbed. Every six feet the gate's designer had included a narrow ledge, intended to provide lateral strength to the heavy iron and keep it from sagging. Here he could rest a moment, but visions of the gate clashing suddenly open and sending him smashing against the wall hastened his climb.

Just below the enormous keyhole there was a slightly wider horizontal beam. It took him several careful minutes to scramble over its lip. A slip here and he would tumble twenty feet to the rock-hard ice below.

"I must have vertigo or maybe it's that acrophobia Master Flarman talked about," he panted, refraining from looking back and down.

"Almost there, Briney Otter!" he encouraged himself.

While he rested he studied the keyhole just above him. It had a richly ornamented escutcheon that would provide claw and paw grips, but he'd have to leap the last six feet, just to grasp its lower edge.

Not giving himself time to think about it, Marbleheart jumped upward and caught one foreclaw on a forged iron ivy tendril. He found a second hold, then purchase for several other claws.

Drawing himself up by his forelegs and twisting his long torso upward, he just managed to hook his right hind foot over the edge of the escutcheon. With a final heave, he shot upward and collapsed inside the keyhole itself, gasping but safe for the moment.

"I need more exercise," he muttered. "Gotten fat, living so easy since I came to stay with Wizards!"

A warm, heavily misted breeze blew out through the keyhole, smelling strongly of rotten eggs. The mechanism of the lock—a great bolt, heavy levers, and a coiled spring—posed no problem to the agile Otter. He slipped past the metalwork and peered cautiously out the other side of the keyhole.

The sulfurous odor was at once explained. The iron gate closed off the lower end of a narrow, V-shaped hollow. The sides and floor of the gorge were dotted everywhere with splashing, roaring, bubbling, steaming and rumbling clouds of superheated white vapor and jets of boiling water.

On level places between dark blue-green pines, yellow birches, and pale green poplars, hot pools of varying shades of aquamarine and turquoise burbled almost merrily. Boiling water gushed from hillside springs or spurted in intermittent geysers. On either side of the stone causeway that led to the gate on this side were puddles of viscous, chocolate brown, boiling mud, popping and plopping like oatmeal cooking in one of Blue Teakettle's Pots.

Marbleheart had never seen, heard, or smelled any place like it.

He half clambered, half slid down the inner facade of the gate and trotted along the causeway, taking cover in a twisted clump of deodars just beyond the mud pots. In the distance he caught a glimpse of three tall stone figures walking slowly away from him between erupting geysers, but there was no one closer by, no watch at the gate.

The Otter hitched up his courage and followed the trio at a safe distance, taking advantage of outcroppings of yellow-stained stone and occasional scrubby bushes for concealment. After a time the statues disappeared over a slight rise. He approached the hill cautiously, swerving now and again to avoid pools of hot blue-and-green water or hissing jets of live steam.

Peering over the crest of the rise, he faced a village of squat, round stone huts, roofed with thick, flat slate. The huts were set in a circle about a rough, stone-paved plaza before a larger, conical building, which was crudely decorated with primitive stone carvings of flowers and fantastic beasts.

Between this and the open side of the square stood a squat, short stone dais or pillar. Seated on its flat top, ten or twelve feet above the ground, Marbleheart saw Douglas Brightglade and First Citizen Serenit.

"Thank goodness!" the Otter breathed. "They appear to be alive, well and whole, and that's a blessing, at least."

At first there were no stone natives in view but as Marbleheart moved cautiously around the edge of their village, individual statues began to emerge from the huts and move toward the larger building beyond the prisoners. They moved in stony silence except for the thudding of their feet on the paths.

From their perch, Douglas and Serenit watched them pass without speaking. In fact, aside from the muted roaring hiss of distant fumaroles and the sudden sharp hiss of geysers, there was no sound at all.

That silence was broken when a clash, loud and sharp, like two dense stones struck together, came three times. The tribesmen increased their pace and filed quickly into the cone-shaped building.

Heavy iron doors crashed shut behind the last to arrive.

Marbleheart slinked between empty huts, listening and watching, until he was on the edge of the cleared square around the stone pillar. Rather than cry out, he took a pace away from his cover and stood on his hind feet, waving his forelegs in slow arcs in the direction of the captives.

Douglas, who had been relaxing as comfortably as possible atop the pillar, sat up at once and waved back. He glanced carefully about, saw no guards or other passersby, and gestured to Marbleheart to come to the foot of the strange monument.

"Welcome to Stony Gorge," said the Journeyman in a loud whisper. "You must have had a pretty grueling trek, following us here."

"Are you well?" asked Marbleheart anxiously, shrugging off the comment.

"We're as well as can be expected," replied Serenit as Douglas nodded. "These people don't feel the cold nor do they seem to eat, but having a Wizard along provides such luxuries as food and warmth."

"Not that it's so cold here," said Douglas, waving at the geysers and hot springs.

"Personally, I've not had a thing to eat since I caught a land-locked salmon, some way back," complained the Otter.

Douglas looked thoughtful for a second, made a gesture, and dropped a picnic basket covered with a red-checkered cloth down to the Otter. Marbleheart caught it quite neatly, spilling nothing.

"Will you come away with me? We can maybe find a place to hide until we can get out of this place," he called up to the prisoners.

"No, I think not. For one thing, hiding places are mighty hard to find, as you can see. And I want to find out just why we were brought here in the first place," Douglas told him.

"They haven't told you yet?" marveled the Otter, lifting the edge of the napkin to see what sort of goodies Douglas had transported from the Wizards' High kitchen. Fried chicken pieces, a container of potato salad, ham, cheese, and warm, buttered dinner rolls!

"No, the statue who brought us here wouldn't say a word," said the First Citizen.

"He expected you. Maybe he thought you should expect him. Still, if you're comfortable and safe . . ."

"Safe as a mouse at Wizards' High," Douglas assured him. "It would be handy if you would hide yourself somewhere, however, and observe a bit as a free and outside agent, if you understand what I mean."

"Perfectly!" chuckled Marbleheart. "Well, I'll find a nook or a cranny somewhere and enjoy what's in the basket, if you don't mind."

"After you've had your bite to eat, you might see if you can eavesdrop on their meeting inside," added the Journeyman, pointing over his shoulder to the building behind him. "Maybe get some idea what these strange Stone Men have in mind for us."

"I'll certainly do that," the Otter agreed, his normal good

humor restored by seeing his Master and the First Citizen fairly safe. "I'll report back when and if I can."

He scampered off between the two nearest huts, avoiding a stream of slow-flowing, malodorous water, and disappeared around one corner of the hall, carrying the picnic basket under his left front leg.

After gobbling the chicken, three ham-and-cheese sandwiches (with mustard—Fire Wizards love mustard), and the potato salad, Marbleheart hid the empty basket and circled the large stone edifice, studying its construction and layout as he went.

It was built of rough-hewn, flat blocks of the dark blue granite laid in even courses to the height of thirty feet. Its walls were pierced with many small slit windows to let in light—the statues might not need air but they needed light to see by, he decided.

Climbing the rough outer wall was no great task. He selected the eastern wall to scale, as there were fewer huts on that side of the building.

He reached the lowest bank of windows but found that his view inside was blocked by the hips and backs of the throng of statues gathered within. He climbed another two dozen courses and peered cautiously through one of the top-row windows.

The interior was just about as he had expected. Circular, its floor sunk well below the level of the plaza outside, the sides of the pit lined with rows of stone benches—really just square-cut granite blocks without backs—on which the Stone Men sat or stood.

Opposite the single door was a low dais on which stood the largest and heaviest of all the statues Marbleheart had yet seen.

As the Otter settled down to watch and listen on a narrow sill above the heads of the crowd, this figure raised his right arm for attention and the low crowd murmur fell away at once.

This Stone Man, Marbleheart decided, was in Authority.

"I am Detritus," the statue chanted in a deep, booming voice that somehow reminded the Otter of a landslide. "I am Chief of Stones!"

"We so recognize you, O Chief!" the gathered statues replied in rough chorus, some sort of ritual response.

"Let us consult together," intoned the Chief of Stones, and he sank to the dais cross-legged and folded his massive arms on his knees.

"Watchman has brought us two Wizards," announced Detritus. "He has done well!"

"He has done well!" responded the assembly, turning to point to Douglas's kidnapper. Watchman raised his hand in acknowledgment of the accolade, but said nothing.

"Without further preliminary," continued the Chief, "we shall interrogate these Wizards."

The throng buzzed and nodded.

The Stone named Watchman rose and went out through the door. Although he couldn't see from his high viewpoint, Marbleheart was not surprised when Douglas and his companion appeared in the doorway, floating casually along on air, followed by a disconcerted Watchman, who had evidently expected to carry or drag them into the hall.

"Come forward, then, Wizards," said Detritus, gesturing imperiously. "We wish to interrogate you."

Douglas floated right up to the platform and settled in midair at the level of the Chief's eyes. If Detritus or the other Stone Men were taken aback by the Wizard's bold move, they allowed no sign to show on their rigid faces.

"I'm ready to answer questions or provide any information in my power," said Douglas pleasantly. Serenit floated down to a bench—with grave dignity—in the front row.

"You are Wizards, we know," began Detritus, matter-of-factly. "How do we address you?"

"If you mean my name, I am called Douglas Brightglade. By profession I am a Journeyman Pyromancer, student of Flarman Flowerstalk of Wizards' High," Douglas replied.

"Never heard of either of you," grated the Chief, shaking his head.

Douglas showed his surprise at this. Almost everyone had heard of Flarman.

"My companion, however, is not a Wizard. He once was, but has since been stripped of his powers and title. He's therefore but an ordinary man and his name is Serenit of New Land. He was formerly known as Frigeon, the Ice King."

Detritus nodded, but said, "I have no knowledge of Serenit nor of Frigeon, either."

"These are fairly recent events," said Douglas.

"Whether he is also a Wizard or not is unimportant, however. *You* are a Wizard, Douglas Brightglade!"

"I am—a Journeyman Wizard, not yet advanced to full Mastery, however."

"But you will right a grave magical wrong," Detritus persisted, leaning forward suddenly. "For such is said to be a Wizard's duty, ever!"

"If I can, of course—or I may be able to find help for you, if your problem requires a full Wizard. Tell me about it."

Detritus gestured to another of the Stone Men, seated in the front row near Serenit. This individual, not quite as tall or as impressive as Chief Detritus, rather bent and much older, rose and bowed to the dais.

"This is Archey, our Tribal Storyteller," Chief Detritus explained to Douglas. "He will tell you our story, if you will please listen."

"Proceed," said Douglas, settling back on a cushion of thin air to listen with evident interest.

Chapter Five

The History of the Stones

THE Storyteller drew himself up as tall as he could, threw up his arms dramatically, and chanted in a high, singsong voice.

"Hear now, stalwart sirs! Lovely ladies! Eager offspring! Hear the Tragedy of the Stone Warrior Tribe, O brave and trusty Stones!

"The tale begins countless ages agone, when we were still true Men in body and stature, dreaded warriors but also lovers of and workers in, even worshipers of, hardest stone, World's very foundation, the Sacred Blue Gabro!"

In those days, he said, there had been a long era of peace—not a peace of progress and prosperity, but a peace of languor, of disinterest, of self-indulgence. Men cared little what happened elsewhere in World at that time. The winters were easy. Larders were ever filled. Maidens danced in spring season's first soft nights. Children played in cool lakes. Men hunted for meat each day, sat before fires at nights, and told fantastic stories of the Beginning of Things.

It seemed peace and contentment would last forever.

But there one night appeared, as a sudden black-ice blizzard from the Star-marked Pole, a terrible and powerful race of Beings who called themselves merely Darkness.

The mysterious, fearsome Darkness gathered about themselves all manner of discontented, evilly disposed and wretched Men and Near Immortals, even some few rebellious Fairies and twisted Dwarfs, Trolls, and Gnomes.

They granted them powers and riches, invincible weapons, and impenetrable armor—and taught them powerful magic spells—in exchange for unquestioning servitude.

Darkness's minions extorted gold, jewels, and the fairest of Men's daughters and sons as tribute, hiding them away betimes in deep cavities and crevices at the very top of World. They sent horrible, shambling armies under suborned princes to conquer Mortals and Near Immortals, Men, Fairies, Dwarfs, Elves, to slay or enslave them as they saw fit.

"How long ago was this, do you know?" asked Douglas when Archey paused for breath and dramatic effect.

"In centuries? A thousand, or close to," replied Archey, startled by the unaccustomed interruption.

"History repeats itself, I guess," sighed the Journeyman. "But go on, please."

The Storyteller nodded and continued his tale of fear, horror, loss of innocence, bloodletting, thunder, vivid lightning, and senseless cruelty.

"All this was not enough to satisfy Darkness, even so," he continued.

Here and there a certain few Beings, a handful of brave individuals, tribes, and nations resisted both the tempting bribes and the sudden, wild attacks, fought with desperate bravery and occasionally with success against the powerful Minions of Darkness.

Often when things seemed darkest, a hero would appear and lead the fight for years, decades, even centuries, to preserve freedom and life awhile longer.

First among these few heroes was a tribe of great warriors who worshiped ancient menhirs, Stones of Vast Power, standing in secret places of World. These called themselves Men of the Stones after the mysterious monoliths and circles of standing stones from the very dawn of life on World.

"We Stone Men," said Archey proudly, "had a firm faith. A tribe or a single man, striving to be as strong and pure as the Sacred Blue Gabro, would be as everlasting as the stone. We had no need for the blandished wealth and power of Darkness. We feared no one, nothing, not even Darkness!"

Darkness demanded these Stone Men become its servants, for they were nearly invincible in battle, ever brave in adversity, willing to fight to the death against impossible odds.

"We were the finest warriors and also the finest builders in World," claimed Archey earnestly. "We had become such by adhering to our bedrock principles for a cause that was right and just."

Darkness sent wave after wave of heavily armed minions to conquer and destroy the Stones—to no avail. At last, the very Darkness itself came down from its hollow places under the top of World to lay siege to the Stones' stronghold here in Stony Gorge.

"It was a time of bitter cold, yet of bright, all-consuming fire, of earsplitting thunder by day and continuous lightnings by night! But we endured!" Archey cried, caught up in his own tale.

The Stones on their benches also sat enthralled by a story they had heard a hundred thousand times before.

"Even Darkness itself could not overcome us by mere force of arms," Archey's voice fell lower and lower until it was almost a whisper. "Faceless Darkness decided that only the most twisted, the most wicked magic could defeat us."

A powerful Mortal Wizard was summoned and paid a great deal of gold and many rare and powerful talismans to destroy the Stones or place them where they could no longer influence other Men. . . .

"His full name we never knew. Wizards had always before been leaders *against* Darkness, you well know. To find that one of them was willing to do evil, cruel enchantment for mere pay and power . . . the thought almost shattered our courage.

"This Wizard stole his power from the very stone we

worshiped! He drew on earthquakes, avalanches, rivers of
white-hot lava, dire secrets locked in the deepest interior of
World, to do his terrible magicking."

"A renegade Geomancer," guessed Douglas, although he
had only read of such Wizardry in his studies under Flarman
Flowerstalk.

"Where we were once ordinary men—brave, strong, and
mortal—in one great flash we became of the very stone we
venerated! The Wizard made us eighteen feet tall, immensely strong, but painfully slow of thought and movement. He
cursed us with almost-eternal life and buried us alive under
Eternal Ice where everything was locked, forever frozen,
still and dark. We knew nothing of World for a thousand
years, except the slow rumblings and gratings of the glacier
that drained the ice field away to the south."

"The way Watchman followed when he brought us here?"
asked Serenit.

"Precisely," agreed Detritus.

"We lived, for a millennium, knowing nothing. Oh, we
heard great but distant explosions now and then and sensed
awful cries of agony. Occasionally the very bedrock beneath
us shifted uneasily, but we never knew what had happened
out in World," continued the Storyteller, deeply saddened.

After the most recent tremors, the ice above and about
the Gorge suddenly began to thin, allowing some sunlight
to reach them. One day it collapsed like a weakened dome
of glass, burying the village in its shards. Then the geysers
and hot springs began to erupt, steam, and flow.

When they finally were able to open the Gorge Gate,
the great outflowing glacier was receding at a remarkably
fast rate.

"The entire ice sheet was actually melting! If this was
so, we saw, the glacier would grow shorter and shorter,
shallower and shallower."

"Ah, I begin to understand . . . somewhat," said the Journeyman. "I can tell you why and how the glacier receded—
and that it will continue to shrink for some time to come."

"We'd like to hear that story very much," said the Chief, "but let Archey finish his story first."

"Of course! Sorry!" Douglas apologized.

"Well, it's short telling, from then on," sighed Archey. "The glacier has indeed shrunk. It has released its grip on Stony Gorge, at least. We are almost free! We could walk out on the surface now, if we wished to.

"We could have free contact with other free Men. But there is still one problem, Sir Wizard!"

Douglas nodded.

"We are still men of enduring stone! We have never been comfortable not being true Men as we once were! We wish to return to our former state. To be no longer frightening ogres to all the rest of World! To be finally disenchanted! Surely you can understand that, Sir Wizard?"

"I *do* understand. But what do you believe I can do?" asked Douglas.

"You must undo the spell that made us undying un-Beings," cried Detritus. "We wish to be flesh and blood again, to live a decent, proper span of years, to bleed when we are cut, to ache when we are struck, to sire sons and daughters and watch them grow, strong, clean! You *must* help us, Wizard Brightglade!"

Douglas sat in midair, elbows on his knees and fist to his chin, pondering the problem for a long time.

"I'll do what I can, of course. There's no spell that can't be broken, but as my friend Serenit here will attest, some enchantments take longer to disspell than others."

Serenit nodded, solemnly.

"When I was Frigeon, I overdid my magicking in much the same way this unknown Geomancer did, and today innocent people are still waiting in terrible agony or, worse, in oblivion, for their release, just because of me."

"What will you do?" Detritus asked Douglas, ignoring the First Citizen's explanation.

Douglas replied at once. "I can call upon a Master

Pyromancer of great experience, and a Master Water Adept, also, as well as a Magician from Choin—I'm not sure what his specialty is, if any. Together we'll surely break your spell, in good time."

"Well," said Detritus firmly, "to make *very* sure, we'll keep you two here with us, until the task is done."

"That's neither friendly nor fair," objected Serenit, leaping to his feet.

On his high window ledge Marbleheart clapped his paw over his mouth to keep from crying aloud in protest.

Douglas gestured to calm the former Wizard—and the unseen Otter as well—and said, "Friends, you've been terribly wronged. It's my duty to right such wrongs, where I can. It's not necessary for you to hold me prisoner. I will not desert you."

"So you shall not," ground out the Chief of the Stones stubbornly. "For you *will* stay hostage here until we are flesh and blood again."

Douglas looked at the Stone Man leader for a long moment, then nodded his head.

"I see I can't do anything to change your mind. However, let me send a message to my Master Flarman Flowerstalk, for he is probably the most powerful of the Wizards remaining in World."

"If need be, you may," said Detritus. "But I want you to try your own powers first. The fewer Wizards we call upon, the less it will cost us in the end."

"There's no fee asked, Sir Chief," protested Douglas, shaking his head. "When I do it, it will be because I wish to alleviate suffering and set your people free, not for any hope of gain."

"Nevertheless . . . ," growled Detritus.

"Honored Chief," spoke a member of the crowd, rising.

"We will listen to the wise Master Dolomit but briefly," snapped Detritus.

"Sir, a word has been uttered here by the Wizard's companion. A word that we may have forgotten."

"I fail to understand, Dolomit," Detritus ground out. "Get to the point!"

"Simply that we perhaps are not being quite fair to this young man. After all, it wasn't he who imposed our ordeal a thousand years ago."

Detritus scowled until Dolomit sat down amid a spattering of approving applause.

"My decision is carved in hardest gabro! We will *not* trust *any* Wizard, since a Wizard betrayed us in the first place," he declared angrily. "We will treat them well and fairly but I will *not* let him go free until they—or someone—work out our salvation."

And that, Marbleheart saw, was *that*.

Several minutes of heated debate followed, but the Chief of Stones refused to crack. At last it became a matter of either accepting Detritus's way or challenging his leadership. None of the Stones wanted to do that, now that he'd led them so close to their goal.

"We may all suffer for your hard-headed distrust," warned the Stone named Dolomit. "The modern Wizards may punish us for wrongfully holding one of their fellows. What if they turn their magic on us?"

"No," Douglas interposed quickly. "I accept your conditions, Chief Detritus. I'll attempt the spell breaking on my own as you wish—and I may well succeed, for all I know."

"You've already found some of your magics will not work against us, I suspect," Detritus said suddenly.

"That's true! The original powerful spell used to enchant you protects you from my powers—at least for the moment. I say again, you need not fear me. My duty and desire is to save you all from the ancient Geomancy. I'll abide by your rules."

"You've no choice," snorted the Chief.

"I'll seek no revenge nor impose any punishment, unless I discover punishment is due for acts you've committed that

I don't yet know about. If so, you'll then be judged by fellow Mortal Men, not by any Wizard. That is a statement of fact."

Douglas and Detritus locked equally stone-hard stares for a long-held breath, and it was the Chief of Stones who snorted and looked away first.

"Take them back to the Column! Give them anything they need to work their magic," he ordered Watchman. "Does that suit you, Wizard Brightglade?"

"Barely. It's warm enough and dry enough up on your Column, so I'll not complain. Allow the First Citizen to go home, however, I pray you. He can do neither good nor harm to you Stone Men, being no longer a Wizard himself."

"We have only your word for that—and his word," snapped Detritus, preparing to step down from the dais. "And we've not yet established whether we can trust *any* Wizard, have we?"

"Well, then I'll begin at once—from the top of the column outside, if you so insist. Anyone may watch who wishes. I have no secrets except as part of my craft. Come one! Come all!" cried Douglas, floating over to Watchman to be led away.

"You must take this seriously!" shouted Detritus after him.

"Oh, I do! Very much so!" cried the pupil of Flarman Flowerstalk with a nod and a wave. "I'll keep you informed of any progress I make, although I must say again it would go much faster if I could call in my Master."

"Not yet," insisted the Chief, sounding weary now. "You must understand that we cannot afford to trust . . ."

But the Journeyman and the First Citizen were already out the door, returning to their strange prison column.

Marbleheart skipped gingerly down the outside wall of the meeting hall, and trotted off to find a cozy place to hole up and finish his picnic lunch. He would go talk to Douglas when the crowd had lost interest in him.

"Which should be around an hour or so," he decided, "judging by what I've learned about Men, even Stone Men. By then it'll be time for a nice dinner from Blue Teakettle's kitchen, I do believe."

Chapter Six

Myrn Sets Out

WITHOUT the Magical Feather Pin, which the Dowager Princess Finesgold had given her, it would have taken Myrn Manstar all of three weeks to reach the High. As it was, within six hours of leaving Waterand Island she whizzed over upper Crooked Brook and zipped down for a light-footed landing at the double front door, where Bronze Owl was hanging from his personal nail in pale gibbous moonlight.

"I rather expected you'd be flying in," Owl said to the beautiful Aquamancer's Apprentice. "You and Augurian obviously take these disappearances as seriously as do Wong and I."

"Of course!" said Myrn emphatically. "I intend to get my Douglas safely back in time for his Examination. I don't want to have to put off our wedding until spring, either. Not with the invitations already out."

"Besides, Douglas may need help," said the Owl, opening the door and letting out the cheery, homey air of the High to wash away her worry and concern like a warm, fragrant shower.

"Come have some supper. Wong is still trying to make heads or tails of this business in his own ways."

"Indeed," said Myrn as she entered the kitchen. She patted Blue Teakettle fondly on the cheek and waved gaily to the neat rows, ranks, and racks of utensils, from stove lid to saltcellar. They clattered, banged, scraped, and rattled their fond welcomes.

"First, let me have a cup of the same tea Flarman drank before he whisked off. And let me see his cup, if you've saved it, dear Blue."

Flarman's teacup was produced at once, still covered by its inverted saucer, along with another cup of freshly brewed Choin tea from Blue Teakettle's spout.

Myrn sipped her tea as she studied Flarman's dried leaves, now looking rather soggy and bedraggled. As she finished, the Choinese Magician appeared from the stairway, wreathed in smiles and bowing double in greeting.

"I see you've already begun your own researches," he said, pointing to the teacups.

"Yes, indeed. Take a cup with me, please do, and I'll look at your leavings, too, just in case," said Myrn.

"My pleasure, Honored Lady," said the Magician, and when he was seated at the great kitchen table—he looked like a child sitting at the vast board, so tiny was he and so huge was the table—he sipped tea while Myrn interpreted what she saw in the other two cups.

"There are always at least two layers of leaves," she explained. "The obvious—and the hidden."

"So I was taught," Wong said, nodding his understanding.

"The obvious indication in Flarman's cup is that he is about to undertake a long, urgent journey. We already knew that. It doesn't say where he is going, however, or why—as far as I can see."

"It never does, does it?" commented the Magician. "Do you see what lies hidden beneath?"

"Contrary to what most people believe, it isn't the tea that provides prognostication," Myrn murmured as much to herself as to the Magician. "It's the water, really. And the water in Flarman's cup has almost dried up."

She peered into the cup for several minutes, frowning and muttering helpful spells.

"This indicates . . . something to do with a deserted land. The direction indicated is either north by northeast or south by southwest."

"But we already suspected that, too," observed Bronze Owl. "From what the Horniad told you, Myrn, and the Otter told the gulls. Douglas is in the far northeast."

"But the leaves don't indicate that Douglas is involved," she added, looking puzzled. "Time may have obscured that part. Flarman read them fresh and departed quite suddenly. Perhaps he was able to see Douglas's name here, but I can't!"

"Perhaps because the Journeyman is no longer in danger," suggested Wong, helpfully. "It might be so, if Flarman has already rescued him."

Myrn handed her own teacup to Wong.

"Here, you can read my leaves better than I can. One should never try to read one's own future, Augurian says."

The Magician took her cup and leaned back in his chair, almost disappearing below the table's edge. His voice floated up to them after a moment.

"Yes, yes! You are promised a long, cold journey to the north very clearly. Under that the leaves say to look for a beacon of fire in the sky."

"Douglas or Flarman?" wondered Owl, clapping his wings together loudly. "It must mean to watch for a signal."

"Certainly my interpretation," agreed Wong, reappearing above the tabletop. "The leaves also say that you will marry, soon and well, my dear."

"Well, that's a revelation!" said Myrn with a slight touch of sarcasm.

"But it does seem to indicate that our present problem will not delay the wedding," insisted the Magician.

"Let me see your cup then, please," said the Apprentice Aquamancer. "Ah, yes, also a long, cold journey! I was planning to ask you to accompany me to look for Douglas and Flarman, Revered Sir."

"I intended to offer my services," Wong answered.

"And . . . here it says something about returning home soon. I had thought you intended to stay for the wedding."

"I had so intended, of course. My country . . ."

"Needs you, I'm afraid," said Myrn, peering at the leaves again. "I see confusion, death, and bloodshed—not a pretty picture—in your homeland."

She put the cup down and looked sadly at the tiny Choin. He returned her concerned look for a moment, and then turned to the Owl.

"We know we are to go north, then, and the two of us shall go . . ."

"Three," said Bronze Owl. "I'll go, too."

"*Someone* must stay here," Wong pointed out reasonably. "Myrn will confirm what I have already sensed. There is a singular blockage of information flow from and to the northeast of us."

"I feel it, too, as did Augurian," said Myrn, nodding.

"What if Flarman sends a message to us here, or Augurian needs to tell us something and no one was here to receive it?" reasoned the Choinese Magician.

Owl reluctantly agreed he would remain at the High to serve as their mutual point of contact. "But how shall I relay any messages to you?"

"Send the gulls to look for us if you don't hear from me first," decided Myrn. "They fly as fast as anyone."

"There remains only the question," said the Apprentice early the next morning as she gathered up her travel kit and slung it over her shoulder, "of exactly where we're going."

"To New Land," said Wong. "Where we last know Douglas, Serenit, and Marbleheart to have been. Serenit's people can set us on their path. Flarman may also have stopped there for the same information."

"Let's go, then!" Myrn exclaimed.

They stepped through the back door into the mist-shrouded kitchen courtyard. Owl, Blue Teakettle, and Black Flame were there to see them off, along with the

Familiar's wives, Pert and Party, the five Ladies of the Byre, who paused on their way to the dew-heavy meadow, the Thatchmice, who were among Douglas's most ardent admirers, and a score of silly doves from the cote above the Workshop door who came just out of curiosity.

Myrn, laying her hand on Wong's arm, whispered the words that activated her Feather Pin. The Magician grasped his lacquered black hat with his other hand while Myrn pointed her free arm up and north.

There was a *whoosh* of displaced air. The pair shot aloft and dwindled to a tiny double speck in mere seconds.

Because Flarman might have stopped to have a word with Bryarmote, too, Myrn shaped their course first for Dwelmland, the Dwarf's subterranean principality.

On her most recent visit, when she was on her way to join Douglas in Old Kingdom, Bryarmote's chief steward, a jolly old dwarf named Fortoot, had showed Myrn the hidden family entrance to Bryarmote's vast system of caverns so that she could call at any time without having to pass through the miles and miles of canyons, gorges, arroyos, passages, and tunnels that marked the other, more formal entrances.

She flew, therefore, directly to a tiny patch of soft greensward high on one shoulder of a peak above Dwelmland and found the heavy bronze door hidden behind a clump of purple rhododendrons. She knocked politely on the proper panel and within ten heartbeats the door swung wide open.

"M'lady!" Fortoot himself greeted her with a broad smile and a sweeping bow. "Welcome back to Dwelmland!"

"How did you know we were coming?" marveled Myrn after she had introduced the Magician. They followed the plump little steward into the mountaintop and down a rapidly moving stair that carried them along much faster than they could have walked.

Fortoot explained proudly the stair had been a present to the Dwarf Prince and his bride from Flarman; one of his own inventions.

"Our Home Guards keep a keen watch on the skies, of course," the steward answered her question. "Little passes over our borders they don't detect and identify. Recently, for example, they reported a large flock of arctic gulls passing swiftly overhead, headed toward Valley."

"Yes, they carried an important message to the High," Myrn told him.

"This morning I chanced to be supervising the tuning of Princess Crystal's new carillon near the doorway when the word came of your approach. The Silver Dwarfs who installed the carillon turned out to be rather badly tone deaf, you see. The chimes were Prince Bryarmote's wedding gift to his bride."

"A different sort of wedding ring," laughed Myrn. She spent the rest of their swift descent into the heart of the mountain explaining the pun to her Choinese companion.

Fortoot led them at once to Bryarmote, who was working in his office. He sat at a huge and cluttered drawing board set before a picture window overlooking one of the most spectacular views in Dukedom—of the deep blue, steep-sided fjord that opened onto Sea near Fairstrand.

"We cannot stay very long," Myrn told him with her hug and kiss of greeting. She waved off suggestions of lunch, dinner, staying the night, and talking the Dwarfs blue in the face, as he put it, then explained their mission.

"No, Flarman didn't come this way or we'd have seen him. My Guards would have spotted him, you can be sure."

"Which must mean he transported himself by a spell of some sort, for he would have flown close over here, in any case, even if he hadn't stopped," Wong reasoned. "I guessed that, of course. I could trace the course of his Transportation Spell but it's a rather laborious process, I'm afraid."

"We'll go to New Land first, and without delay," Myrn said firmly.

"Give me five minutes to speak to my foremen and my wife and mother," the Dwarf Prince insisted, "and I'll go with you. My people came originally from Far Northland,

you know, and I'm familiar with its ways and dangers.
Not a place for the unwary, especially at this time of
the year."

"Why this time of year, pray?" asked Wong.

"It'll be snowing heavily up north soon and the cold will
be very intense, if it's not already. You can get as lost
flying in a heavy snow as you can over Sea in a fog. No
landmarks visible!"

While he instructed Fortoot and his staff, Myrn took the
Magician to meet Lady Finesgold, the Prince's mother, of
whom Myrn was particularly fond, and Bryarmote's shy
new bride, Princess Crystal.

"How I wish I could go along!" cried Finesgold after
hearing of their mission. "I know just how you feel about
that handsome boy. I'd do the same if it were my man lost
in the Northland wilderness!"

"You are certainly welcome to come along," said Myrn,
trying not to let her dismay show. Her party was already
too large for her best comfort. Finesgold was as tiny and
delicate looking as the Choinese Magician—and probably
just as tough. "The Pin can carry us all."

"No, no! I won't burden it or you with a little old lady.
Besides, I'm in the middle of repotting my flowers for
winter, and that can't wait longer."

"Myrn is burdened enough with a little old Magician,"
agreed Wong, who felt immediately at home with the
Dowager Princess. They were both of the same age as
well as size.

"Now you two!" cried Myrn. "Any more of such nonsense and I'll leave you both behind!"

"I go along with these adventures just for the amusement," Wong confided in Finesgold. "I haven't lifted a
hand in spell since I first came to Wizards' High."

"That's not true!" Myrn objected. "He's to be a member of Douglas's Examination Board. I have to be nice
to him."

Shy Crystal, who had said very little, was shocked by
her teasing words.

"My dear mother-in-law tells me that I should learn to tease, as you do. I find it quite difficult. May I come and stay with you for a while at Wizards' High, someday? Perhaps I could learn such affectionate impudence from you, pretty Apprentice."

"As soon as we are wed—well, perhaps not *immediately* after, but soon," promised Myrn with an amused, embarrassed chuckle.

"How wonderful it is to be affectionately teased," sighed Wong. "My people, Princesses, forgot how to tease each other gently over seven centuries ago—and it's a fault I regret to this day."

Finesgold left her pot gardening long enough to order them a picnic basket to carry on their way and returned them to Bryarmote's study, where he waited for them.

"Send us word of Flarman and Douglas as soon as you can," requested Finesgold.

"And the cuddly Marbleheart," added Crystal.

"The Sea Otter would love you, ma'am," Myrn told her. "If he likes anything better than eating, it's being cuddled."

Chapter Seven

A Column of Wizards

AFTER midnight—the arctic late-summer days were still very long, the nights short—Marbleheart left his den under one of the huts and stole softly to the Stone Column. If there were guards, they weren't keeping very close watch.

He found Douglas sitting cross-legged before a tiny flame with another hovering over his head. The First Citizen slept, wrapped in several blankets. Douglas was reading a small, thick tome of excruciatingly tiny print.

"Hoy!" whispered the Otter from below. "Care to chat a bit?"

"Come on up," called the Journeyman, marking his place with a forefinger. "I just remembered this little book in Flarman's library, so I sent off for it. It has a footnote mentioning a wicked, old-time Earth Adept named Obsydion. He seems to fit the Storyteller's description of the Stones' enchanter."

Marbleheart leaped and scrambled nimbly to the pillar top and curled himself in front of the tiny fire. Serenit slept away, snoring lightly.

"Huh! He's some help!" chuckled the Otter, pointing his nose at the First Citizen.

"He's bereft of Wizardly powers but not Wizardly opinions," said Douglas. "It's better to have him asleep than trying to help."

"Oh? Well, I think I hear you saying 'go away' to me, too," said Marbleheart, pretending a huff.

"Don't be silly! I was about to call you, anyway. Are you safe? Have you had dinner?"

"Yes and no," replied the other, curling up again. "I found a hiding place under yon hut, lined it with some sort of soft, dry moss, quite warm and snug. I've learned that Stone Men rumble and mutter in the night, although I don't think they actually sleep. Habit, I guess. And no, I haven't had a thing to eat in a terribly long time, beloved Master."

Douglas made a quick gesture and a steaming platter of juicy pork chops and curried carrots appeared before the Otter, who was so used to this kind of magic by now that his only reaction was to wiggle over onto his belly and begin to eat with gusto.

"Tell me," he said around a mouthful of hot, spicy carrots, "if you can bring a book from Flarman's library and gourmet cuisine from old Teakettle's kitchen, why can't you send a message to the Wizard and ask his help on the Stone's enchantment?"

"Good question, Familiar!" said Douglas. "Mainly, because Bronze Owl says Flarman is nowhere to be found. He's evidently already on his way here, so I don't need to call him. And the first thing he'll say when he arrives is going to be, 'What do you know about Geomancy, me lad?' So, I'm studying up on a sort of magic that isn't practiced much these days."

"The kind of magic that did for the Stone Men?" asked Marbleheart, reaching for a third chop. "Do you want a bite of this?"

"No, we dined as soon as we got back from the tribal meeting. What did you think of it, by the way?"

The Otter sat up to sip a bit of hot, sugary coffee.

"It had the feeling of family," he said thoughtfully, "and in the end, it was Papa Detritus who told everyone what was going to happen, or else."

Said the Journeyman with an approving nod, "He did let them debate, however."

"Oh, I guess so. But he'd have gotten his way even if

they had all opposed him. Is that democracy? I felt most of the Stone citizens disliked the idea of holding you hostage, for example."

"There is that," conceded the young man. "Even the most democratic societies work that way, however. After all, the Chief is responsible. They were probably right to let him try his way. If that fails, it'll be Detritus's neck, not theirs, you see."

Douglas raised his head and seemed to be listening to the wind blowing over Stony Gorge. The sky was overcast and through the pervasive reek of hydrogen sulfide they caught the smell of snow in the air.

"What is it?" inquired the Otter.

"I need a way to signal," Douglas told him.

"Easy enough," said his practical Familiar. "Build up the fire a bit. There can't be another fire within ten days' ride of this forsaken place, can there?"

Douglas nodded as if to say, *Why didn't I think of that?* and waved his hands over the tiny flame between them.

It sputtered gleefully and flashed a bright yellow shaft of light high into the air, pencil thin but considerably taller than the surrounding hills.

From far down the Gorge a Stone guard cried out in startled alarm, and a moment later Detritus poked his Stony face out of the hut nearest the Meeting Hall.

"Hey, you! Put out that blasted fire!" he bellowed.

"Sorry, Chief! Just part of my magicking," called Douglas, mildly. "Relax. You'll be happy to know I'm making progress, if slowly."

"Hmph!" growled Detritus, scowling, but he withdrew into his hut, letting the leather curtain fall back into place across the opening.

"Think Flarman will see it?" murmured Marbleheart.

"Without a doubt," said Douglas. "Eat up and get back into hiding. I may need you free tomorrow. Just in case, old friend."

"Here I go. Mind if I take the bones to gnaw?"

He scurried back to his hiding hole—apparently under

the Chief's own hut—and Douglas resumed his study of
the ancient chronicle.

"Did you see that?" cried Wong Tscha San.

Myrn's party was spending the night at Serenit's rustic
lodge not far from where his Ice Palace had once stood.
Clangeon, Frigeon's steward, had made them welcome, but
had been unable to give them any news beyond pointing
out the path his master and the Journeyman had taken to
the glacier five days before. They planned to follow that
trail, via Feather Pin, to the Face as soon as it became light,
despite the threat of snow.

"Did I see what?" growled the Dwarf from his bed.
"What's to see?"

"A bright, yellow shaft of light in the sky to the north,"
explained the Magician. "It shot straight up and stayed for
several minutes, then disappeared. Right over there!"

"Northern lights, probably," said Bryarmote, but he rose
from his bed and began to pull on his clothes. "Better wake
the Lady Apprentice."

"If it was just aurora borealis," asked Magician, "why
should she get up?"

"Because it's time we were on our way, of course. Nights
are longer here than they are in Choin. It's past my fast-
breaking time, as it is."

Myrn had not seen the light in the sky, but she at once
reminded them of the tea leaves' advice to look for fire in
the sky.

"Keep the proper direction firmly in mind, please," she
told the Magician, "while I borrow some warm coats from
Clangeon. We'll go check on it."

"A distress signal, do you think?" Bryarmote asked Wong
while Myrn was talking to the steward. "Does it mean one
of our Fire Wizards is in trouble?"

"A beacon, rather, I would think," said Wong. "They are
both more than capable of taking care of themselves."

"Then why are we here?" grumbled the Dwarf. He was
a slow awakener.

"Well, sir Prince, there is always the possibility we can be useful," Wong replied quietly. "My people have a saying. *'Better sure than sorry.'* "

Bryarmote nodded in agreement, inhaled a cup of very strong, very black coffee when it was served, and felt more able to face the snowy skies over New Land. Myrn came and ate heartily but quickly.

"Ready to go?" she asked.

Her two companions were, and in a few minutes they were skimming swiftly up the smooth-sided valley carved by Eternal Ice over countless ages.

In less than an hour they pulled up just short of the towering blue-ice Face, and landed gently on a gravel mound beside a deep, still tarn.

The Dwarf ranged back and forth on foot, bent almost double, searching for confirmation of the gull's story. Myrn and the Magician sat back to back on a frosty rock beside the lake, studying the area closely in their own special, magical ways.

"It hasn't snowed enough yet here to cover any tracks. I see the Otter's paw marks in this patch of sand, easily," called out Bryarmote. "And two sets of prints that have to belong to Serenit and Douglas. Douglas is wearing the stout Dwarf traveling boots I gave him years ago."

"A stout Dwarf's boots? Why not a thin one?" wondered Wong. "Sorry! Anything else?"

"Not much—signs of gulls roosting, of course. Fishing in the lake from the looks of the mess they left."

"You've missed one other sign," Wong spoke up, pointing to the flat shingle beach before them.

Bryarmote came to look at once.

"No Man has feet that big!" he exclaimed. "He must be twenty feet tall!"

They slowly circled the giant's footprints. They led out of the tarn and returned to it again, clearly. But the marks made by Douglas's boots came just so far, then stopped.

"That confirms it," said the Apprentice. "The gull Aurora had it right, sirs."

"And the Otter followed the statue right into the lake," said Bryarmote. "Brave fellow! He followed the statue, or whatever it is, right under the glacier ice, beyond."

"So I see it," agreed Wong. "But how are we to proceed? I suppose we can travel under the water, too."

"No, we'll fly in the direction of that beacon you saw before dawn," decided Myrn. "I'm sure it was made either by Douglas or by Flarman, to show us the way."

"No need to tarry here, then," agreed the Dwarf.

They joined hands once more and shot up and over the Face, following Wong's memory of where the light signal had been seen.

"There's my Douglas!" cried Myrn in relief as they glided over Stony Gorge several hours later. She put on a sudden burst of speed, arrowing straight at the two figures on the stone column in the cobbled square.

"No, now, wait . . . ," protested Wong. "Perhaps . . ."

But Myrn's momentum carried them straight to Douglas and Serenit. Seeing them coming, Douglas waved cheerily, and Serenit quickly straightened his robe and brushed at his thinning hair. He was a bit vain about his appearance before ladies and strangers.

"Ahoy!" Myrn called out happily. "Are you mates captives? Are you in danger? We come to help you escape durance vile, my dear!"

Douglas gathered her in his arms, gave her a kiss and a tight squeeze.

"Yes and no, as my Familiar said a few hours ago."

"Yes to what?" asked his betrothed, forgetting to let him go.

"Yes, we're prisoners. Hostages, really."

"Hello, Serenit!" Myrn said. "May I present Wong Tscha San of Choin, a Magician? You already know Bryarmote, of course."

Everybody bowed or shook hands before Myrn returned to the matter of being hostages.

"You really *are* captive here, sweetheart?" she asked.

"As I said."

"But you said no, also."

"I meant, 'No, you can't rescue us from durance vile,' " said Douglas calmly.

"But come on! I can fly us out of here in a second," Myrn protested.

"You could, but we can't," Douglas said, and he sat them down by the fire and explained about the Stones and their enchantment.

"I've given my word I would help them, you see," he concluded. "I was just doing my homework when you came dropping down out of the snowclouds. I'm certainly glad you're here, sweet, and that you brought Wong, for you both certainly can help puzzle out this strange spelling. Bryarmote, you're always welcome on an adventure, of course."

"I will be delighted to assist you, Master Douglas," said Wong, with a formal bow. "It won't count against your Journeying this time."

He referred to the Journeying rules that applied when the Journeyman had gone recently to Old Kingdom to investigate the Coven of Black Witches. To qualify for his Master's Examination, he had had to carry out that task without help from other Wizards.

"No, this time I'll take all the help I can get. I can't find very much anywhere about Geomancy. It seems to be a blind spot in Flarman's library and my training."

"Not surprising," said Wong. "There . . ."

"Say," interrupted Bryarmote, who had been studying the stone village with great interest. "Where's Flarman, after all? He should've been here well ahead of us."

"Haven't seen him," admitted Douglas. "I hoped he would see the light and come."

"Well, *we* saw it, instead," said Myrn. "Where's Marble-heart?"

"Around somewhere. Probably looking for some lunch,"

said Douglas. "He should be within call, anyway."

"So he's safe, is all that matters," said Myrn. "Now . . . what can we do to help here?"

Snow soon began to fall steadily and after noon temperatures plummeted. The Journeyman, the Apprentice, and the Magician sat earnestly discussing the magical matter of the Stones.

Bryarmote and Serenit, used to the ways of Wizards, listened patiently and silently, keeping their eyes peeled for signs of hostility among the natives.

Several times various Stones passed through the square but paid them no attention whatsoever, even though the number of prisoners had more than doubled.

Twice Detritus came from his hut and stood glaring suspiciously at them, rocklike fists on his hips, but he made no comment. He was content, it seemed, that something was being done on the Stones' behalf.

"This ancient book I found in the library at Wizards' High," Douglas said, "has only a short footnote that mentions a rock-hard Wizard named Obsydion. He was evidently a creature of Darkness, a long, long time ago. No other details."

"I was going to say," Wong said, "that I know little or nothing about the craft of Stone Wizardry—Geomancy, as you call it—but I have a slight knowledge of the man Obsydion. Ten centuries ago, he lived. He was eventually destroyed by his own evil Dark Master, so there's no hope of finding him today."

"His tomb, his remains? Perhaps they would provide further clues?" asked Myrn with a slight shudder.

"No, Lady Apprentice! *If* his body was preserved, it was hidden by the Darkness, perhaps under the top of World. Even I would hesitate to travel there and, beside that, an intruder in such a place might well stir up more than he bargained for. Best to let dead Wizards lie," warned Wong, shaking his head vigorously.

"A bit like the barrow-wights in Old Kay, eh?" mused Douglas. "Well, what then? I admit I'm stumped."

They sat in silence made even deeper by the blanket of snow about them. Douglas dug out a handkerchief from the sleeve of his gown and, with a long-familiar spell, arranged and enlarged it as a tent to cover them all.

Myrn in turn summoned a small, warm, dry breeze and blew all the snow from beneath the tent until their perch was completely dry and comfortable.

Marbleheart appeared through the thickening whiteness and joined the party, greeting them all cheerily. He reported that the Chief had spent the afternoon in his hut arguing with his advisers about the hostages.

"As I thought, the others aren't too happy about possible consequences of capturing a Wizard," the Otter said.

"The quickest way to solve that is to solve this riddle," said Myrn, and she set about preparing supper for the party.

Wong was so still and silent for so long it was apparent he'd been in a "seeing" trance, an important tool of his craft. The smell of roast pork and fried rice, his own recipe sent along by Blue Teakettle, at last recalled him to the Gorge.

While he ate daintily with ivory chopsticks, he began to speak.

"Yes, Obsydion was almost certainly responsible for the spell cast on the Stone Warriors a thousand years ago. His Earth Magic is the most ancient of all the disciplines of Wizardry. Earth came long before even Water and Fire. Its spells are incredibly complex and unbelievably strong, for they include safeguards against disspelling by any other powers than those of a Geomancer."

"Which explains," said Myrn, "why we can't make a crack in this Stone business."

"Correct, my dear Apprentice! Usually, one discipline has at least some entry into all the others, and vice versa," Wong went on with a pedantic nod. "You recall? Fire can boil Water. Water can quench Fire. Air can attack or support them both. But Stone, Earth, is all but invulnerable to the others, except over a tremendously long time. The

most ancient Geomantic enchantments . . . they're like . . .
well, like stone walls."

"And there are no longer any Geomancers alive?" asked
Marbleheart.

"There *was* a Geomancer who belonged to the Fellowship
of Wizards, before the war that ended in Last Battle three
hundred years ago," said Wong. "I don't know his name,
but perhaps Flarman or Augurian will remember. He may
still be alive."

"I've never heard either of them mention the craft, let
alone the Wizard," mused Douglas, sounding quite discouraged. "And the Fellowship scattered far and wide after Last
Battle—this one could be just about anywhere in World!"

Myrn reached out and took his hand.

"I think we must get in touch with Augurian. At least we
know where *he* is. Goodness knows where Flarman is!"

"I begin to worry about Flarman myself," admitted
Douglas. "Yes, we must speak to your Master about
this. I don't think anyone else knows more about the old
Fellowship than he does, not even Flarman."

"I'll try to call to Master Augurian, then," decided the
Lady Apprentice. "If it doesn't go against your promise to
Detritus, Douglas."

"No, I consider only myself bound here by my word in
that," said the Journeyman. "How will you get in touch with
Augurian?"

"Unlike some Masters," Myrn said pointedly, "and their
Apprentices, my Master and I long ago set up a way to
keep in close communication. I should be able to let him
know where I am, even with this blocking spell we feel. It
seems to block incoming messages. Perhaps it won't stop
an outgoing one. I'd go to him, except even the Feather Pin
would take a couple of days or more, I'm afraid, from this
distance."

While the others watched in fascinated silence, the
Apprentice stood facing south on the edge of the column,
her arms folded across her chest and her eyes closed. An
aura of power shimmered about her that all could feel and

which Douglas and Wong could see as a faint blue glow
against the snow-filled night.

"Magister!" called Myrn, although Marbleheart was sure
she didn't move her lips to speak. "Magister, your Apprentice Myrn Manstar calls you."

Silence for a long minute.

"Yes, Master. I am with Douglas as well as Serenit, Magician Wong, Prince Bryarmote, and Familiar Marbleheart.
This place? It's known as Stony Gorge, I'm told. Six or
eight days' foot travel due north of New Land. Yes. Yes!
Thank you!"

There was a sharp *click!* and the aura dispersed from
about her.

Before she could drop her arms and turn back to the
waiting men and beast, a translucent image of Augurian
materialized beside her, wavered twice, then became seemingly solid. He seemed to have trouble making contact with
the stone surface. Even after they'd begun to talk to him, he
would drift slowly downward into the stone, as if he were
sinking into thick mud, and had to pull himself up to the
surface of the rock again with an effort.

Now he smiled at their welcoming shouts.

"What can I do to help, friends?" he said in his very deep,
rumbling voice, which always reminded Douglas of waves
breaking upon green rocks.

Chapter Eight

Summit Meeting

AS Douglas opened his mouth to begin, he was interrupted by an angry shout out of the snowy darkness.

"You blasted Wizards!" shouted Detritus. "I'm keeping an eye and an ear on you! Don't think I'm going to feed all that great crowd you've got up there. You can all starve for all I care!"

"Our kindly host," explained Douglas with a wry grin. "Name's Detritus and he's Chief of Stones, the people I was about to tell you about, Magister. They need our help."

"Gracious!" said Augurian, a little startled. "I must meet him shortly, Douglas."

"You undoubtedly will, Magister. But for now, tell us . . . how go your researches?"

Augurian shrugged his shoulder. "I must admit I'm as ignorant as I've been since Myrn brought me the Horniad's brief message. It's clear the danger the Sea creatures spoke of was to you, Douglas. I would not have been so concerned had not Flarman disappeared at the same time."

"Yes, where *is* Flarman? I wonder," interrupted Douglas. "I thought I felt him nearby but now I believe it was Myrn's presence I felt, not Flarman's, just before I sent up the flare."

"I suggest that we start at the beginning, young Journeyman," murmured Wong from deep within a pile of furs. "Master Augurian needs to be brought completely up to the

73

moment. It wouldn't hurt the rest of us to hear it straight from the beginning, either."

Douglas nodded and began with the discovery of Watchman at the Face of Eternal Ice Glacier.

The tale took quite a while to tell, ending with the Choin Magician's faint recollection of a Geomancer in the original Fellowship of Wizards.

"Ah, yes!" cried Augurian at that. "Now that you mention it, I do recall an Earth Wizard among us before Last Battle. Litholt, if I rightly recall the name."

"I can't recall," said Wong. "I was never a close member of the Fellowship in those days."

"But your memory is correct, Revered Sir!" the Water Adept said. "Litholt was—I hope, still is—the last of the wartime Geomancers. The craft was dying even then. It is by far the hardest of the Mysteries, you know."

"And the most durable, as witness these poor Stones," Douglas said. "Their spelling is at least a thousand years old!"

Marbleheart shook his head sadly. "If this Litholt person is dead, as it might be, our best hope of disspelling the Stones is gone."

"I hope it's not so, for their sake, and for the sake of an important and useful branch of Wizardry," said Serenit. "Perhaps . . . there may be Apprentices? Most of us had Apprentices, in the olden times, even I. You've met him, Douglas?"

"We met Cribblon in Old Kingdom," the Journeyman answered. "He spoke well of you as his Master, Serenit— except as a cook, as I recall. He's even now working toward Journeyman, over in Old Kay."

"Ah, yes, so Flarman told me," said Serenit. "But pardon my interruption, Master Aquamancer. Pray continue!"

Augurian was considering, chin on hand, staring into the snow curtain that surrounded them.

"Perhaps there was an Apprentice. But I think not. Flarman was the first of us to take on a student after the Chaos. The thing to do to begin, at least, is seek out

Litholt. A Geomancer, I agree with Master Wong, should be able to undo the spell on the Stones."

"And Flarman?" asked Myrn.

"The Fire Wizard has given no indication he needs our help, of course," said Augurian, gravely. "I believe the search for this Litholt should take priority, don't you?"

"I agree, seeing that my freedom depends on settling this enchantment business," said Douglas.

"Then I'll begin at once," said the Water Adept, and with a nod to them all and an affectionate pat on the arm for his Apprentice, he disappeared.

"Then it's just a matter of waiting," sighed Marbleheart. "Why didn't you go with your Master, Myrn Manstar? No need for you to shiver here on the rocks."

"Oh, I would have, if I had my Magister's power to project myself back to Waterand. Not yet, anyway! Perhaps he won't take long to find our old Geomancer, now that he has a name and a memory to go on."

" 'Project'?" wondered the Otter, snuggling down between Myrn and Douglas under the furs. "What do you mean? Augurian wasn't really here in person . . . ?"

"Exactly," said Myrn, sleepily. "We saw but his image here. His body never left Waterand. It's similar to what Master Wong does when he's entranced."

While Marbleheart pondered this latest magical feat, the others settled down to sleep, to await the results of the Water Adept's search.

They were breaking their night-long fast when the Aquamancer appeared once again, bobbing up and down through the surface of the rock before he managed to find equilibrium once more. He looked even more weary and drawn than before, Myrn thought.

"I've found it!" he announced. "I know where Litholt is, right now."

"Catch your breath," Myrn ordered him, as a fond daughter might order a hardworking father.

"There are some problems, however," added Augurian,

after a pause to steady himself.

"Always are," grumbled Marbleheart, softening his words with a grin. "Nothing is ever simple and easy, is it?"

"Long before Last Battle in Old Kingdom," began Augurian, "the Wizard Litholt left Old Kingdom and the councils of our Fellowship and retired from active participation.

"We never knew, never had time to find out, where the Stone Wizard had gone . . . but now I know. A place called Serecomba . . ."

"Serecomba!" exclaimed Wong. "That's a great, terrible desert in the far south of Choin!"

"Correct!" said Augurian, nodding. "Do you know it well, then?"

"Hardly at all! It's regarded as impassable, totally without water or any living thing. A deadly desert."

"But is it so, Magician?" asked Douglas. "According to Flarman, no desert is ever completely deserted."

"I . . . I . . . I admit that I never set foot there or even questioned the facts when I learned them as a young man," the Choinese said. "I never had occasion to travel into Serecomba. No one lives there, as far as I know, so it held no interest."

"Yet it sounds like quite a perfect place to go and become a recluse, an eremite," observed the First Citizen. "If this Litholt wished to be left alone, that is."

"Evidently just what was desired," said Augurian. "The dark, stark, terrifying years of the War affected even us Wizards very strongly. As you well know, Serenit."

The former Ice King nodded solemnly and sadly. "I find that I have blocked out most of my own memories of that time. I don't even recall the name of Litholt."

"You must project yourself to this desert, then, and ask the Geomancer to come help us," Myrn said.

Augurian shook his head.

"That's the problem, my dear young Apprentice. I have tried and tried but I can get no answer. Litholt's not taking calls."

"Maybe the Wizard *is* dead," Marbleheart said, wringing his forepaws.

"No, someone has set up a live spell barring all interference from outside," said Augurian. "Similar to the spell shrouding *this* place, actually. No, someone will have to go in person to Serecomba."

"No problem, then," said Douglas. "I will go—if I can convince Detritus it's necessary in order to save his people."

"How will we go?" wondered Marbleheart. "By the Feather Pin?"

"Yes, if Myrn will take us," said his Master.

"Of course!" she cried. "I want to go. I've never been to Choin."

"I shall go, also," said Wong. "It is my country. And the tea leaves suggested there would be danger, as I recall."

Douglas warned him, "Your life will be in danger if your Emperor's advisers find you!"

"But who could better guide you? Not only is Serecomba a tremendously vast wasteland but Choin itself is huge beyond most men's comprehension. You might take years to cover it all, even by the wonderful Dwarfish Pin."

"Once we are on the desert, we can locate any Wizard by his aura of power, however faint it may have become," said Myrn. "Of course, the Feather Pin is the only way to fly."

"Douglas, yourself, and me, then," decided Wong, rising from his snug nest of furs. "We can drop Serenit off at his home. Augurian is not really here. The Dwarf Prince . . . ?"

"I shall go with you, if you can carry the additional load, Mistress Myrn," said Bryarmote. "You may need a strong right arm, and remember that I have great experience of deserted places."

They agreed, and Douglas called out to Detritus's hut. In a moment the Stones' Chief was standing beside the column, looking at them irritably yet hopefully.

"We're making good progress, Chief," Douglas told him, after introducing his companions.

"About time!" said the surly Stone. "When can we expect results?"

"First I must take a trip to find a certain Geomancer. Only a specialist can unravel your spell," Douglas explained. "When I come back, the actual disspelling will begin."

Detritus shook his massive head stubbornly.

"No! You have sworn to remain here until we are saved, Wizard Brightglade. The others may go where they please, but you must stay!"

"Be reasonable, please," tiny Wong blinked up at the giant. "Douglas must go, for it is his duty to assist you. Mistress Myrn must go, for she controls our means of swift travel. The Otter will go with his Master . . ."

"Even if he hates waterless deserts," muttered Marbleheart under his breath. "No water! No fish!"

" . . . and the Dwarf is sworn to protect the party by force of arms, if necessary. And it is to my country they go, so I must guide them."

"That leaves Serenit, and he is no longer a Wizard," sneered the Chief. "No! I will have to have at least one Wizard to hold as hostage, against your returning. I trust no one!"

They argued the matter for almost an hour, until at last Detritus turned to walk away in an angry, stiff-necked huff. "You *will* stay, Journeyman," he said finally. "Or at the very least, another Wizard!"

He disappeared into his hut.

A number of Stones had gathered to hear the discussion from a distance. They stood about the square, looking rather downcast.

"What's to do?" asked Marbleheart.

"Well, I'll just have to stay, I guess," said Douglas. "Myrn, my dear, you and Wong, with Bryarmote's help, can find this Litholt, I'm sure. I'll be fine here. I'll spend my time trying to trace Flarman."

Myrn shook her head firmly.

"No. I have a better way."

She unhooked the Feather Pin from her blouse deep

underneath her warm furs and, reaching over, quickly pinned it to Douglas's lapel. "I give you the Pin!"

"No, no!" he protested in surprise. "It's *your* Pin, given you by Dowager Princess Finesgold! Keep it!

"Too late," said Myrn with a laugh. "I've already given it to you, willingly and completely. Finesgold told me that, once given, it becomes the sole property of the recipient."

"That's certainly so," said Finesgold's son. "You have the Pin now, Douglas, like it or not!"

"Suppose I give it back, willingly and completely?" asked the Journeyman, ducking his chin to look at the golden feather.

"Won't work," said Bryarmote flatly.

"I'm very sorry you did this," said Douglas, taking Myrn's hand tenderly.

"I'm not," said she, giving him a quick kiss on the cheek. "It's yours now and, as I'm yours, too, in effect I still have it. Call it my engagement present to my husband-to-be! *That,* and the right to finish what you've started."

She taught him the magical phrase that activated the Pin— "*Cumulo nimbus*"—and the Journeyman recalled Detritus.

"I think you are being unreasonable, stubborn, stiff necked, hard jawed, and wrong headed," Douglas said to him sevcrely. "But we accept your compromise. The Wizard Manstar will stay in my place. She's not only a Water Adept, but my betrothed wife. You can be sure I will redeem her as quickly as possible."

Detritus for the first time looked pleased—and even a little ashamed of himself. He at once accepted the offer.

"She will be safe and comfortable here," he promised Douglas. "No harm will come to her that a whole tribe of Stone Warriors can prevent."

"Nothing to worry about in that regard. She is a Wizard's Apprentice, you must recall," said Wong, also quite severely, "and her powers are sufficient to protect her person, even from arctic storms, avalanches, and sudden eruptions of lava."

"However," added Bryarmote, glowering darkly, "be

warned that if anything untoward befalls our pretty Myrn, you will be held solely responsible, Chief Detritus, not only by the Wizards, but all my Dwarfs, and I suspect the Fairies, the Dragons, and all sorts of good Men, also!"

"I must do it, however," said the Chief with downcast eyes before the Dwarf's smoldering anger. "I am compelled by circumstances. But hurry back with this Geomancer person, and all will be set aright."

"We intend to," said the Journeyman briskly. "Bryarmote, stand on my left, and take Master Wong by his hand on the other side. Familiar, stand touching my leg, here. Serenit, take the Magician by his other hand."

When they were so arranged, Douglas bent and kissed his bride-to-be on her lips and said good-bye softly. Myrn hugged him reassuringly, hugged the Otter, and then each other member of the flight in turn.

"*Cumulo nimbus!*" whispered Douglas, getting it right the first time.

This strange flying company rose steeply into the snow-filled darkness and, with a final wave, shot off southward at a tremendous clip, making the air whistle with their passage.

"I'll stay with you for a while before I return my image to Waterand," declared Augurian. "I need to rest and recharge my Being from the exertions of projecting all this way against the pressure of Obsydion's spell, twice in one day."

"My poor Magister!" cried Myrn, fluffing the furs about his tall, thin frame. "Rest here as long as you like. I'll be happy for the company!"

"While we rest," said the Water Adept, drawing a heavy, deeply embossed leatherbound book from his left sleeve, "maybe we can use the time to study? You have your own advancement to Journeyman to think of, my child."

He held the book up for her to read its impressively long, gold-stamped title: *Studies in the Hydrographic Cycle Including Various Means to Utilize Its Great and Mysterious Powers without Changing Its Nature to the Detriment of Its Many Other Benefits.*

Myrn laughed, nodded, and groaned all at the same time, and Augurian began to lecture.

A worried score of Stone Warriors stood in stony silence, listening.

Chapter Nine

Choin

DESPITE his brave face on the matter, Douglas was unhappy to leave Myrn a hostage in Stony Gorge.

"She's capable of countering anything the Stones might do," Wong pointed out, sensing his distress, "and she can always leave, if she is seriously threatened. Detritus believes he has the strength to hold her against her will, but he's mistaken."

"Very true, I suppose," agreed the Journeyman. "But I know Myrn. She'll abide by our promise, if she possibly can. And I feel terrible about her giving up her Feather Pin."

"As she said," Marbleheart said with a sudden laugh, "when she gave the Pin to you, she kept it in the family."

"In that case," said Douglas, in mock asperity, "when we get back from this adventure, I'll give it to you!"

The Otter squawked in consternation and changed the subject.

"Here's New Land," he pointed down the long U-shaped glacial valley. They were just passing over the Face, and could feel the warm southern wind bounding up at them, bearing a heavy burden of swirling mist.

"If you need me," offered Serenit, who had borne the high-speed flight stoically but without much pleasure, "I'd be happy to tag along."

"You're needed here," Douglas told him. *In addition,* he didn't say aloud, *you're still under banishment. To allow you to cross the New Land borders would sit badly with the Beings who sentenced you.*

"At least let me offer you luncheon," said Serenit, secretly relieved his offer had been refused.

"Not a bad idea, that!" cried the ever-hungry Otter.

Douglas angled down into the flat-bottomed valley and landed on the veranda before Serenit's lodge, set pleasantly in a forest of young pines and cedars, overlooking a shallow but fast-rushing stream that flowed where once the glacier had piled up hundreds of feet thick.

They were met by Clangeon, much relieved to see them again, and shortly the capable steward had set a tasty meal before them: fresh-caught, broiled Sea bass, watercress salad, spicy crab-cakes, and excellent corn bread, all of which Marbleheart declared were superb.

While they ate they discussed the best course to follow next.

"Myrn said she doesn't know the top speed of the Pin," Douglas said in answer to a question from Bryarmote. "Beyond a certain speed it becomes difficult to breathe, she found. But she's never timed her flights very carefully."

"We flew from Wizards' High to Stony Gorge in less than fourteen hours' flying time," observed Wong. He plucked an ivory-beaded abacus from his right sleeve and began to calculate furiously.

"The distances between the High and Bee-Wing, which is the capital of Choin?" he muttered as he worked. "The distance from Bee-Wing to the edge of the Serecomba Desert? The time from the High to Serenit's house, here . . . ?"

He drew a chart with his chopstick on the rough plank tabletop, showing them the way he recommended they go.

"Here we are in New Land, you see? Ten hours at most to Wizards' High, for that was our time on the way north, less the time we spent in Dwelmland. Overnight at the High. Check with Bronze Owl for word from Flarman."

"Good idea!" said Bryarmote. "Owl can send word to Crystal that my trip has been extended. And I've got some useful tools, a sword or two and some stout chain-mail hidden behind the big fireplace at the High. They might come in handy."

"You have a cache of weapons at the High?" exclaimed the Journeyman Wizard. "It shouldn't surprise me. Flarman says there are things about his cottage and workshop caves even he doesn't know."

Bryarmote looked pleased and proud at the compliment.

"It'll take us at least three full days, I'm afraid, to fly over Sea from Dukedom to my poor homeland," Wong estimated. "Closer to four days, unless we can find ways to add to our speed. We should stop and call upon my good friend Captain Foggery on arrival."

"If you think we should take the time," Douglas said, sounding doubtful.

"We must, for Foggery has all my maps and charts hidden in his garden. I feared the Bureaucrats would ferret them out and steal them if I left them at my house. They are most accurate and, therefore, most valuable."

"Bureaucrats?" asked Marbleheart, finishing his third serving of crab cakes.

"I refer to the hereditary professional managers who actually rule our vast Choin Empire," Wong explained. "Their posts were once earned by competitive examinations. In those days, Choin had the best, the most efficient, most humane, most honest of all World's governments. But several hundred years ago they persuaded the Emperor to make their positions hereditary, passing from father to son."

"With what result?" Marbleheart wanted to know. His curiosity was only a little smaller than his appetite.

"The downfall of my wretched country! A certain Minister of Finance might be capable and honest enough, but his son or his grandson might be a thief—or even worse, a fool! The best clerks are released to make room for know-nothing nephews and cousins with neither ability nor training—and no tradition of devoted public service."

"I see the picture you're painting," said the Sea Otter, looking shocked. "Why have not the Choinese risen and changed the system back?"

"A very good question," sighed Wong, pushing back from the table and folding his napkin neatly into the shape of a flying bird. "You have to experience the cruel and overweening power of a hereditary Bureaucracy to understand. Any man not in some magnate's favor can be trampled into the dust, buried in procedural confusion, or even hanged on the Imperial gallows as an example to others."

"That's awful!" cried the Otter in dismay. "Will it change, ever?"

"I devoutly hope so," said the Choinese Magician, but said no more, for Douglas was signaling that it was time to depart for Wizard's High.

The cottage beneath the tall, treeless High, when they slanted down to it just at dusk, looked empty, forlorn, and lonely. The meadows were sere and yellow, and the trees, except for the hardy old willows along Crooked Brook, had already dropped their leaves as tribute to approaching autumn.

It was worrying that there would be no plump, cheery Fire Wizard waiting to greet them when they landed at the kitchen door. There was still no explanation of his strange disappearance—unless Owl had heard word.

"Nary a peep!" said Bronze Owl. "Augurian did send Deka the Wraith earlier today to say you were on your way here. Will you have supper and sleep here tonight, Douglas? I realize from what the Water Adept said that you're in a hurry to find this missing Geomancer."

"The rest would be worth the delay," replied a weary Douglas—he had gotten little sleep the night before. It seemed as if a week had passed since he had last closed his eyes.

At least Blue Teakettle's marvelous kitchen was brightly a-light and filled with cheer, warmth, welcome, and wafted cooking odors. Knives and Forks exuberantly chased tin-

kling silver Spoons three times about the great table before
falling into their proper places on either side of the more
sedate Dinner Plates.

Pots at home on the range clanged their lids together
like cymbals in time to the pure chiming of crystal Goblets
marching in place before Decanter, the somewhat haughty
Master of the Feast.

"Bean soup, weary sirs? Get it while it's hot!" cried
Tureen. Its Ladle performed miracles dipping the thick,
savory liquid into the waiting Soup Bowls without a precious
drop spilled.

"Such a lovely Ladle!" shouted Marbleheart in glee.
"And Blue Teakettle! Your dinners have kept us well fed
and happy in many a strange place, Blue dear, but none so
delightful as your very own kitchen. Pass the potato cakes,
please, and let me have the rest of those sausages, if you
don't want any more for yourselves."

Douglas was lifted from a bleak mood to good cheer
and ate everything on his plate before he excused himself,
yawning.

"We'll leave at dawn, sirs," he said to the Dwarf and the
Magician. The Otter was already fast asleep, curled into a
ball of soft fur on the stone hearth of Bryarmote's famous
Dwarf's Fireplace.

"Owl, I know you'd be happier going with us, but I still
think someone should be here, in case messages arrive and
need to be passed along."

He didn't even hear Owl's assurances he'd stay on duty
at the High. The Journeyman was asleep almost before he
collapsed into the middle of his down comforter.

The Thatchmouse Family peered down from their lofty
nest under the thick thatched roof and hushed their children.

"Let the Wizardling sleep," Mama Mouse whispered gently. "Poor Man-child! He didn't even pull off his boots!"

South of the High and a bit west the next morning, they
soared high over bustling Perthside on Farango Waters.
Douglas pointed out to his friends the house in which he'd

been born, and the shipways where his father, also named Douglas, built strong, fast sailing ships for Thornwood Duke's growing merchant fleet.

"Five keels laid down, I see!" counted Marbleheart. "Your father's a busy man!"

Once they'd passed over the southwest point of Dukedom and were well out to Sea, Douglas increased their airspeed to just below the point Myrn had warned of, where breath became hard to catch.

Once in the air it was no longer necessary for them to hold hands in order to fly together. Marbleheart dozed while Wong and Bryarmote chatted of the deep caverns and very old mines where the Choinese had once found rich deposits of jade, white gold, and diamonds.

Douglas kept his mind and eyes on their progress, trusting his old sense of direction once he'd determined their course toward the distant Choin coast.

Clouds swept by like full-rigged ships, laden with dignity and purpose. Occasionally the fliers passed between towering autumn thunderheads glittering with lightning, swollen with rain and hail falling onto the roiling surface of Sea far below.

Sea here was very deep and islands were scarce. Where they did break the surface they were little more than black, sharp rocks, the summits of submarine mountains, ringed with creamy white surf. They were good places for all manner of Seabirds to roost and nest at other times of the year, but in the last days of summer they were deserted and lonely.

They met a flock of Frigatebirds gliding on their immensely long, tapered wings, coasting down the wind and calling saucily to each other as they went.

"Hoy! Hey!" the birds shouted to the fliers. "Ahoy! There's Douglas of Brightglade, the shipwright's son, the Pyromancer's pupil. Ahoy!"

"How's the weather ahead," Marbleheart called as they passed. He knew the Frigates of old. They were World's best weather forecasters.

"Rain on the Choin coast, but quite warm and quite light. Warmer winds ahead, friend Sea Otter! It's still midsummer in Choin waters. We're going off Highlandorm way to find winter feeding grounds in Lasting Mists, where the grunnion will be running soon. We salute you, too, Honored Magician! Welcome back!"

"Have you ever flown over the Serecomba Desert?" asked Douglas, circling the flock of Frigates to keep from shooting on past.

"Never! Too far inland," the grizzled, old flight leader told him. "Some of them silly Skylarks go that far, and occasionally you'll meet a Robin Redbreast who has been there. Their sort don't mind the dry climate, but it's much too dry for us Seafarers."

"Well, thank you anyway," the Journeyman called, speeding south again.

"I'm not in favor of dry myself," observed Marbleheart, thoughtfully. "What kinds of beasts like to broil under a desert sun? I wonder."

"You'll find out shortly," chuckled Bryarmote.

"Lizards, of course," Wong answered the Otter's idle question. "Snakes, too. Many Dragons live in the endless empty places at the center of the Serecomba."

"I've met a few Dragons myself," said Douglas. "Rather haughty at first, but good hearted. Fiery tempered when roused, I found."

"They're sacred to our Empire," said Wong. "Not that anyone ever tries to harm or even go near to them. I've never met one myself, but I'd like to."

"I'm not at all sure I'd want to," said Marbleheart. "What would you talk of with a Dragon as big as a humpback whale with wings?"

"History, mostly," Wong told him. "Dragons live a great long time, being Near Immortals, and remember everything that ever happened since the Earliest Times and before even that, I'm told."

Chatting and dozing—even Bryarmote took a long nap in the afternoon, which was unusual for him—they sped on across the endless plain of Sea. They lunched on ham, cheese, and spicy sailor's sausage sandwiches on the wing without stopping, merely slowing down for comfort as they ate.

Ducking under a dark patch of rain, Douglas had them open their canteens to replenish their water supply. He and the Dwarf used the opportunity to take a shower bath, which refreshed and cooled them. Wong was too modest to remove any of his clothing in public.

"I'm getting stiff from being so still," complained the Otter.

"Let me show you some useful exercises," Wong offered. "My ancestors developed them for living in crowded cities where physical exercise was difficult."

For an hour or more they all stretched, bent, twisted, and swung their arms and legs. Passing birds, seeing them so, laughed aloud and called advice.

"Flap your wings!" they shouted in glee. "Wriggle your tails!"

By then they had all shed the heavy Northland cloaks and boots. The Magician, happy to do some little magic task, reduced the bulky New Land clothing to tiny bits of wool, fur, and leather and stowed them in his wide left sleeve.

Nightfall came suddenly, for these were subtropical waters where the sun plunged over the horizon with startling speed.

"We need an island where we can stop, have dinner in comfort, and stretch our legs," the Journeyman said to the others. "Keep an eye open for a suitable landing place, won't you?"

Marbleheart, with the sharpest eyes of them all, spotted an island long before anyone and guided Douglas down to a worn and rounded mid-Sea peak high above thundering surf.

They dined on chicken and dumplings, hot from Blue Teakettle's pot, and drank sparingly of new-brewed, nut brown Trunkety ale drawn from one of the huge casks

Flarman laid in each year from the cellars of the old Oak 'N' Bucket.

Douglas had intended to continue the trip immediately, but when his stomach was full, his will to move on weakened. He proposed they nap on solid ground until moonrise. A fat, waxing moon would light their way until a bit before dawn.

They slept. Marbleheart, who'd napped several times during the flight, explored the isolated pinnacle of rock he'd named Marbleheart Isle, quite immodestly, from top to bottom, looking for someone to talk to. He met no one, except thousands of silvery sardines schooling where the cliff plunged into the deeps, providing them shelter.

The little fish, assured the Otter wasn't hungry, talked lightheartedly of their life in mid-ocean. They asked the Otter for news from distant dry land, so he gave them a quick history lesson covering the last twelve or twenty years, from the rise of Frigeon Ice King to the death of Emaldar the Witch in the eruption of the volcano Blueye.

Being isolated in mid-ocean, the sardines had little news to tell in return. The Otter left them to their schoolwork and climbed back up the island summit to waken the travelers with fresh, hot coffee just as the moon rose from Sea.

"You have any idea how much farther we have to go?" the Dwarf Prince asked after they'd taken off.

Wong was squinting at the moon and measuring angles from the horizon to certain stars using his fingers and arms as an astrolabe. He consulted an enormous gold watch he pulled from beneath his broad, red silk sash, and again produced the ivory abacus. His tiny fingers flew in calculation.

"I learned celestial navigation from our friend Seacaptain Foggery. I calculate we've passed the halfway point," he said at last. "We have close to a thousand miles yet to go. If my mathematics have not entirely deserted me, we will fly half a thousand miles this day, unless we stop for some reason, and will fly most of tomorrow, again, before we reach the Choin coast."

"Well, I suppose it's faster than one of Thornwood's ships," said Douglas, "but it's not half so interesting."

He found that while he could easily maintain the speed of the first day, it was uncomfortable for him and his passengers, especially the Otter, who tended to suffer most from drying out in the wind. Douglas reduced his speed by a third and flew much lower, where the air was moister and warmer. There they encountered occasional rainsqualls to wet them down—much to the Otter's relief.

During the afternoon Douglas conducted class for his Familiar. Since returning from Old Kingdom in midsummer, he had little time to instruct the Otter in his duties and the lore he needed to serve a Wizard.

The Choinese Magician, who'd never adopted a Familiar for some reason, listened with great interest, occasionally contributing a comment or an anecdote.

Bryarmote, who had picked up a smattering of Magic here and there in his long life, also commented and demonstrated—his lore concerned mostly weapons and fighting or delving and locating precious metals or water underground.

Later everyone took turns napping, even Douglas, now completely at ease with this novel means of travel.

Another night at Sea. This time they dined and napped on a low-lying coral atoll, a ring of sandy islets barely above the waves, crowned by groves of tall, graceful coconut palms loaded with fruit.

Remembering the Great Sea Tortoise Oval, Douglas showed them how to crack the tough, fibrous nuts with one of the Dwarf's short swords. They shared the sweet meat and drank the refreshing, wholesome milk for their supper and again for breakfast.

They all took a morning swim, enjoying the rainbow-colored fish swarming in the glass-clear shallows. The Otter offered to catch a few for the frying pan, but had to agree with the others that the fish were too pretty to eat—especially as the Otter wasn't sure which were safe and which might be poisonous.

"Out of my element, really," he explained, and settled for a double armful of big, juicy clams that he discovered buried in the coral sand at the low water mark.

Their third night approached with storm clouds and winds that buffeted them about the sky—to Marbleheart's delight and the Dwarf's dismay. Just before full dark they saw a scattering of lights ahead and below.

"Land!" cried Douglas, glad the over-Sea portion of their flight was over.

"Not just lantern lights, either," observed Wong. "It's as if they built bonfires to greet us . . . but that's not possible, is it?"

"No, not for us," said Marbleheart grimly. "Those are buildings a-burning!"

Douglas circled warily over the great fires, keeping just within the lower fringe of the storm clouds.

"Can you make out what's going on?" he asked the sharp-eyed Otter.

"Yes and no," was Marbleheart's reply. "A number of houses burning dreadfully, I can see, and occasionally crowds of men rushing about, shouting and waving sticks and torches. You can just hear them from here."

"So I can," said Wong. "But I can't make out their words. I'm sure they are shouting in Choinese."

"Well, they *would* shout in Choinese here, wouldn't they?" asked the Dwarf. "Unless we've gone far astray. *Very* far astray!"

Wong asked Douglas to fly lower while he peered through a brass spyglass he drew from his right sleeve. They dropped with the falling rain beneath the scud of low clouds.

"Ha!" Wong exclaimed at last. "A palace fortress, there! I know where we are, now. My home is a bit farther east, away from the coast a few miles. Go east until you see a large seaport city on an almost landlocked bay. Then I'll direct you to Captain Foggery's house."

The Journeyman turned east along the coast.

■   ■   ■

"What a splendid surprise!" exclaimed the ancient Seacaptain when they dropped into his rain-washed garden and knocked at his door. "A wonderful relief, also! I was afraid you might be the Constables."

All was quiet in this neighborhood—*as a graveyard at midnight,* Marbleheart thought, remembering the silent barrows of Last Battlefield with a shudder. Wong had guided them swiftly and unerringly to the retired Westongue sailor's rambling wood-and-paper house not far from the port city of Choin Harbor.

"Has the Governor's Constabulary given you trouble?" asked Wong, worriedly. "What of the fires and men running about in the night, over to the west?"

"I know something about it," admitted Foggery, ushering them through a sliding door into his large, pleasant parlor, where they left their shoes by the door. "Perhaps the Governor's policemen have forgotten me in the confusion of the riots. Come in! I'll tell you all I can."

When they were seated on cushions and each had been brought a bowl of hot water, soap, and towels, followed by tea laced with mint, the old Sea Captain explained.

"The old Emperor is near death."

"Ah!" sighed Wong. "It is a mixture of good news and bad, then. He has been failing for some time."

"Yes. Of natural causes, we believe. He *is* quite elderly, as you know."

"But from what our friend Wong has told us," said Douglas, "the Emperor is merely a figurehead, not a powerful leader at all."

"So the Bureaucrats always believed," said Foggery. "Not true! The people of Choin insist that power flows from the Emperor. The succession, they are crying, must be directly from him. Unfortunately, there are a dozen or more men who claim direct descent!"

"And the Bureaucrats are divided, each wishing to name his own candidate, of course?" asked Wong softly.

"Yes, one who each thinks he can control," Foggery declared flatly. "That's bad enough! These days a number of our Bureaucrats have the military and police power to pull it off. The Ennobled Bureaucrats are actually fighting among themselves! That's what the fires are. Faction against faction, and the poor commoners are caught in the middle."

Wong rolled his eyes in horror and the others shook their heads in sympathy.

"Our own Governor was assassinated just a week past when he attempted to march his Guards and Constables to Bee-Wing. He was the Emperor's Great Grand Nephew, and had a valid claim to the Dragon Throne. There was bloody slaughter, I hear. A grandson of the Governor's wanted his Constable thugs for himself, to press his own claim. The grandson's force was victorious . . . but he himself was killed by one of his own officers, I hear!"

Douglas threw up his hands in dismay. "Is it that bad? Is there nobody to bring order to this bloody mess?"

"I don't know!" exclaimed Foggery. "I've been trying since you departed, Master Wong, to organize some sort of communication with my friends about the area. One friend, named Fong Wei—you know him?—was taken and thrown into prison by the Minister of Education. He cleverly trained a rice rat to carry messages out to us. That's how we heard that much. Fong Wei has since simply disappeared! I've sent my young men to find other Scholars and Sages, but they have all gone into hiding, I fear."

"Poor Fong!" said Wong, shaking his head slowly. "Can he be helped, do you think?"

"Nobody knows where he is," Foggery told him.

The retired Westonguer mentioned a dozen other names, but in most cases he admitted he had no news. Most appeared to be fugitives, running from this or that faction of Minister or Nobleman, hiding in farmer's hovels or in forests or open fields disguised as peasants, waiting for the storm to blow over.

"Eventually the Bureaucrats will sort it out, of course," said Wong. "They always have in the past, at the cost of much blood and gold."

"But if I recall," protested Foggery, "was it not Wong Tscha San, a Magician, Scholar, and Sage, who once said that in such a time the small farmers, the town merchants, and the villagers must organize to throw the Bureaucrats out and reinstate the Ancient and Honorable Ways—a Choin where a man's life had value and government meant justice, harmony, protection from criminals, and a fair share of the wealth each labored to produce."

Wong acknowledged the words as his own.

"And it was ever my worst fear that when a Time of Confusion came, we would be caught without a single leader all of us could agree to follow. Is it not now so, Seacaptain? Who could—who *would* lead the disenfranchised? Who will they follow?"

"You, for one," declared the Seacaptain, thrusting out a blunt forefinger at the Magician. "They will rally to Wong Tscha San."

"I *can't* do that. It wouldn't be good for the country at all," said Wong, sadly shaking his head. "White Wizards and Good Magicians are sternly and wisely warned against accepting or imposing political leadership."

"Yes, Flarman Flowerstalk says that good Wizards make the worst kings," Douglas agreed. "His most recent example was Frigeon, the Ice King, who was a Master Aeromancer."

"Wisdom from the Fire Master," agreed Wong, nodding. "Well . . ."

They heard a thundering like a great herd of cattle being driven past Foggery's front gate. Men and boys—even women—cried out to each other, clashed rice hooks, butchering knives, and scythes, filling the rainy darkness with roars of violence and fear.

Bryarmote hitched his Elvensword closer to hand and jumped up, while Douglas prepared a useful spell or two, just in case. The fur on Marbleheart's back stood on end and he bared his sharp teeth in a silent snarl.

But the crowd passed on and their tumult faded into the night.

"No telling what's going on out there," sighed Foggery.

"Someone who can lead? Someone everyone respects?" asked Wong. He looked piercingly at Foggery for a long moment.

"I am a foreigner myself," reminded the retired Captain. "Nobody would follow me."

"Perhaps not. But perhaps they would! Absolutely no one else is remotely qualified that I can think of," said the Magician sharply. "The prohibition of magickers against accepting crowns is a good one . . ."

"Unfortunately, it's a rule followed only by White Wizards and such," said Douglas, recalling his history lessons on the summertime lawn of the High, taught by Bronze Owl. "A teacher I know said once, 'The only thing necessary for evil to triumph is for good men to remain idle.' If we don't act soon, Wong, a wicked, selfish, unscrupulous trickster might put himself forth—and be successful!"

"True!" agreed the Choinese.

"We must help," Douglas declared.

"You, Douglas, have the important matter of the enchanted Stones to concern you, not to mention your Examination for Mastery, and your wedding," objected Wong.

"What's more important?" demanded the Journeyman Pyromancer, looking about at his friends. "The Examination can be put off, as can the Wedding. Even the Stones' disenchantment! Here, thousands of innocent people could die! I don't want that on my conscience, nor would Myrn. We must do what we can to help Choin!"

"No, no!" exclaimed Wong. "Consider the consequences, young Wizard, should you fail to break the Stones' spelling in a short time."

"Chief Detritus may try to harm Myrn," Marbleheart insisted. "He wouldn't be able to do it, of course. Myrn is already too powerful, if just an Apprentice. And she's sharp as a Sea Nettle! She'd easily save herself, if the

Stones should break their promise."

"But then, what?" asked Wong. "What would you expect Detritus and his Stone Warriors to do when their patience runs out? Sit at home and sulk?"

"Hardly," retorted Marbleheart. "I listened to them in council. To Detritus. He's aggressive and ambitious. He'd lead them out to do battle for their cause, sometime, somewhere."

"Exactly my reading of the Man and his people," agreed the Dwarf, sliding his short sword in and out of its scabbard. "They're warriors, after all!"

"And who would they attack?" asked Douglas.

"New Land!" cried the Dwarf instantly. "Destroy everything Serenit has accomplished, perhaps shock him back to his old wickedness in his disappointment and frustration."

"Our friends agree with me," said Wong to Douglas. "All sorts of bad things would follow. How would Tet, his Highlandormers, and their War Dogs stand against Stone Warriors in pitched battle? Or Thornwood's Dukedom, for that matter, especially without you or Flarman to advise them?"

"We're stuck in a dilemma, then," Douglas sighed. "What's to do?"

Wong lifted his hands again, this time in supplication.

"The Stones' problem should be simple, compared to quelling the unrest in all of Choin when the Emperor, poor old man, dies. I really believe we must pursue our goal in the Serecomba—the sooner the better. Find the Geomancer! Then we all can turn our full attention to Choin and the empty Dragon Throne."

Foggery was confused by their talk of Stones until Douglas told him the story from the beginning. When he was done, the Captain agreed with Wong.

"Get this Geo-whatever-it-is and take care of the enchantment first. We Choinese must fight our own battles, or they'll never be won. Oh, you Wizards can help, but someone here has to take the helm and set our course."

He stood and paced about the sparsely furnished sitting room, staring blindly at his collection of exquisite paintings of flowers, mountain landscapes, and bright-plumaged birds, and delicate jade sculptures in tiny, softly lighted wall niches.

He turned at last to Wong and said, "Well! You must help Master Douglas. In the meanwhile, I'll gather the core of an opposition party and get them to agree on a single candidate for Emperor—and fight for him, if need be."

"Good, my old friend! I will return to help my country as soon as we have the Stones disspelled, Douglas examined and confirmed in Mastery, and Myrn and he married. No later than the first the new year, say?"

"It'll have to do. Take some time for us few to organize even a small party of trusty men," said Foggery, and he drew himself up, looking decades younger than he had when he'd answered his door and admitted them to his house.

"I . . . guess I just needed someone to say it. This is my beloved adopted country, even though I still love Dukedom and Westongue of my youth. It's time I did something to repay Choin's hospitality and respect."

Wong applauded and shed tears of gratitude. The rest crowded around and vowed their assistance and advice, at least.

"You may use my name and Flarman's, too," said Douglas, quietly. "With Wong Tscha San's name, that might be enough to rally your party and give them the needed confidence."

Wong signaled a change of subject by asking Foggery to return his maps and charts of the Empire. They would plan the next phase of their search for the Geomancer.

Chapter Ten

Serecomba Search

"YOUR boy'll never come back for you, now he's escaped me," sneered Chief Detritus, pushing his enormous, craggy, stern face close to the Apprentice's as she sat on her pile of furs atop the Column.

"He will. Why do you doubt it? It's my word and his against yours, Chief of Stones. Time will tell!"

"It's your *life*, really," snorted the Stone, stepping back and looking off down the Gorge, where a fifty-foot-high geyser was roaring into the frosty air in billowing, bellowing clouds of steam. "If you fail us . . . If Wizard Douglas fails me, I am finished as Chief. That would be intolerable! The shame! To be toppled just when I have a chance to free my tribesmen from this Obsydion's spell! To have to slink along behind some other Chief who will undoubtedly build on my foundation!"

"Nonsense!" snapped Myrn angrily. "If something goes wrong, how can anyone blame you? You're what my mother calls a worry-wart, always looking on the dark side. Give my Douglas a chance! He can hardly have reached Choin yet! I guarantee he'll be back, and with your Geomancer, too, or some other way to disspell your people."

The giant stormed about the cobbled square, kicking three feet of soft, new snow high in the air and glowering at his worried villagers and at his hostage. The more he stomped, the angrier he got.

"I'll tell you this, missy," he shouted, "if your poor excuse for a Fire Wizard isn't back very soon, I'll teach him to throw us Stones over. I'll see to it he never finds *you*, his beloved, his betrothed! I may not be able to destroy you, Myrn Waterspiller, but I know places to hide you away, forever and a day!"

He plowed through the deep snowbanks at the side of the square and slammed into his hut.

His words sent a chill down Myrn's back, more from the tone he used—almost madness, she thought—than his words. She refused to let it show.

"Don't you dare test me, Stone Man!" she called after him, not shrilly but with calm authority. "I am Water Powered, an Adept, an Aquamancer! Pupil of Augurian of Waterand! In a contest between us, water wears away stone every time. You can be eroded, ground to pebbles, and split to splinters and shards! Beware of water, Detritus!"

And shame on me for such an outburst, she thought to herself. Lifting the book Augurian had sent for her to study, she drew several deep breaths and calmly resumed her reading where the Chief had interrupted with his tirade.

"Patience, Water Adept," came Augurian's voice from beside her. "His type of stone doesn't always stand up well under pressure."

"Magister!" exclaimed the Apprentice. "He got me to boil over a bit, as you heard."

"Understandable," said Augurian, wavering at her elbow. "He's a hard man; I saw that when I first met him."

"Have you any word from Choin?"

"Not yet. Owl sent word by Deka that the travelers came to Wizards' High three nights back and left the next morning. They should be somewhere in Choin by tonight or tomorrow. I've tried to follow them in the Crystal Pool, but there's a great deal of interference in the ether between us. Even Deka couldn't find her way across Sea in that direction."

"Oh, dear!" cried the girl.

"It happens now and then, of course. Have some patience, foster daughter! I'll keep trying and you'll be the first to know what I see and hear."

"I'm sorry, Magister! I know you'll do everything you can. The question here is, what shall I do if I have to run? I can't break through the shielding that Obsydion put around his spell. All I can do is head for home or for the High."

"If you can, you should stay close to Detritus and his warriors. In his anger, Detritus may attack the nearest Men, and that would be . . ."

"Of course, Serenit and his New Land settlers. Should we warn them of their danger?"

"It doesn't exist yet, but if it comes, Myrn, it must be you who warns them. Tell them to take ship and seek deep waters. They are a strong and self-sufficient group, but I don't think even they could stand long against these Stone Warriors in a fight."

"And then what?"

"Send for me. I'll see what we can do together to render them less harmful, despite Obsydion's magic. If I were to withdraw the warm south winds, for example . . . ?"

"I think I see, Magister. If we can't affect them directly with out magic, we may be able to affect their actions indirectly. Maybe slow their advance?"

"Think about how you could do it, Apprentice. That's what I had in mind," her Master said with a broad smile of confidence.

Myrn asked for word of the elder Pyromancer but Augurian had heard nothing new. They talked for a long while about her Apprentice's lessons and as the arctic dusk fell, Augurian's image departed, promising to see her the next day, if his work permitted.

Myrn adjusted the fire Douglas had left for her warmth and light, ate a lonely supper, and read until she felt sleepy enough to pull the furs about her and settle down to slumber. At least it had stopped snowing and blowing.

Darn it, Douglas! Here I am close to freezing my . . . and there you are where it's still summertime, hot and nice! Hurry back, not because I'm cold, but because I need you beside me, no matter what powers and magicks I learn to wield.

"The snow and ice of Stone Valley seem almost inviting just now," Douglas said to the Otter.

They were standing on a barren bluff overlooking an endless sea of drifted sand and broken stone ridges, the northern edge of the Serecomba. Behind them, the dry rolling hills were scantily clad in brittle grey-green shrubbery and cactus armed with wicked barbs.

Nothing, as far as the eye could see. A perfectly flat, treeless, plantless, grassless expanse all the way to the southern horizon. The sky had a harsh coppery hue. A steady, hot wind blew constantly, dry as sticks, hurling sharp bits of sand to irritate their faces and eyes.

The harsh sun seemed motionless, unrelenting, a giant kiln firing the landscape like a clay pot.

"Even with water a man, let alone an Otter, wouldn't last two days out there," Marbleheart said with utter distaste. "Ugh! Give me even a brackish stagnant swamp, rather than this."

"But there *is* a Wizard out there, I can tell," Douglas said. He took a sip from his canteen and stopped himself before he took a second. The water was blood warm and left a foul, metallic taste in his mouth, but the last source of water was a muddy pool ten miles behind them.

Nearer, Bryarmote was enlarging a shallow cave for an underground camp. They could hear his tough Elvensword cleaving the stone—and his thunderous Dwarf curses.

Even with his best Aquamancer-taught magic, Douglas knew the water from the pool would still taste of green slime and bitter salts. He planned to transport water from the well at the High that evening.

"I feel it, too," agreed the Otter, his nose raised to the hot wind, his eyes slitted against the glare. "There definitely is a Wizard out there. Fairly strong, don't you think?"

"But still a long way off," Douglas answered with a frown. "Something else, too. Do you catch it?"

"Yes, but I don't know what it can be."

"You've never met a dragon," his Master said. "That's dragon smell—maybe many dragons—you feel, young Otter! Remember it!"

"Desert scorch and dragon scent!" muttered Marbleheart, trying to spit but failing entirely. "Give me a sip of your water, Douglas, and tell me what we're going to do next."

While the animal carefully wet his mouth and tongue, Douglas said, "We'll fly out over the desert. It'll be cooler a mile or so up. Maybe several miles. Maybe five miles!"

"And from up that high maybe we can see how wide this desert is," agreed Marbleheart, handing the canteen back. "But will we be able to see a Wizard from that height?"

"I'm hoping that he isn't just sitting in the middle of the desert right on the sand. He must have some sort of shelter. Maybe even water. He must have a source of water."

"Maybe he imports it, as you're going to do. Soon, I hope! Before we're fairly broiled."

"Actually, that's one of the things I'll be looking for— magic used to import water, food, maybe clothing. We don't actually have to see the Wizard. Just his habitat and his aura."

"Habitat?" repeated the Familiar as they started back for the cave. "I guess I see what that means. Say! Why just bring water to drink? Why not send out for a block of ice from Serenit's glacier. He has plenty to spare."

"Now that, I say, is a splendid idea, old Familiar!" laughed Douglas, bending to pound his furry friend on the shoulder. "Inspired!"

"Only a Fire Wizard could find something to smile about in this place," grumbled Bryarmote as they approached. "What's up?"

"*We* will be—tomorrow morning," Marbleheart told him. "But before that, Douglas is going to bring some ice from New Land and some water from the Old Fairy Well at Wizards' High, and we're having sherbet for supper."

"The heat is getting to him, poor rodent," Wong, who was beginning to learn to tease, said gently. "I must admit that, without my chrysanthemum parasol and a fresh breeze from my lotus-flower fan, we'd be crazed, also. Whew!"

He was sitting in the deepest shade of a rock overhang in one of the last folds of the desert-edge hills, a gaily hand-painted silk parasol over his head, even so, and a flowered fan stirring the air near his left ear.

"He was good enough to let it blow on me while I toiled under the ground," said the Dwarf. "His 'whew' should be 'phew' for I stink like a Troll after only two hours' digging."

"Douglas's going to bring in some water, so we all can bathe," repeated Marbleheart. "Come, show us this hole you've bored."

The Dwarf Prince proudly led them down into comfortable quarters cut into a sandstone outcrop. He'd done it all with his Elvensword and a handy stone-cutting spell he'd learned, ages back, from a younger Flarman Flowerstalk.

"Originally intended to let you carve your way into fortresses and such," Bryarmote explained, "but just as good for making a tunnel in rocky ground."

Twenty feet beneath the desert, the air in the new-carved cavern was filled with fine rock dust but cooler by many degrees than the air outside—quite comfortable, indeed.

To make it even more so, the Dwarf had hewed a flat-floored living space with a raised fire platform under a narrow chimney, already drawing up a thin trail of smoke from a blaze on the hearth.

"I'm rather surprised it draws," said Douglas, craning his neck to look up the chimney. "I would expect a strong downdraft."

"Secret of the trade," the Dwarf responded with a grin. "When you have only a few magic tricks, you tend to keep them to yourself. My chimneys always draw well, as you should know."

He had just finished chopping three wide niches in the chamber walls, each serving as bedroom for himself, Wong, and Douglas. The Otter preferred to sleep near the hearth.

Douglas and Marbleheart admired his workmanship—the smooth, vertical walls, the gently rounded corner, and even the packed rock dust that formed the level floor.

Now, at the Fire Wizard's request, the Dwarf drew his sword again and, with a dozen well-placed, loud-clanging swings, excavated a large, square pit in the floor and a smaller, round one beside it, connecting them at the bottom with a channel.

Douglas sat on the cool floor and wove his best teleporting spell. The square pit immediately filled with a huge block of crystal-clear glacier ice, streaming cold vapors out across the cavern floor. The ice block was straight from the Face of Eternal Ice.

A moment later in a rush and a splash, several hundred gallons of sweet-smelling well water filled the round cistern and seeped into the space around the block of ice in the square one.

"Cool, clear water!" crooned the delighted Otter, and they each gulped a cup or two at once. "There will be plenty to drink and bathe and cook in for the rest of our stay."

"And how long will that stay be, I wonder, Sir Wizard?" asked Wong.

He spread his maps on a rock table while Douglas told them his plan to sweep the desert methodically in an attempt to locate the Geomancer's hideaway from the air.

"He is there, I know," said Wong. "I feel a strong Wizardly presence here."

"Do you feel the Dragons, too?" wondered Marbleheart.

"Is that what it is? Rather daunting, I must say. So that's what a Dragon feels like! Well, well! Maybe I'll meet one or two yet, Otter."

"I'll forgo that pleasure, if there's a choice. Anything that big and powerful should be avoided, I say!"

"Oh, but you've met whales, I know," reminded Douglas, beginning to set out supper near the ice pit, where the air was nice and cool. "And they're quite huge and very powerful."

"Not the same thing," the Otter insisted. "Why, whales are mammals, just like you and me! Dragons are . . . reptiles, aren't they? I steer clear of reptiles, when at all possible."

When the sun dropped behind the distant sand dunes, the air outside cooled rapidly, but the cavern retained its even temperature overnight. By dawn, when Marbleheart arose to check above ground, the glacier ice in the pit showed little sign of having melted. He took a long drink and splashed his face and feet generously before he went up to see what a desert morning would be like.

He was prepared to hate it, as he had the white-hot noontime and endless afternoon. To his surprise it was delightfully cool, dry, and still. The air was as clear as a bell and Otter eyes could see almost forever. But there wasn't much to see.

Did he catch a tiny bit of movement out over the flat floor of sand? A crow flying along? Hardly! Crows might be disrespectful and raucous, but they had more sense than to cross a baking wasteland like this.

A vulture? Bronze Owl had lectured him about the families of birds, and he recalled the metal bird's distasteful description of the habits of such necessary scavengers.

The speck disappeared before he could decide. His imagination told him it might have been a Dragon.

Chapter Eleven

Mountains in the Desert

THE Sea Otter laughed aloud when he considered how strange they must look, if there had been anyone or anything to see them.

He flew close beneath the Journeyman, keeping in the young man's shade as much as possible. The sun, even this high over the ground, burned down on them with steady ferocity.

Above him, Douglas glided along at a medium speed, his black-and-orange Wizard's gown hitched up to his knees to keep the skirts out of the way. His bare legs were beginning to get sunburned, Marbleheart noted.

He warned Douglas of the potential pain and trouble. For protection Douglas floated his cloak like an awning over them both.

A most strange sight, indeed, Marbleheart thought with a chuckle.

As far as his eyes could see they were the only moving objects in the desert landscape. No clouds scudded across the intense blue firmament. No birds—or dragons—flew over the desert floor. If there were small beings such as mice or insects living in or under the baking sand, Marbleheart couldn't see them from this height.

"Something as big as a Wizard, however," he remarked to Douglas, "I would see easily, even from this far up. Unless, like us, Litholt has gone to ground."

"It's something I've already thought about," conceded the Journeyman. "We may have to rely on our Wizard sense alone, if it comes to that. But right now I want to see if there is a castle or a fort, a hut or even a dugout cave somewhere out here, where Litholt might be living."

The "sense" of Wizardness was still there, but so scattered they couldn't home in on it. As the morning progressed, Douglas found it grew slowly stronger the further southwest they flew.

"Lithold came here for much the same reason Flarman retreated to Valley long ago, and Augurian fled to an island in Warm Seas," mused the Otter.

"Yes," Douglas lectured with a nod. "Cribblon also fled after Last Battle, but to the far west of Old Kay. And actually, Frigeon, too, settled as far as he could get from Old Kingdom when he built his Ice Palace. They all wished to escape the horror and fear of the terrible conflict."

"Then Lithold may not have hidden completely. Even Cribblon practiced a little magic for the benefit of his neighbors. And certainly Flarman and Augurian did, too. I mean, even if this Geomancer was horrified, terrorized, demented perhaps, stripped of most of his magic powers, it doesn't mean he'd completely disappear, forever and ever."

"According to Augurian," said Douglas, "Litholt fled some years before Last Battle. Maybe it was just too much for him, even that early. That it took marvelous, stupendous, reckless courage to even *think* of facing the Darkness, I can believe. You know what it was like facing the Barrow Wights, even three centuries later!"

Despite the heat, Marbleheart felt a chill, as he always did when he remembered his captivity under the burial mound beside Bloody Brook. With that kind of mindless fear, a man—or even an Otter—might do almost anything; none of it remotely sensible.

They flew on and on.

"High noon," observed the Journeyman, squinting at the sun. "With the sun directly overhead, we can't see anything at all. No shadows. What do you think we should do?"

Marbleheart shook his head. His eyes were burning from hours of staring down at glaringly white sand and an occasional bed of rock polished so highly by sand-bearing winds they reflected the sun's rays like mirrors.

And the mirages! The first time he had cried out in surprise and pure delight. *You guys were wrong! There's a lake here in the middle of the desert!*

But as they flew on, the lake receded and receded before them, until he had to admit that it was a trick of sun and shimmering heat. Most discouraging!

"Well, we have only three choices, as I see it," he answered at last. "Go back and cool off in Bryarmote's cave, or fly on and take a chance we'll miss something in the glare, or land and try to find a spot to rest until the sun moves down the sky enough to cast decent shadows."

"Going back is tempting, but I don't think we'll accomplish much if we do that every noontime. As Wong says, we could take years scouring the Serecomba like this, day by day."

They flew on for several minutes in silence.

"The least sensible thing to do is land and rest, have some lunch, maybe take a nap," thought Marbleheart aloud.

"Maybe the least sensible thing to do is the best thing to do, after all," Douglas responded. "To just go on is no good. Even a good-sized castle we might miss in this fierce light. Maybe if we look at the desert from ground level for a while . . ."

"Whatever you say," sighed the Otter, and Douglas let them down easily, swooping gracefully to the sand.

On the ground he pitched his handkerchief as a canopy for shade over them and brought cold water from the cave to drink and wash their hot faces. Once as comfortable as they could expect to be, they ate a light garden salad and some ice cream with strawberry sauce.

Under their canopy the temperature proved surprisingly comfortable. To step out of its shade, however, was to be pounded mercilessly by the sun's near-vertical rays. Douglas experimented with disks of blue-tinted glass and discovered that wearing them over their eyes as spectacles was a help in the glare, greatly improving their ability to see clearly and easing the strain on their eyes, also.

He fashioned a pair for the Otter and another for himself. Marbleheart exclaimed over them when they again lifted off to continue their search.

By now the sun had glided to an angle at which they could see low sand dunes and ripples, even the infrequent outcrops of sharp stone, by noting their shadows, not the stone or the dune itself.

"An hour more, then we head back," decided the Journeyman Wizard in late afternoon. "We could stay out here overnight, but I yearn greatly for the comfort of Bryarmote's cave and the taste and feel of the glacial ice water."

"Not nearly so much as I do," groaned Marbleheart hoarsely. "I am, after all, a water animal. I've an idea. To find where we left off when we come back tomorrow morning, we must mark the desert floor somehow. No use going over sand we've already looked at when we start out again."

"That's why I keep you as my Familiar," Douglas said. "You occasionally come up with a really bright idea."

They discussed how to mark a desert that was a million square miles of total sameness, and in the end used the most abundant material they had—sand. Skimming over the surface, Douglas created a gentle but insistent wind that swept the loose grains before it into a circular berm several feet high. He repeated the process four more times, linking the great circles together.

"There!" Douglas said as he finished. "We can see that from five miles up and fifty miles away, I should think."

With that, they mounted as high as they easily could, where the air was thin and quite cold—it felt good—and at top speed dashed back the way they had come.

The Magician and the Dwarf had spent the day in the cool of the cave, amusing themselves with alternate games of chess and gin rummy.

Twice more the young Wizard and his Familiar left before dawn, located their circular end-marks, and flew straight on, fairly slowly so as not to miss anything.

On the third morning it took them as long to reach the marks of the night before as it would to search.

They had yet to see a single sign of life, present or past, upon the desert floor. Yet the feeling of Wizardly presence was growing stronger each day. The Dragon smell seemed to fade away, however.

Now the far side of the desolation became visible—a range of blue mountains at the desert's far edge, serrate and tumbled against the horizon. In the clear air the range seemed only an hour's flight away, but all the third day they flew on without seeming to get closer.

"Are you sure the mountains are not an illusion, too? A super-size mirage?" the Otter asked, wearily.

"I'm sure they're not," said Douglas, who really wasn't all that sure, in fact.

"What next, once we reach the mountains?" asked the Otter at the end of that third day.

"I wonder? . . . I mean, Augurian's information was that the Geomancer was hiding 'in the midst of the great desert of Serecomba.' What if what we've crossed so far is only half the desert?"

"Ye Gods!" cried Marbleheart. "What are you suggesting, Wizard?"

"That these mountains are in the *middle* of the desert, not at its far side."

"I see, I think. You're saying that this Geomancer lives not on the sands but in the mountains, which are in the middle of the sand? Wow!"

"It makes sense, if you think of it," Douglas mused, "that a Wizard who derives power from earth, rock, and stone would prefer to settle in mountains rather than in a place where his resources are pretty scarce."

"I see! Yes, I think you're making sense. Which means either we are both crazed by the sun, or you've hit on the answer."

"A possible answer, anyway," said Douglas cautiously. "Worth checking out, at least."

"Not before tomorrow," his Familiar said quickly. "We can shoot over there at top speed in the cool of dawn and start fresh."

Douglas agreed, turning toward home. They flew in wearied silence for more than an hour before Douglas said, "What are you thinking?"

"About a drink of water, a cold bath, and supper, of course. Well, and that if I had a choice between mountains and desert, I'd live in mountains, too."

"Take us with you, then," said Wong when they had explained their new plan. "We're doing nothing useful here. We weary of waiting."

"I'm five rubbers ahead at gin," Bryarmote said to tease the older man.

"And I've cornered your King so often he must be considering abdication," shot back the Choinese gentleman. The two were getting on just fine, it seemed, despite the heat and boredom.

"No reason why not," agreed Douglas, much to their relief. "It'll mean establishing another camp."

"So be it," cried the Dwarf. "Something constructive to do, at any rate."

"And I may be able to help you search, if I can climb some of the peaks and look around. I have certain powers and spells that might help, under those circumstances," Wong added.

"I almost hate to leave our cozy cave, and our block of ice is not yet melted away," complained the Otter, half-seriously. "But it'd be pleasant to have two more creatures to talk to. Douglas and I are reduced to six or seven sentences a day, as it is."

■ ■ ■

The change in venue proved heartening to them all, weary as the searchers and the waiters alike had become. The most welcome thing they discovered when they arrived at the edge of the mountain range was that there were numerous springs of fresh, sweet-tasting water, and grass and even trees along deep-cut water courses.

Bryarmote picked a campsite halfway up a mountain not so tall as many others, but graced with springs and their runnels, green grass, and brush to break the visual monotony.

A natural cave, with few alterations, served as their new headquarters. While daytime was as hot as ever, the elevation made the nights quite cold. In the morning, their stream-fed pool had a delicate edging of ice crystals.

Marbleheart was enchanted with the tiny waterway. He could swim once more, roll and slide over worn, moss-slippery rocks, dive and splash, and roll to his heart's content.

Here also there were signs of animal life. That first evening Douglas took his old leather case from his right sleeve and, while the others watched with interest, removed two crystal vials, mixed very carefully a drop of clear green liquid from one and a pinch of white powder from the other, forming a tiny green-and-white bead, which he then dropped into the fire.

"Summoning Spell," Marbleheart explained from past experience to the Magician and the Dwarf. "I saw him do it twice in Old Kay."

"An interesting variation of a delightful old charm I often use to find lost objects," murmured Wong. "Yes, I can see how it has been cleverly altered to find guidance and information."

For what seemed a long time nothing happened, but just as Douglas was about to admit failure, they heard sharp, excited barking, and a long, low, iron-gray dog trotted up to the fire, sat hip-shot before them, and lolled out a long pink-and-black tongue, grinning at them in a friendly fashion.

"Someone called?" the dog inquired, cocking its head to one side.

"I called any nearby Fire friend," answered Douglas, hiding his surprise. "I am a Pyromancer, and my name is Douglas Brightglade."

"Pleased to meet you, Pyromancer Brightglade! Not many of your calling in these parts for many, many years, I'm afraid. Still, we Fire Dogs remember our duties to the Fire Wizards quite well."

"Fire Dogs!' exclaimed Marbleheart. "What's a Fire Dog?"

"Long ago we were cast from meteoric iron to control home fires. Some of us settled here in the Wyvern Hills when we lost our Wizards. But we remember our duties, still."

"I remember the Firefly in the Forest of Remembrance," said the Otter to his companions. "And the Fire Lizard in the canyon below the Great Falls of Bloody Brook. I suppose a Fire Dog shouldn't surprise me."

"Of course not," explained the Dog, tiring of sitting on its haunches and flopping onto its stomach before them, short legs tucked underneath its long body. "I was just going off to howl a bit at the new moon when I felt you calling, so I came by to see how I could help you, Pyromancer."

"And we thank you for your courtesy," Douglas said gravely. "You're a good Dog!"

"Thank you! Thank you! All dogs love to please, you know. Do you want me to support those lumps in your fire? It isn't burning as well as it might. Coal fires are more particular than wood ones."

Without waiting for an answer, the Fire Dog wriggled on his stomach under the larger chunks of soft coal Bryarmote had found on the mountainside and from which Douglas had made their fire.

At once the flames burned brighter and taller, gave off more heat and less smoke and smell. The Dog looked quite pleased with his effect.

"What's your name, I wonder," asked Wong, intrigued by the strange animal.

"I am Tongs," replied the Fire Dog. "My mother named me after a good friend who worked for a blacksmith on the far side of Serecomba. Smithing is only one of the things we Fire Dogs help at extremely well."

The travelers chatted with their visitor for a while, until Tongs reminded them he had been called for a purpose.

"We seek a Stone Wizard we believe lives in these mountains. Called Litholt," Douglas told him.

The Fire Dog's eyes lit up with interest.

"Ah, old Litholt! Yes, I've heard that name. Where? Well, that's a problem, I'm afraid."

His eyes took on a sad, hang-dog look so comical they all laughed. Tongs ran his tongue over his nose to hide an embarrassed grin.

"I wish I could help. I know I've met someone called Litholt a number of times, but I just can't remember where or anything about him!"

"The Geomancer's hiding spell again!" Wong guessed. "Litholt really must desire to be left alone! And like that of the other Earth Wizard, Obsydion, this magic making is very durable, very hard to crack!"

"I'm terribly upset," confessed Tongs, rolling over in the coals, sending up a fountain of sparks. "My duty is to help you, Wizard, but the—something—prevents me! I really wish I could tell you. I do! I do!"

Douglas soothed the iron animal as best he could. Shortly, as the fire died down, the Fire Dog fell asleep in the embers, sleek head on his paws.

"We almost had it!" Bryarmote said, shaking his head and beard in regret. "We've come so very close!"

"We've made great progress, really," Wong insisted. "But I am at a loss for what to suggest next. We can no more break the Fire Dog's amnesia than we could break Obsydion's spell on the poor old Stones, in the time we have."

"We at least know the Geomancer is somewhere nearby, probably in these very mountains," the irrepressible Marbleheart insisted. "That's something!"

"I think we concentrate on sensing the Wizard's aura, now that we know we're close," said the Journeyman as they crawled into their blankets.

"I can help you with that," said the Choinese Magician.

"You'll be a very important part of it, indeed," Douglas replied with a yawn. "Very important part, I promise you!"

"It relieves me to hear it, Douglas. I have felt quite useless so far on this adventure."

"You forget your charts and the maps and our introduction to Captain Foggery," said Bryarmote to his elderly friend. "But I know how you feel."

By then Douglas had snuggled down inside his blanket and resigned himself to slumber.

The Otter lay on guard in the cave mouth, watching the stars wheel overhead in the clear air. After a while he rose and laid several lumps of fresh coal on the embers next to the sleeping Fire Dog, to make the fire last until morning.

Tongs mumbled thanks in his sleep.

Chapter Twelve

Directions and Diversions

"NOW!" said Douglas after breakfast. "My idea is this: If I stand on *that* peak up there"—he pointed—"and you, Master Wong, stand atop the farthest peak over there, and we both concentrate and let our Wizard sense tell us in what direction lies our hidden Wizard's center of power and mark that direction carefully . . ."

"Where the two lines cross will be the Wizard!" cried Bryarmote. "I've used a similar method tunneling blind through rock."

"And sailors use such a way to locate themselves off a strange coastline by converging lines of sight," Marbleheart said. "If you get a strong enough signal, and mark it with care, it might just work."

"As there will be no active spelling involved, the Geomancer's magic shielding won't block our attempts. I hope!" added Wong. "Well, shall we try?"

"What can *I* do," asked Bryarmote. "I have no feel for this Wizard sensing, at all."

"Stay with me, Dwarf friend," the Magician invited, "to help me mark my sighting. Douglas will have the Otter help him."

Douglas flew them to the top of the farther peak.

"Snow!" exclaimed Marbleheart as they set down on this high vantage. "Who would have thought there'd be snow here so close to the desert!"

"Wait a moment, please," said Wong. "We'll need warm

clothing if we are to stand about up here for very long."

He removed the miniaturized Northland boots and coats from his sleeve, made them full sized once more, and quickly passed them out. The wind was blowing ever more strongly.

"We'd better hurry!" called Douglas as he and Marbleheart launched themselves into the air. "It's going to snow, I think. We have an hour, I would say, at the most."

The little Magician and the burly Dwarf waved their understanding and were shortly lost to sight as Douglas set his course for the tallest mountain on the eastern edge of the range to take his own bearings. The sun, looking rather pale and wan that morning, was just then clearing the mists from the horizon.

"Watch your step!" yelped the Otter, who'd jumped to the ground as soon as they arrived. "This wind is truly fierce and there's ice underfoot!"

Heeding his warning, Douglas firmly grasped a handhold as soon as he touched the icy summit, for the gale threatened to whip him away before he could find a safe place to stand.

"Give me a few moments to catch my breath—the view is truly breathtaking, isn't it?" puffed the Journeyman.

"I'll admire the view. *You* get yourself in position to point out the Wizard."

The Otter fell silent, crouching down flat against the thin covering of snow, waiting for Douglas to find his bearings.

"That way!" the Journeyman said soon after.

The "sensing" came to him like a low murmur, as if someone not far away were humming softly while he worked, not realizing anyone was listening. It was clear and quite strong, Douglas felt. He held his right arm outstretched, pointing.

Marbleheart hastily scraped a line in the snow crust with a forepaw, parallel to the young Wizard's upraised arm. He added an artistic arrow's point, to show which way it ran.

"How will you carry the direction back to compare it with Wong's?" he wondered aloud, scrambling back to where

Douglas was clinging to the mountaintop with both hands.

"It's simple navigation now," replied Douglas. He carefully drew from his sleeve a flat, metal circle made of brass. Marbleheart looked at it curiously. It was engraved about its rim with evenly spaced tick marks. Every fifth mark was longer and labeled with numbers that ran from 0 to 355 by fives, clockwise.

"It's called a protractor," Douglas explained. "We point the zero line directly toward the rising sun—which is due east, of course—and note which degree mark corresponds to the line pointing to our hidden Wizard."

He suited action to words and announced that the vector—another new word for the Otter—was exactly 170 degrees around the protractor from east.

"Now what?" his assistant wondered.

"Return to Wong and Bryarmote and see which way their line points," Douglas replied, and in a moment they were off again. "Remember the number, Familiar. One hundred and seventy degrees from east."

"Not soon forget it," said the Otter, but he recited "one hundred and seventy degrees" over and over to himself all the way back to Wong's peak.

They found the other two companions hunched close together behind a sheltering rock, out of the worst of the blowing snow. They could still see where Bryarmote had used his Elvensword to make a deep incision in the rock to indicate the direction of Wong's line of strongest "sense."

"Let's see from here," said Douglas. Wong and he struggled to the summit.

They knelt in the snow. The Familiar slithered here and there about them, trying to comprehend what they did. The Dwarf stood over them, sheltering them as best he could from the rising wind, ready to catch them if they should slip.

"You heard it best at one hundred fifty-seven degrees, I see," said the Journeyman. He scratched a diagram on the bare stone, using a sharp shard of rock as a scribe. He and Wong studied the result carefully.

"There are at least two higher peaks blocking our view," the Magician pointed out. "We must go aloft and look at it from more directly above."

"And quickly, for the snow is increasing and we'll soon lose your sun if we delay over long," Bryarmote warned.

"We'll freeze in this mountain air!" protested the Otter.

"Nonsense! No halfway fair Magician would come out without his warming spells. Let's go!" insisted Wong, who, for his age, had proved himself to be extremely hardy.

By the time the Journeyman and his Familiar had made their sightings from high above and returned everyone to the warmth of the cave, the weather had turned even colder. It was snowing heavily.

"Might as well have stayed with old Detritus," snorted the Otter.

"Unless this clears in an hour or so, we'll have to wait until tomorrow to find where our lines cross," Wong predicted.

"Well, we might as well make ourselves comfortable and cozy, build up the fire, maybe break out some hot buttered rum," suggested Bryarmote, who loved being snowbound as much as anybody. It would give him a chance to explore the cave, as well.

"I've never experienced this much snow in my whole long life," sighed Wong in some awe at the snow drifting about the cave entrance. "First in Stony Gorge, now here. Is it magic, do you think, Douglas? I can't detect any magicking in it."

"No, just plain, ordinary mountain weather," Douglas answered. He and the Dwarf went out to gather a fresh supply of coal chunks before the snow got too deep for easy walking.

The Fire Dog appeared through a veil of white snow and invited himself to the party.

"Not very often there is a fire to dog around these parts," he said with zest.

"You're most welcome!" said Marbleheart. "What's your

prediction of the weather, Tongs?"

"Oh, it's hard to tell," answered the cast-iron beast, carefully placing several lumps of coal just so on the hearth. "It could pass in an hour—or it could snow for a week. I'm no prognosticator."

"Well, I am," claimed Wong, and he dug several instruments and other curious items from his sleeves and began to cast a weather forecast while the Dwarf and the Otter set the supper table.

"Not before midnight will the snow cease, and then it will get intensely cold for a day or two," announced Wong, rather portentously. Then he laughed at his own tone. "Sorry! I'm so used to making a show of weather predicting to our rice farmers. They always like a little dramatic license with their weather."

"So, let's just settle in and enjoy the forced rest, the food, and the company," said Douglas, although he was more than a little disappointed. They all wished to find the Geomancer immediately and head for Stony Gorge, snow or not. But nothing could be done. Even strong Fire Magic could do little to turn aside an alpine storm of this intensity.

"If I tried anything it might just turn all to rain, and that might be even worse," Douglas decided. "A heavy rain on these slopes could be pretty destructive, I fear. Besides, it would undoubtedly alert Lithold to our close presence. He might choose to move away."

Marbleheart, with his sharpening magical skills, ordered up a feast of broiled steaks and plump baked potatoes, a crisp cob salad, bacon-flavored green beans, and chocolate layer cake. Meanwhile, Douglas sent for Deka the Wraith to carry messages detailing their progress to Augurian, Myrn, and Bronze Owl.

"The barrier I experienced here doesn't slow me when I have a known location at either end," explained the Wraith. She winked out with Douglas's messages and brought answers before they finished Blue Teakettle's scrumptious chocolate cake.

"Bronze Owl says he has nothing to report. No word from Flarman," the Otherworlder told them, sipping delicately from a cup of hot lemonade. "Augurian is concerned about Myrn. He knows that Detritus is, as he put it, 'chomping at the bit.' "

"It must be serious, when Augurian uses slang. What does Myrn say, though?" Douglas asked anxiously.

"Oh, the Lady Apprentice says not to worry. She has the situation well in hand."

The bridegroom clucked with concern.

"Mistress Myrn could handle seventy Stone giants and sew a fine seam at the same time," claimed Marbleheart, loyally.

"You're right!" admitted Douglas with a wry smile, "but somehow I can't help worrying about her."

"A normal part of being in love, I understand," Wong consoled him. "Not that I know much of love, mind you. I've never met a lady willing to share her house with crucibles and thuribles and such, not to mention the sometimes nose-twitching odors of magical dabbling."

"What? Never!" scoffed the Dwarf. "A handsome man like you, Master Wong? A good provider, too! I'd think the pretty and dainty Choinese maidens would trip over their own toes to catch your eye."

"Perhaps . . . at one time it was so," admitted the little Magician, actually blushing. "There *was* once a beautiful young poetess . . ."

Through the stormy evening and on into the night they sat about the slow coal fire, ate and drank and told stories until they fell asleep—all except the Fire Dog, who kept the fire going as the outside temperature plunged. He hardly slept, just rested from time to time among the comfortably glowing embers.

Myrn Manstar discovered to her surprise that Chief Detritus had an insatiable appetite for stories. The more magic and monsters, the better.

"Tell me again about the Beings who came to fight the Battle of Sea with you and Augurian, Flarman, and

Douglas," he all but begged, although he had obviously come intending to browbeat her once again.

"Not tonight, sir," she said, with an unfeigned yawn. "I must get my sleep. I still have a lot of studying to do if I am to pass to Journeyman before too terribly long."

"When can I come back and hear your story of the Destruction of the Ice Palace?" Detritus asked.

"Come for lunch tomorrow, if you please," she replied.

As he left the Column—he'd been standing in a freezing rain all that time, listening and exclaiming in wonder as she recounted the war against Frigeon—he asked, almost apologetically, "Do you think we'll hear from your Wizard soon?"

"I had a message from him this very afternoon," Myrn said, turning down the firelight so she could sleep. "He is—they are—within a few miles of the Geomancer Litholt, even now. Maybe tomorrow, or the next day at the latest they'll find him. You must practice greater patience, Detritus. Your people certainly are patient and long suffering. Why not you?"

"I am . . . responsible. I've promised them they would not much longer be hard, heavy, unliving rocks," he replied very slowly. "I must not disappoint them!"

He strode away through the downpour.

I have come to respect and even like the stubborn old rockhead, thought Myrn. *He's not as bad as he would like everyone, even himself, to think. It'll be more of a problem keeping him out of trouble of his own making than getting myself out of this gorge and back to my Douglas.*

She took a moment to jot these musings down, so that she would remember to give them to Deka, the next time the Wraith came with reports from the search party.

Then she slept.

"Strange request from an Aquamancer's Apprentice held hostage in a far land," Augurian said to Stormy, his Petrel Familiar. "Let me see! She wants me to send her *Tales of the Queen of Faerie* and a copy, if I can find it, of

Adventures of the Fair Young Maiden and perhaps *The Wonderful Wizard of Oz.* Now, there's a hard one! Where can one lay a hand on a copy of *that* classic?"

Stormy cocked his head to one side and squawked quizzically.

"*The Lord of the Rings*? Never heard of that one," Augurian went on. "Maybe Flarman has it in his library. He always did favor odd and little-known histories of that sort."

He gathered together the requested volumes, some ancient and worn, others gaudily printed and illustrated in color for the pampered children of wealthy men in far-off lands to stimulate their imaginations and teach them of the real World beyond their fathers' walls.

He slipped a note to Myrn under the flyleaf of the copy of *Maiden,* which happened to be on top of the pile.

"What Worldly use do you have for this sort of literature, if I may ask?" it read.

Back shortly came an answer, in Myrn's clear, careful, and feminine hand.

Dear My Magister,
  Thank you for the adventure and history books. As for my reasons, they are twofold. First, my captor, as he calls himself, Chief of Stones Detritus, is an absolute pushover for stories of Heroes, Fairies, Magicians, wicked Witches and all that sort of things. As long as I can keep him asking for—and as long as I can provide—such tales, he is tame as a library lion! He can't think of sending me away or hiding me under the Ice Cap, for then he would miss my stories.

The second reason should be more obvious. These poor people have been imprisoned in this Gorge for a thousand years! Think of all the history they've missed in ten centuries! I tell Detritus what I can of the past and I think he spends his evenings retelling it all to his people in the Meeting Hall.

I like to think they are learning a more civilized view of life, also. They have good souls within their stone-hard hearts but their World, long since passed away, was one of harsh cruelty, selfishness, war at the drop of an insult, and bloody fighting just to survive.

They find the ideas of keeping peace and working hard for the satisfaction of accomplishment totally foreign. They will soon be rejoining our World. Perhaps I can help show them attitudes that will serve them something better than their old ideals of bitter conquest, cruel barbarity, and bloody strife.

Thus the books. In the end, someone will have to teach them to read for themselves. Perhaps Flarman's Valley neighbors would lend them Schoolmaster Frackett, a former Wizard himself.

—Myrn, your Apprentice

Chapter Thirteen

Litholt's Dome

FROM high over the mountaintops Douglas peered down at a certain curious peak. It rose at the intersection of the two lines of Wizard power he and Wong had marked the previous morning.

Unlike the other peaks about it, this one alone was softly rounded, falling smoothly to a circular vale surrounded by the more angular peaks and rougher slopes.

It had no snowcap. About its base stood a forest of great trees, some perhaps fifty feet tall, with dark green or grey-green leaves in wide-spreading crowns. Where the sun's rays struck them, their leaves glistened a bright spectrum of colors.

"That's the Geomancer's home," he declared with certainty.

"There?" asked Marbleheart, who had come along for the ride. "I don't see any houses or castles or even caves."

"No, it's the whole mountain. See? The rounded one with the tall, dark trees."

"Ah, yes, now I see. That must be the place! Something strange about those trees, though. Do you catch it?"

Douglas circled the rock dome slowly.

"No, I don't see . . ."

"Their leaves don't blow in the wind. There's still a pretty strong wind and a pretty cold one, too. But see! The leaves don't move at all in the gale!"

Said Douglas, "We'll find out when we get down there."

He directed their course back to the cave to pick up the other members of the search party. An hour later the four of them stood on a mountain slope above the circular vale, staring at the remarkable dome opposite.

"Look for a gate or a door," Douglas suggested quietly. "There must be a way in."

"None that I can see from here," whispered Marbleheart. "No roads lead to this spot. No goat paths on its flanks, even. No cave openings. What do you think, Bryarmote?"

"Never seen a hill quite like it," the Dwarf admitted. "I think you're right, Douglas. It's hollow. I smell smoke, don't you?"

"Yes, I do," replied the Journeyman. "But I don't see where it's coming from."

Wong, perched on a ledge nearby, was slowly scanning the domed mountain with his wise old gray eyes, missing nothing.

"We must pass through the wood," he said. "These are not normal, usual trees, dear friends."

"I thought as much," said the Otter. "Yet . . . they don't seem menacing to me."

"We can tell better when we reach them," said the Choinese Magician. "The Wizard sense is very strong here, do you notice? I wonder that Litholt has not yet noticed our presence."

Said Bryarmote, "Well, come on! We'll never find the way in by standing out here."

They could have flown down, but Bryarmote preferred solid ground beneath his feet if anything dangerous should happen, and Douglas agreed. Wong, rather than clamber awkwardly down the scree-slippery slope to the edge of the trees, opened his parasol and, using it as a parachute, floated gracefully after them, three feet above the rough ground.

Marbleheart slid down a bank of new snow and splashed merrily into the brook in the bottom of the vale.

The great trees grew so close together it was difficult to find a way between their boles. There was no underbrush, either, only bare rock and gravel underfoot.

"If there *were* underbrush, I bet it would be thick and thorny," grumbled Marbleheart. "What is it about these trees, Master Wong?"

"I've discovered their secret already," Wong told him.

He laid his small hands on the nearest trunk and gazed up at its crown, forty or fifty feet above.

"Quite remarkable! Feel this," he said to the Otter, and when Marbleheart had pressed his forepaws to the bole, he started back in amazement.

"They're not wood at all. They're stone! Stone trees!"

Bryarmote and Douglas felt the trunks of several near-by trees.

"This one isn't stone, however," called the Dwarf. " 'Tis metal! Iron, I believe. Magnetic, at that!"

His steel dagger had leaped from its sheath and slammed with some force against the iron tree, stuck fast.

"Hmm," said Douglas to Wong. "That would explain . . ."

"Yes, the barrier to magic. Magnetism is very effective in throwing spells awry."

Bryarmote drew his Elvensword, which was made of some other metal than steel or iron, it seemed, and struck the trunk of one of the stone trees a terrible blow.

The tree and the blade rang like bells, and a shower of intense blue sparks flew every which way, falling to the damp ground where they glowed and hissed for several seconds before winking out. Other than that, the tree bole showed no sign of damage from the magic blade, nor was the blade marked.

"Well, maybe that'll tell the Wizard we're here," said Douglas, accepting the inevitable. "Did it dull your edge, Bryarmote?"

"Nothing, not even cast magnetite or carved stone can damage an Elvensword," said the Dwarf, returning the blade to its scabbard with some satisfaction and then wrenching his dagger from the iron tree's bark. He slid the dagger into his sheath and hooked it in place with a loop of leather.

"I ask myself," murmured Wong Tscha San, "why the trees are here at all?"

"They are quite beautiful in a hard and unyielding way," observed Marbleheart. "Certainly quite durable, they'd be."

"I imagine such creations would delight a Geomancer," agreed Douglas.

Bryarmote snorted in practical derision.

"Nonsense! I'm an expert on fortifications, excavations, and construction of all sorts, and I say these trees were placed here to screen the entrance to the Wizard's house."

"If that's so," said Wong, "we have but to pass through them to find Lithold's entrance."

For better than an hour they tried to find their way through the belt of close-set trunks. Each time they caught a glimpse of the cleared ground beyond, some circumstance forced them to take a different line, and they found themselves drawing further away from the mountain rather than closer.

"I recognize a Mazing Spell when I see it," said Douglas to Wong. "The Geomancer has enchanted the trees so they prevent anyone passing them, although the way seems easy."

"You're right, of course, Fire Wizard!" exclaimed Wong with a chuckle. "Do you know the Universal Mazing Solution? I'm sure Flarman taught it to you early in your training."

"Yes, I remember it," said Douglas, stopping to think. "Yes, I have it now. But that's so simple!"

"Mazing is a complex spell, worthy of our Geomancer," Wong said, stretching out his right hand. "It begs for a simple solution. Follow me, honored sirs!"

Douglas fell in line behind him. Bryarmote, wise in the ways of Magicians and Wizards, made no comment but got in line behind Douglas. Marbleheart, who was learning not to make hasty judgments where magic was concerned, brought up the rear.

Wong set his left hand on the nearest stone tree and walked about it to his right, slowly. Before he had gone half way around his hand was stopped by an adjacent tree, pressed so close against the first at this point that they could not pass between them.

Wong transferred his left hand to the new tree and, keeping it lightly brushing its iron bark, moved forward around the new bole.

By many ingenious means the great trees always passed the Magician's gentle hand from one bole to the next, in a twisted, convoluted path, often seeming to turn back on itself, but always leading to a brand-new way in the end.

Nobody spoke except in whispers—Marbleheart realized they had been doing so since arriving in this strange grove. If Wong lost touch, the Otter thought, they'd probably have to begin all over again.

"What's happening?" he whispered to Douglas, unable to contain his curiosity longer. "What is Wong doing, Master?"

"The Universal Solution—it'll solve any maze, anywhere, if you give it enough time. You put a hand on one wall and follow that wall without lifting your hand. Never fails! As long as you keep that same hand to the wall— tree-trunks, in this case—it'll eventually lead you to the center of the maze—or outside the maze if you started from the center. I've read of it many times, and even worked it out on paper, but I've never actually seen it done."

"Is it working?" the Otter asked.

"Hush!" said Bryarmote, who had built a few subterranean mazes in his day and was very interested to see if the solution really worked. "Don't take his mind off what he's doing."

"His hand, rather," corrected Marbleheart. "Well, I'll be hornswoggled!"

For they had rounded a particularly large ironwood trunk and walked out into the wide and neatly mowed lawn between the inner edge of the forest and the foot of the rock dome.

"Aha!" cried Douglas in delight. "You did it!"

"A clever way to disguise a maze," conceded Wong. He was quite pleased by their sincere compliments. "I must commend Litholt for its ingenuity when we at last meet him."

They walked some way around the dome, looking for an entrance both with their eyes and with the Wizards' sharp magic senses.

"This may be a tougher problem than just the maze of trees," said Wong, frowning. "There is certainly a way in, but there are many ways to hide a door."

"I know quite a few of them," claimed Bryarmote. "I've hidden some entrances, too, in my day."

He took the lead, stopping frequently to examine what seemed to the others to be plain, smooth rock faces, or tiny cracks or narrow clefts. No snow had fallen here, at least, which made the walking easy.

The air was chilled, but it was not the intense cold they had felt outside the ring of stone elms and ironwoods. Little sunlight penetrated the stone leaves, casting the clearing in a soothing twilight.

At noon they stopped to rest and eat roast beef sandwiches, radish roses, and carrot sticks.

"If the entrance is higher up the mountainside, I would think," said the Otter, "there would be steps or a ramp leading to it."

"Unless the Wizard always flies in and out the front door," said Bryarmote. He sounded discouraged.

"So close!" said Marbleheart. "So far, yet!"

"Don't give up so easily," Wong Tscha San said, patting the Otter on the back.

"It's not me! I just hate to see the Dwarf lose his confidence," said Marbleheart with a laugh. "He's beginning to turn bright red even now, you see."

Aside from a sip or two of Trunkety ale with his roast beef sandwich for lunch, Marbleheart had not drunk anything since he had gobbled a mouthful of new, clean snow early in the morning. He tried to ignore his thirst, but it grew and grew until he thought he heard it grumbling in his tummy, saying all manner of nasty things about his mouth being out of order.

The stream in the vale, of course, was outside the solid ring of trees. He had no desire to find his way back in by himself, even if he could find a way out.

"I'm going ahead to look for water," he said at last. "Catch up with me later."

"I was thinking the next step, now that we've just about circled the whole mountain," said Bryarmote, "is to circle it again by air, around and around, high and higher. Cover it all that way."

"Well," said Douglas doubtfully. "If that's what you suggest, I'll go along with it. Don't go too far off," he added to the Otter.

"I never get lost," claimed the beast, and he *gallumped* off ahead of the rest.

"He's a restless creature," Douglas reminded the Dwarf, who had plopped to the ground, angry with himself and the whole business.

"Let 'im go," growled Bryarmote. "I need to sit a quiet while and perhaps I can think of something. It makes sense that a main doorway be at ground level. Yet . . ."

"If you decide to fly," said the Journeyman, "just let me know."

Wong wandered off to examine an ironwood tree, wondering if they bore fruit and thus had seeds and how long they took to reach full size. Iron trees would be handy things to grow in Choin proper, where metals were extremely scarce and mining a monopoly of certain greedy Bureaucrats who charged prices so high common folk couldn't afford to buy them. Iron tools were extremely expensive as a result. Steel was almost as dear as silver.

Marbleheart, meanwhile following around the curved wall, cried out with satisfaction. From a nearly vertical crevice flowed a sprightly little stream, leaping in tiny waterfalls from ledge to ledge. At its foot it splashed merrily into a deep, clear pool.

First the Sea Otter took several long, refreshing gulps and then a joyful swim. The water was sweet and cold. He tried sliding off the lowest ledge into the pool, making a happy splash. He did this several times over again, then laid on the mossy brim to catch his breath and wait for the others to come along.

Only then did he realize, with a sudden start, that he'd made an important find.

"This pool drains back *into* the mountain," he said to himself. "It might provide us a way to get inside!"

He swam across the pool to inspect its outlet under the dome wall. The water flowed under a low arch perhaps four feet high in the middle and as black as the inside of a boot beyond.

He was tempted to explore on his own—he was completely unafraid of the dark, but he remembered the Barrows of Old Kingdom once again. He wasn't prepared to face a possibly irate and undoubtedly powerful Wizard alone.

He retraced his steps, surprised at how far he had come, and found Douglas napping on a soft bed of sunlit ferns under an overhanging bit of outcrop. Bryarmote busily scribbled in a notebook with a chewed stub of pencil, drawing up a list of known ways to hide doors and entrances. Wong was seated in a shaft of warm sunshine, his legs crossed and his hands folded in his lap, eyes closed, humming softly to himself.

"How's it go?" Marbleheart asked the Dwarf, hugging his secret for a moment longer.

"Blasted and beswizzled!" swore the Dwarf, throwing down his pencil and then stooping to retrieve it to return it to his jacket pocket, along with the notebook. "No ideas at all! Sorry for being such a grump!"

"I completely understand," soothed the Otter. "Did your list include hiding a door under a waterfall?"

"Oh, yes, I covered that possibility some time ago. But there are no waterfalls, here. No water at all . . ."

He stared hard at the sleek animal, still soaking wet from his swim.

"Where?"

"Just a way along," responded Marbleheart with a broad Otter grin. *"And the stream runs back into the rock!"*

"Hoy!" shouted the Dwarf, leaping to his feet. "Hey, fellows! Come on! This super Familiar has found us an entry."

Wong stirred at once and rose gracefully to his feet without touching the ground with his hands. Douglas rolled over on his right side, groaned at his stiffness, and blinked a moment before he climbed to his feet.

"A waterfall down the side of the dome," explained Marbleheart quickly. "Into a nice little pool that drains back *into the dome*! Come on! It'll get us into the innards of Litholt's Mountain."

Chapter Fourteen

A Most Surprising Kind of Wizard

THEY waded into Litholt's Mountain along the tiny burn, bent almost double—except for the Otter, who went on all fours or swam happily in the rippling current.

At first it was as dark as Marbleheart had said, and Douglas had to light their way with a flame floating in the air over his forehead. After a quarter mile straight into the rock, a dim, sourceless glow from the ceiling and walls made the flame unnecessary. The glow became brighter the farther they went. The tunnel ceiling rose to three times the Journeyman's six feet.

"No signs of habitation," commented the Otter, looking around curiously.

"You wouldn't expect signs of life in an aqueduct, would you?" snorted Bryarmote. "Which is what this obviously is. Besides, you're wrong. This tunnel may be natural, but there're touches of good hardrock chiseling here and there."

He pointed to a high water mark well above his head on the tunnel side. "Just as well it's not spring," he observed. "With the snowmelt, the water must get pretty deep through here."

They found their way easily down a shallow cascade and around a catch basin below. The stream disappeared into a narrow cleft in the rock, too narrow for even the Otter to follow. To one side of the catchment was a landing, however, and a steep, narrow rock-hewn stair mounted upward to and through a hole in the ceiling.

They climbed through several levels where passages branched right and left. Douglas led them upward.

"How can you be sure this is the right way?" asked Wong.

"The Feather Pin," Douglas explained. "It guides its wearer through underground places. It served us well when Myrn rescued me from the erupting Blueye, you'll recall."

"I recall," said the Magician. "Do you sense, as I do, we are very close to our Wizard? The emanation is remarkably powerful. Twice what I would normally expect, actually."

They came to an iron grille that blocked the stair before them.

Said Bryarmote, "Here, my blade will hack it down in no time!"

"Wait," Douglas urged. "Don't damage the Wizard's property, if you can help it. You yourself taught me lock picking—something every Wizard should know, you said. Let me see if I can get it open."

He examined the grille carefully. It was set right into the rock on top and sides, without a handle or visible hinges or lock mechanism.

"On the other hand . . . ," he started to say to Bryarmote.

There was a startlingly loud *clang* behind them. A second grille dropped heavily into place, trapping them on the steps between the two gates.

"*Now* can I smash it?" yelled Bryarmote, whipping out his bright Elvensword.

"I guess you'd better," replied Douglas, skipping nimbly out of the Dwarf's way.

"*Hist!* Listen!" whispered Marbleheart as Bryarmote raised the sword. "Someone's coming!"

"A Wizard cometh," warned Wong.

"Wrong, Wong! *Two* Wizards!" said a familiar voice.

Flarman Flowerstalk pressed his round, smiling face against the other side of the grille.

"I was right to let them in, you see," the older Pyromancer said to a figure standing in the shadows behind him. "They're old friends! In fact, this one was once my Apprentice, and is about to become a full Master Pyromancer, if he can pass the Examination!"

"Magister!" cried Douglas. "What in World are you doing here?"

"I have the seniority over you, Journeyman, so I get to ask questions first," Flarman said, and laughed, his usual jolly self. "Let me introduce my long-lost friend and fellow Master Wizard, Litholt Stonebreaker. Litholt, this is Douglas Brightglade, of whom I've told you quite a little. With him is the famous Choin Magician, Wong Tscha San, and the fierce-looking Dwarf—who was about to slice up your fancy grillwork with his Elvensword—is Bryarmote, Prince of Dwelmland. And there is Douglas's Familiar, of course, Marbleheart, Sea Otter of the Briney."

He stepped aside to allow the stranger to greet his friends.

All four gasped in unison and utter surprise.

The long-missing Geomancer was—a Lady!

"There is quite a bit to sort out and set straight here, I can see," Litholt Stonebreaker said pleasantly after she had raised the grille to allow them to enter her home. "I'm so pleased to meet you, every one! I feel as though I know you all, from Flarman's tales."

She led them into a large, tall, rather ornately luxurious yet quite comfortable home under the top of the dome. In a great sitting room as filled with heavily carved furniture, bric-a-brac, scientific curiosities, mementos, souvenirs, and strange artifacts as Flarman's study at Wizards' High, she served brisk Choin tea from an ancient teapot.

It was painted with intertwined dragons in red and black and gold, which hissed good-naturedly at them as she poured.

"Flarman never once told me that there was another *Lady* Wizard in World, ma'am," Douglas told her. "Forgive me for being quite . . . flabbergasted."

"Nothing to forgive, young Journeyman!" Litholt smiled graciously, patting him on the arm. "Flarman was but honoring a long-ago request I made of him and of the other Wizards of our Fellowship. That was over three hundred years ago."

"Before Last Battle, then," said Marbleheart, showing off his knowledge of World history.

"Yes," Litholt sighed sadly. "I was the youngest member of the Fellowship."

"As far as I'm concerned, you're still young and still a member, dear Litholt," said Flarman, contently lighting his pipe with a blazing forefinger.

"Even though I deserted the cause just when things were getting really dangerous?" the Lady Geomancer asked, turning to the Fire Master.

She was a strikingly handsome woman, somewhat angular, but well proportioned, for all of that. There was nothing soft nor gently curved about her, not in the way that Douglas found so wonderful in Myrn Manstar. Her hair was the color of darkened amber, and her eyes jade green. Her demeanor was dignified yet warm; her smile was quick, kind, and merrier as she came to know her visitors better.

She gently stroked the deep, soft fur of Marbleheart's shoulders and neck—he would have purred if he'd been a cat—saying as she did so, "I had a beloved Familiar myself once. A Golden Cockerel."

"I remember brave Aurelius," said Flarman softly.

"It was his cruel, most horrible destruction by the Darkness"—the Lady Wizard shuddered in revulsion at the memory—"that caused me to leave the Fellowship when I did. Most of my powers were stripped away by my grief. I would have been a hindrance, not a help, in the terrible battles we knew were coming—Flarman, Augurian, Frigeon, and I."

"You don't have to explain further, madam," said Wong, bowing to her deeply. "I myself failed to be present at the War against the Darkness. I was only a half-trained Magician's Assistant when it began."

"Well, there's certainly a lot to tell, as I said." Litholt, straightening her shoulders, shook off her remembered grief and reached for her teacup. "Where shall we begin?"

■   ■   ■

Flarman pointed at his Journeyman to begin the tale.

In as few words as he could manage, Douglas told of the statue in Eternal Ice, and the thrall under which the Stone Warriors had been held for ten centuries.

"Go on to the end, before we stop you to question and explain or make comments," Flarman urged, waving his pipe.

Douglas did so, briefly telling of their visit with Captain Foggery and their search of the Serecomba for the mysterious Geomancer. Litholt and Flarman sat forward in riveted interest, but said nothing until the Journeyman had related how they at last located Litholt's Mountain.

"It's my fault," said Litholt. "I forgot to lower my defenses. But Flarman and I were unaware of the other events and of your coming to find me."

"My presence here is unconnected with your adventure," Flarman explained. "Shall I tell it, my dear, or shall you?"

"I want you to tell it, Flarman Flowerstalk—did I tell you how much more I like your new surname? Please go on! I shall interrupt from time to time, as is a woman's due."

Flarman knocked the cold dottle from his pipe bowl into a fieldstone fireplace and turned to face the others.

"When I glanced into my teacup no one was further from my mind than Litholt Stonebreaker. Imagine my shock, after more than three hundred and twenty years, to discover her message there!

"I was so surprised, and her message was so unexpected, that I rushed off without even packing a toothbrush. And without telling anyone where I was going. That was quite inexcusable, I know. I must have caused you some worry."

"Especially as Douglas disappeared at almost the same moment," Bryarmote agreed. "We—Augurian, Myrn, Wong, Owl, and I—were sure the two events were connected."

"I kept looking for you to come zipping along to share the

new adventure," Douglas said. He added, a little ashamed to say it, "I'm sure Myrn feels the same way about me, just now, stuck on that bare column in the Northlands with winter coming on!"

"We'll see that she's relieved sooner than soon," promised Litholt.

"To go on, if I may," said Flarman, "the message said our old friend realized she could no longer hide from her responsibilities. She called on me to enlighten and then assist her return to World. We would have come to Wizards' High before now, but for a turbulence in the magical ether between here and there. You may have noticed it yourself, Douglas my boy."

"Deka told me of it, actually," the Journeyman admitted. "It didn't seem to affect the working of the Feather Pin we used to come here."

"Well, I know something of that, for Finesgold asked me to redesign the Pin ages ago," Flarman said, nodding his head emphatically. "It was made originally by Cloud Fairies, you see, and their magic would be virtually unaffected by any worldly phenomena."

"I don't blame you for delaying your departure from here!" said Wong. "I have come to the conclusion that the disturbance you—we all—felt arises from the pain and confusion of recent events in Choin."

"We must hear of that, too," said Litholt. "Choin is my adopted land. The stability of her government was what attracted me to Choin centuries ago. I'm distraught that I was unaware of the fighting affecting the poor Choinese now, Master Wong! Yes, that would explain the trouble even Deka had penetrating the area."

Flarman continued, "When I arrived here Litholt told me she had begun to hear whispers of hints of fears of civil war in Choin. But we thought no more of it, thinking we would hear further details as time went by."

"I've been watching Choin all the years I've lived here," explained Litholt. "I couldn't do much, of course, because of the Prohibition. I certainly regret that now, because I saw the great Empire beginning to crumble and slump. I heard of the dishonesty, the greed, the cruel selfishness of some of its leaders, especially the Imperial Bureaucrats. I saw the people allowing it to happen, which was even sadder. You know better than I, Wong Tscha San, how it has been."

The Magician bowed deeply to the Lady Wizard.

"When Litholt learned, some days ago," Flarman said, "that the Emperor was on his deathbed, beyond all medical or magical help, she decided it was time to return to an active life in World. I'm flattered to say she first sent for me."

"I didn't know Augurian's whereabouts, and I would have sent for you, also, Wong Tscha San, if I'd known where you were. My rather tenuous contacts said you had fled—and who could blame you? Flarman tells me you were with him, even as I sent the tea-leaves message."

"Truly honored madam! If I hadn't taken a long and delightful walk in the springtime fields of Valley that morning, I would have been by Flarman's side when he read your message in the tea leaves."

"I agreed that we must do something to stabilize Choin," Flarman went on. "Do you realize how many good people are bound to be badly hurt, starved, even killed, if a war between Bureaucrats begins in earnest?"

"You must also remember our constant, ages-old concern," added the Geomancer, "that remnants of the Darkness still in hiding on the very top of World might take advantage of such a chaotic situation to rebuild their power. Especially if it could gain domination over so important a part of World as the Choin Empire."

"While the Emperor yet lives, Choin's troubles are a matter of mobs and riots," Flarman nodded in agreement with her words. "An occasional burning, perhaps. An unfortunate murder. But once the Dragon Throne is empty and no one with sense, integrity, and a clear vision of Choin's future standing by to fill it, the Bureaucrats will be at each other's throats in earnest! The worst sort of war will rage all over this vast land. Brother against brother, and neighbor against neighbor! Peasant against merchant against scholar, and so on!"

"What shall we do, then?" asked the Magician of Choin. "Or, rather, what *will* we do, for I am at your service, Wizards."

"Thank you, Master Wong," smiled Flarman. "Mistress Litholt and I have been consulting and trying to get a handle on the complications of Choin politics. First, I had to bring her up to date on recent history, of course."

"My self-imposed exile was much too long," sighed the Geomancer. "I didn't even know who won Last Battle, although I might have guessed."

"We have advanced to the questions: Whom, if anyone, to support? Whom to nudge a little? Whom to suppress, ever so gently, so that a worthy and capable Emperor-candidate can be found? Who can that man or woman be? With you here, Wong, perhaps we can begin to sort it out."

"It sounds like we've been fencing the winds," put in Litholt, "but the unfortunate fact is, our hands are tied until the old Emperor actually passes away. I wish it were elsewise, but . . ."

"We're agreed, without my even asking the others, that Choin deserves and shall have our help," said Douglas stoutly. "If you can give me the key to disspelling the Stones, I can retrieve my bride-to-be, pick up Augurian, and we can give our full attention to matters here."

"Of course, the Stones' disenchantment must come first, by all means," insisted the Lady Wizard.

"And I agree. Both the Master's Examination and the Winter Solstice Wedding are of utmost importance to World and to all us Wizards, not just to Myrn and Douglas," said Flarman.

"Douglas," said Litholt slowly, "I cannot quickly teach you the disspelling. I'll go with you to this place of the Stones' long imprisonment. The spell, from what I've learned from you, isn't going to be difficult for me to smash, but certainly it cannot be effected from this great a distance."

"But you can do it?" asked Marbleheart eagerly. He was greatly impressed with this wise woman who knew the difference between "effect" and "affect."

"No doubt about it! I've studied for years and years the wicked enchantments wrought by Obsydion Grindstone. Although he was long gone when I was born, when I chose Geomancy for my craft, I willingly accepted responsibility for seeking out and reversing his many wickednesses. In fact, I have devoted my last three hundred years, here under my mountain dome, to just that work."

"Obsydion made Frigeon look like a rank amateur," claimed Flarman. "For one thing, he lived a considerably longer time. He was one of the very first of all the Great Wizards."

"I suspected that from what the Stones said," said Douglas.

"Well, someone tell me what is to be done now," pleaded Marbleheart. "I think there's been altogether too much talk and not enough action."

"I'll agree with my whole heart to that!" cried Bryarmote. "Find me a battle to fight. I'm ready!"

Douglas summoned Deka the Wraith and sent messages to Myrn, Owl, and Augurian. To his beloved Apprentice Aquamancer he said, among other private words:

We're on our way, as soon as we get some sleep and Mistress Litholt gathers together the spells she'll need to take care of the Stones. We must stop and confer with Foggery on our way past, Flarman says, but that shouldn't take long. We'll go by Feather Pin, as Flarman's Teleporting Spell is worn thin by his coming here, and Litholt's is dangerously uncertain through lack of use.

They arrived at Foggery's pleasant seaside house in a rush of wind, a thudding hail of hand-sized stones, and a flashing cloud of red-painted, black-fletched arrows.

The Seacaptain's house was under attack by a troop of soldiers in red-lacquered leather greaves, breastplates, and helmets. They were bombarding Foggery's thick outer wall and tiled roof with three stone-throwing machines.

"Good of you to drop by!" the elderly Seacaptain said, grinning despite a bloody bandage over his left ear. "As soon as we drive off the Minister of Finance's bullies, we'll have tea and talk politics."

"Leave the nasty ballistae to me," cried Litholt. "Stones have plenty of good uses, but throwing them at people's houses is just not one of them!"

With surprising agility for a woman of her age and dignity she climbed to the top of the wall, disregarding another shower of arrows, and raised her arms dramatically above her head, chanting a strange string of harsh words that not even the other Wizards present quite understood.

Stones already in midflight completely missed their targets, shooting instead straight into the evening sky a hundred, two hundred feet in the air. As tiny black specks they curved gracefully back on their trajectories and came screaming in vengeance down on the very machines that had launched them.

The shrill war cries of the soldiers turned to screams of fear and pain. Jagged wood splinters from the heavy machines flew like spears. Rock missiles shattered on impact, shards ricocheting about the scene like a swarm of deadly hornets.

In a single blow every ballistae had been reduced to useless kindling. The lacquered attackers fled in wild panic, throwing down their pikes and powerful, recurved bows to make flight faster.

"Gather up those bows and arrows," Foggery ordered his orange-robed young men. "There'll be use for them later, I'm afraid."

"Why so?" asked Wong. He introduced Flarman and Litholt. Douglas and Bryarmote went off to inspect the damage done to Foggery's stout villa.

"You haven't heard the news? It came from Bee-Wing this noontide. The Emperor is dead!"

"I'm really very sorry to hear it," said Litholt, "although he was a poor excuse for an Emperor in a land once famous for its great rulers."

"Was death from natural causes?" asked Flarman. "Or . . ."

"I doubt even the most ambitious Minister would have dared hasten his death by even a few hours," Foggery replied.

He led them through a gaping hole where once his sliding sitting-room door had stood. A group of Choinese maidens in the orange of Foggery's livery were already busy removing the debris of destruction wrought by direct hits.

"That can wait, ladies," called the Seacaptain. "Tea for our guests, and supper soon after—if there's anything left of my galley."

By the time Douglas and the Dwarf returned, reporting no serious damage to the wall and roof, and no one badly hurt, there were hot tea, sugared cakes, and salted almonds glazed with honey awaiting them.

The orange-robed men, having collected and stored away all the arms dropped by the fleeing soldiers, set about at once repairing the paper wall and sliding door, working swiftly, skillfully, and silently so as not to disturb their revered Seacaptain and his guests.

"Serious fighting began even as the word spread," Foggery said, shaking his head. "As we feared it would, good Masters. I knew the Minister of Finance was anxious to stop my newborn Peasants' Grange and the Artisans' Guild, but it came as a surprise that they struck at me so soon and in such force."

"I'm sorry we didn't arrive a little sooner, Captain," said Litholt, greatly upset by the beautiful Choin art objects and ceramics that lay smashed on the floor.

"Thank you kindly, Mistress, but even I didn't know they were coming or for what purpose."

"And what was their purpose, can you guess?" asked Wong, who was seated comfortably cross-legged on the floor while the others chose low stools.

"They shouted 'Death to the foreign dog,' or words to that effect, I'm told," said Foggery, sadly. Then his face brightened.

"I've been urging various groups to resist the cruelties of the leading Bureaucrats all about our countryside. Response has been astounding," he added, glowing with enthusiasm. "We've already set up a Civil Guard to protect our towns and roads against the illegal private soldiery or to warn victims to flee, at the least. One such patrol sent word to me just in time to bolt my gates and be on guard this morning."

"Lucky for you those raiders didn't have sense enough to use fire, rather than arrows and stones," said Bryarmote.

"It wouldn't have done them any good," said Douglas. "When I saw the paper walls on our first visit, I wove a Fire-Prevention Spell all about here."

"I have you to thank, then, Douglas Brightglade! That explains why they bothered to haul up their precious artillery," said Foggery, nodding his approval.

Flarman, who'd been absentmindedly shooing shards of delicate pottery together and encouraging them to mend themselves, said, "I see you were wounded, Captain Foggery!"

"Just a scratch," protested the Seaman, but he allowed Litholt to undo the makeshift bandage about his left ear to examine the gash made by a flying rock. She quickly and expertly cleansed and rebandaged it.

"It feels quite well already! Thank you, Mistress Wizard."

"Change the dressing tomorrow morning," instructed the Geomancer. "After that the wound will be healed and no damage done. Not even a scar, I guarantee."

"We fly on at once to Stony Gorge," declared Wong over a light supper that evening. "But only if we know you will be safe here for a few days, friend Foggery. What can we do for you? Take you to safety?"

"No, no!" cried he. "Those professional soldiers were minions of the Minister of Finance . . ."

"Ah, Wong Ti Wang?" inquired Wong. "No relation of mine, I hasten to add. Always was a scoundrel."

"Yes, a scoundrel and a monstrous thief! While his soldiers were here trying to silence me, my new Sons of the Soil were burning his country seat. If they succeeded, it will drive Wong Ti Wang from the vicinity. He'll either have to take to the field—which I don't see him doing; he's too fat and it's too dangerous!—or retreat to Bee-Wing. He doesn't dare to be cut off from the capital at this time, nor to leave his bullies behind, either. We'll have no further trouble from Wong Ti Wang. At least not here!"

Foggery insisted, now the local province had been organized into several tongs, or brotherhoods, things would be quiet. The important action was shifting to the capital.

"I'll leave in a day or two to assist the new brotherhoods in Bee-Wing province itself. If nothing else, they can give us useful information on the various Bureaucrats' movements and alliances."

Douglas nodded his understanding and admiration.

"But," he said, "you indicate you expect a full-blown fighting war at any moment."

Foggery shrugged and smiled ruefully. "That's true, and I don't see how we can avoid it, as long as the Ministers, Princes, Imperial Uncles, and Nephews—and even several Imperial Nieces, too—insist on vying for the Dragon Throne with armed force and secret murder. Our policy for the moment must be to guard Choin's subjects from the violence as much as possible, and gather information. Later we plan to publish our joint selection of a candidate for Emperor, within the old-time qualifications of both blood and capabilities, if possible. When the right time comes, that is."

Flarman and Litholt had withdrawn through most of this discussion, talking softly for some minutes. When they rejoined the group at tea, Flarman clapped his hands for attention.

"Litholt has a grand idea!" he announced. "No, we'll say nothing just yet. When we return to Choin, we'll bring it into play. Wong—you, Douglas, and I, with Litholt's experienced assistance. Augurian and Myrn, also. If all goes well, it'll halt the war in a single move."

"Do it immediately!" urged Douglas. "The Stones and Myrn can wait, if they must."

"The scoundrels must be all in a single place, to make our plan work," the Lady Geomancer said, shaking her head. "Which means nothing can be done, just yet."

Though they pressed them for details, she and Flarman refused to elaborate, saying that too many details had yet to be worked out.

"I think I have a smidgen of an idea what you are thinking," claimed Douglas.

"Well, you know me better than most people, my son," said Flarman with a chuckle. "I won't be surprised if this has occurred to you, too. And to you, my dear Wong," he added.

"I can't say that I have any idea," the Magician told him. "But I'm content to trust your instincts and skills, Flarman Flowerstalk."

"As do we all," agreed Marbleheart.

"Foggery," said Flarman, "tell your people to continue as you have planned. Try to keep the conflict from spreading beyond the capital. We will return to Choin in a few days, a week at most."

"We already trust in our Master Magician Wong and you, Flarman Flowerstalk, you can be sure!" said the Seacaptain gratefully. "More cardamom-sugar rice balls, anyone?"

Chapter Fifteen

Stormy Weather

WONG Tscha San stepped into Foggery's pleasant garden for a quiet moment to consult the stars, but returned hurriedly to say that a new problem was approaching.

"A great Sea storm is about to descend upon us," he announced. "The wind is already picking up and I see lightning flashes out to Sea!"

"Oh, oh!" Douglas groaned. "We can't use the Feather Pin until it passes. No protection from wind and lightning. It's a grueling three-day flight to Valley in good weather, as it is."

Flarman and Wong conferred with the Sea Otter to determine the extent and duration of the storm. Douglas, Litholt, and the Dwarf helped Foggery and his crew complete repairs to the red roof tiles. A pelting rain was beginning to fall and a rising gale shook the paper-thin walls of the Choinese-style house and bent the beautiful cherry trees in the garden almost to the ground.

"I can tell you," Marbleheart said, "it'll be a whiz-bang of a storm! On the Briney we call them hurricanes. This one feels exactly the same, but from the opposite direction, strangely."

"Typhoon, it's called, here," nodded Wong. "I recognized the signs at once. Too strong for even our combined powers to safely avert, Flarman Flowerstalk. All we can do is practice patience and find shelter in which to wait it out."

"How long do you think it'll last?" the Pyromancer asked the Otter. He respected the animal's understanding of weather. Only Bronze Owl was more accurate at weather prognostication.

"If the storm's clear eye is close inshore? Perhaps a day," Marbleheart considered, looking worried. "Otherwise it could blow for as long as a week. Perhaps you can tell, Magician?"

Wong closed his eyes and sat very still for a long while. The others waited silently.

"It is obscured by its own tumult, but experience teaches that such a typhoon will bring high winds and tides and a deluge of rain for at least three days," he answered at last.

Litholt came up to them in time to hear this.

"I must use my own Teleporting Spell, it seems. We can't abandon poor Mistress Myrn any longer, even if she is able to cope with her captors."

"It'll be very dangerous for you after all those years without practice," Flarman objected. "Perhaps . . . if Douglas and I coupled our spelling with yours—and Wong's, too— we could generate enough power to get you to Stony Gorge safely. It must be done within the hour, however. Such storms are highly charged. Lightning is a terrible disrupter of spells and fiercely resistant to a Pyromancer's demands."

"Let's do it," decided the Geomancer.

Douglas was reluctant. He felt he should be the one to go to Myrn, if anyone went. Flarman reminded him that the Earth Wizard alone had the lore to dispel the enchantment and gain the Water Apprentice's release from captivity. Litholt must go at once, alone, despite the dangers of distance and the wild weather.

"So be it!" the Journeyman agreed after a moment. "Give Myrn my love and tell her I'll be there as soon as the storm abates."

The two Pyromancers, Journeyman and Master, joined by the Choinese Magician, sat in a triangle about the Lady Geomancer and began the difficult and demanding business of interweaving their powers.

The rest of the company sat well across the room about a glowing charcoal brazier, breathlessly watching, listening to the storm's increasing rage and bluster.

"I can manage shooting myself a hundred miles in an instant with such a spell," Bryarmote whispered. "Flarman taught me the trick years ago. But this will be thirty times as far! That's the kind of power we're talking about here!"

Marbleheart, who was concentrating on the whirling, swirling spell-words heard from across the room, made no reply.

Foggery sat on a pillow, surrounded by his young men and maidens in orange, looking greatly concerned and listening anxiously to the angry young typhoon outside.

"At least there'll be no battles fought as long as this lasts," he muttered to the Dwarf over the tumult. "That's a bit of a blessing!"

"As my good Lady Mother says," replied the Dwarf, " ' 'Tis an ill wind that blows no good.' "

"When the Lady Wizard is at last on her way . . ."

Litholt flashed from their sight.

There was a sharp clap as air rushed in to fill the void left by her departure. All about the room lamp flames leaped and fluttered wildly for a long moment.

" . . . we should seek safe refuge ourselves, preferably far inland," finished Foggery.

"Preferably far underground," growled the Dwarf in agreement.

Foggery knew the storm might completely destroy his beloved home as no red-lacquered soldiery ever could with puny arrows and stone-throwing machines. He rose and calmly began gathering his followers and friends about him, with instructions ready on what to do, wear, expect, and where to go.

Less than a quarter hour later the villa, with stout wooden storm shutters tightly closed, stood empty.

They fled the coastal plain that very night, soaked by sheets of warm rain and buffeted by insane winds. The

retired Seacaptain led them into the low, limestone hills
a few miles to the south.

"Here are caverns enough even for a Dwarf," he said,
poking Bryarmote in the ribs.

"None too soon for me," growled the Prince of Dwelmland.

He was watching the approaching storm-wrack over his
left shoulder as they hurried along. Foggery's neighbors,
farmers and country craftsmen, had preceded them into the
hills, knowing from long, sad experience the best places to
shelter from a typhoon.

"Do you get anything from the Gorge?" Douglas anxiously asked Flarman as they walked.

"No! I find the ether between us clogged with lightning
and thunder. Don't worry, m'lad! She'll be safe. Both Lady
Wizards, I mean. Our spelling was powerful and clear.
Litholt made it to the High, at least, I'm confident."

The Journeyman hunched his shoulders against the rain
stabbing him in the back right through his coat and shirt.
He tried to concentrate on keeping his feet on the slippery path.

Twenty weary miles later Bryarmote unerringly pointed
the way to the low, wide entrance to a great limestone
cavern under the low coastal hills, large enough for them
all—several hundred people by then—to find dry shelter.

Marbleheart and Douglas went about setting campfires
to warm and dry the refugees. Flarman and Wong began
piling up food drawn magically from the stores at deserted
Bureaucrats' castles and fortresses throughout the area.

Soon all was quiet, except for the drumming rain and
shrieking wind and the distant roar of tremendous surf
pounding unmercifully at the Choin coast, felt as much
as heard through thirty miles of shore.

Wong sat gazing calmly into their campfire near the cavern mouth. Flarman, Douglas, and Marbleheart sat nearby,
but said nothing to disturb his meditation. Bryarmote had
gone exploring deeper into the cave, satisfying his Dwarfish

curiosity and love of the underground. There seemed little else to do.

"Flarman Flowerstalk," said Wong, suddenly, "it seems to me this storm is not entirely a natural phenomenon."

"But you said such typhoons were fairly common here," protested Douglas.

"Wait, laddie," cautioned the older Pyromancer. "Hear him out!"

"Thank you, Fire Master," said the tiny Magician, sitting up straighter. "I have sensed a hidden presence in this storm. An emanation I have not felt for hundreds of years. Darkness seems in the center of it all . . ."

"Yes, by Tophet! You're absolutely right, Master Wong! It's faint—but only because it surrounds itself with multiple lightnings, thunderings, and terrible constant winds. Now that it is passing over us *its* stench remains in the air."

Douglas strained across a thousand wavelengths of sensation, sampling emanations and disturbances brought to him by light, heat, smell, texture, movement, sound, and the subtler forces of the innermost and outermost regions of World.

Very faintly he caught a strange, uneasy mood, what Flarman had referred to as a stench, although it wasn't really an odor. It was like a tiny, incredibly black hole in time and space, a state of un-being, spinning at a tremendous rate, pulsating like the panicked heart of a rabbit waiting in dead-sure dread for the stooping hawk.

As he examined it he felt it grow larger, slowly, until he might almost describe it as the size of a fist clenched tightly with tension and menace.

"I think I sense what you mean," he murmured to the Wizard. "Black emptiness. Right from the heart of the storm's eye, I believe."

"Good lad!" Flarman exclaimed. "Yes, that's it! Haven't heard or seen or felt that . . . whatever it is . . . for three hundred years. . . ."

"You mean Darkness?" sputtered Marbleheart, horrified yet filled with curiosity.

"Exactly!" breathed Wong softly. "I never have seen—heard—felt it so close before. It terrified a lowly Assistant Magician once. It frightens me even more now, Master Wizard!"

"Well it should," said Flarman grimly.

"What does it mean?" gasped the Otter, who had caught a corner of the Darkness from Douglas's mind, just at that moment.

"What can we do?" asked Douglas at the same time.

Flarman began to draw circles and triangles in the fine, white sand of the cave floor, carefully but quickly.

"These are secret charms and wards," he said, rubbing the symbols away, smoothing the sand with both hands, then beginning again. "Help me now, Journeyman! I need a better grasp of the Outrider's strength, position, and purpose."

For an hour the three magickers and the Familiar huddled about the sand drawings, muttering strange words, intoning low-voiced, frightened chants that, fortunately, only they could hear. Drawing and redrawing the circles, triangles, rhomboids, pentagrams, rectangles, sine curves and twisted ovals of infinity, they smoothed them away once again, and began again.

"Well!" said Flarman sharply, after what seemed to be days and nights of struggle.

He fed twigs to their dying fire. Around them the storm refugees had settled down to sleep, to await the passing of the shrieking wind and the roaring rain.

"Well?" the Pyromancer repeated. "We were lucky, I guess."

"It's gone?" asked Marbleheart. "Are we safe?"

"Feel for yourself," suggested Douglas, rubbing his weary eyes.

"I don't feel anything," agreed the Familiar, much relieved. "It's either deeply hidden again or it's departed. Which is it, Magister? It's important to all of us to know."

Said Flarman, "What do you think, Journeyman? If you aspire to Mastery, you must have an idea of what has passed over us just now."

Douglas closed his eyes to aid in concentration, and began to speak slowly, feeling his way.

"It was not full Darkness, I gather. A probe, perhaps. Attracted by the rumors of chaos and tragedy from the bloody-minded ambitions and cruel slayings here in Choin."

"The Darkness was always deeply interested in Choin," agreed Wong, opening his eyes just then. "When it first struck a thousand years ago, Choin was too well governed by good and able men, too strong for *it* to attack directly. Or so I was taught by my own Masters."

"That's how I see it, also," Flarman agreed. "Go on, Journeyman. You have it right, so far."

"It—the Outrider, did you call it?—stirred up the great storm to cover its spying. It sought to discover if it might be time, perhaps, to spend greater power on Choin; if the—*chaos* is all I can name it—is enough to allow it to seek control of Empire as it once tried to snatch Old Kingdom."

"As I think, too," said the Pyromancer.

"But its own storm blinded it to our presence—yours and mine and Wong's, I mean. It didn't sense us until it had passed close overhead. It felt *us* just when we felt *it*."

Flarman spread his arms and Wong bobbed his head several times.

"And it passed back out to Sea at once, having been—affrighted, perhaps? Surprised?—by the presence of our powers, and our awareness of it," finished the Journeyman Wizard. "It fled from us! As far as I can see, it has departed into the far Northlands."

"Yes, we were lucky! Lucky to be here at all, and to present it with a sharp pause to *its* evil, deadly desire for poor Choin," said Wong. "I am grateful for you, Flarman, and Douglas, and you, Marbleheart. If it had come when I was alone in my ignorance and weakness it would have flung me aside like a bit of froth on the wavetop. It or its Dark Masters would have soon captured or suborned someone or some group and remolded Choin into its own, dark shape. Choin would have become the new battleground of Darkness, as Old Kingdom once was. And been all but destroyed, as was unhappy Old Kingdom, even in victory!"

"No doubt of that!" cried Flarman. "The lesson to be learned is this: we Wizards must be eternally vigilant if we're to preserve freedom and keep the peace!"

He pulled his blanket about his shoulders and squirmed one hip into the sand to make a shallow groove to rest it in, preparing himself for sleep.

"Well, yes, we were lucky. But we were also prepared and well skilled. That the three of us could have shooed it off at all tells us its power is still a tiny fraction of what it once commanded. In earlier times it would have attacked us on first contact," he muttered.

"What in World is this Darkness thing?" Marbleheart whispered to Douglas as they settled down, also.

"A most difficult question, Familiar. In the first place, it's not of *this* World. It comes from some extremely distant Elsewhere—sent or driven away, we don't know. It feeds and grows strong on its victims' wickedness, the unthinking foolishness and greed and cruelty of Mortals and Near Immortals to each other. When we offer them such sustenance, *Darkness* comes among us and eventually rules us by our own weaknesses."

"You're frightening me, dear Master!" shuddered the Sea Otter, pushing hard against the Journeyman's thigh under his blanket.

"Don't be too frighted," murmured Douglas, half-asleep. "Remember the word Flarman just used: vigilance. As long as the Fellowship of Wizards is basically good-hearted, brave, kind, honest, sensible—as the overwhelming majority of us Men, Elves, Dwarfs and Fairies are—we'll never be conquered or enslaved by Darkness. So go to sleep. It's easier to be honest and good-hearted and sensible when you've had a good night's sleep."

To his own surprise, Marbleheart fell immediately to sleep, cuddled against his Master's back. Wong slept sitting cross-legged yet completely relaxed. Flarman snored for a while, then turned more on his stomach and slept silently.

Bryarmote, returning from his exploration, smiled fondly at them all and looked about for a smooth stone to use as a pillow.

Then he, too, slept.

A cool autumn rain fell on Valley, swelling the little pasture runs to overflowing. Pleased to be once more too wide for the shepherds to jump, they skipped excitedly down to find Crooked Brook, on their way picking up the fallen poplar, birch, sugar maple, and willow leaves, until in places their waters seemed plated with copper or gold. The water of Crooked Brook then became what the Fairies called Brook Tea. Black where the stream was deep, amber as good beer in the shallows. Crooked Brook foamed around rocks and bubbled about the jet of Augurian's Fountain, just downstream from Wizard's High, before it and its burden of leaves dashed off to race merrily under the stone span of Trunkety Bridge. After that it slid along quietly through the smooth, deep stretch above Perthside, merging at last with salty Farango Waters.

This scene was placidly surveyed by Bronze Owl, who, untroubled by the damp chill, swung on his nail in the middle of the great double front door of Flarman's cottage. Everyone else, that late afternoon, was within, gathered around the blaze in the Dwarf's Stone Fireplace, Bryarmote's pride and joy.

Blue Teakettle flopped her lid and burbled, peacefully napping on the back of Range. Salt and Pepper whispered and giggled together in the center of the great table. They were constant companions, seldom apart.

A long, lean Pushbroom, interrupted in its task of cleaning the kitchen yard by the coming of rain, leaned comfortably against the broom closet door, playfully teasing old Sugar Caster, who was concerned that the damp would cake his contents and clog his holes. Sugar Caster was something of a hypochondriac.

Pert and Party catnapped on either side of Black Flame, but the tom, at least, was alert, although purring contentedly for the ladies' comfort. They deserved their rest, as the last of their most recent litters had been found happy and comfortable homes in Valley farmhouses and village kitchens or as mousers on Duke Thornwood's ships out of Westongue.

In Hutch, a great, heavy cupboard made of mellow old walnut planks an inch thick, a gay young blade, a Paring Knife, flirted with abrasive old Sharpener, promising her they could really make sparks if he rubbed her the right way. Sharpener scoffed at the blade's blandishments, saying, "Oh, you'll be dull and useless again in a few days, Beau. Then you'll come running to me for a stroke or two, I know."

"But, my darling," protested Paring Knife, stiffening in pretended umbrage, "I'm not that sort! Believe me!"

If a whetstone could snort, this one would have, but just then their attention was distracted by one of the Bread Pans on the sideboard near the stove, who began to croon softly, calling to Blue Teakettle and saying, "Oh, Kettle dear, will you knead us!"

"Who needs you?" sniffed a muffled voice from within a large, stoneware bowl covered with an embroidered dish towel. "Let poor Teakettle have her nap."

"I'll knead you, Dough," offered Butter Churn, unctuously. "And later you'll need me, after you've baked well."

"*Shhhhhh!*" hised Blue Teakettle, wakening abruptly. "Get ready, all! Someone's coming!"

Owl was surprised by a sharp and quite close-by clap of thunder, but thought nothing more of it than to say to himself, *Thunder's unusual in autumn showers, isn't it?*

Shortly after, however, he jerked to full attention, rattling his wings in surprise. Crossing the ancient plank bridge from Priceless's neat rows of apple, crabapple, and peach trees, he spied someone coming along at a brisk pace, cowled head bowed to the raindrops, straight for the cottage gate.

"Ho, a visitor!" Owl called to those within, and a moment later he was joined by Black Flame, who pushed one of the door leaves ajar to come and see for himself.

"A lady, I see," murmured Owl. Black Flame nodded calmly and glanced at the bird for a moment.

"Not just *any* sort of woman, however? Yes, I agree," replied Owl.

The traveler hesitated at the gate, studying the house and its surroundings with lively interest from under her hood.

"Come up, ma'am!" Owl called, fluttering noisily from his nail toward the gate. "Welcome to Wizards' High! Come right in out of the rain and chill."

The amber-haired woman in slate gray hood and cloak opened the rickety gate and approached, first carefully closing the gate behind herself.

"Sign of good breeding," Owl muttered to the cat. "Closes gates without being asked!"

"This *is* the home of Flarman Flowerstalk, I see," said Litholt Stonebreaker to Bronze Owl. She showed no surprise at all to be speaking to a metal bird. "How fortunate for me! For a moment I thought I'd lost my way."

"This is Wizard Flarman's cottage," replied Owl. "I am Flarman's doorknocker, adviser, and friend. I'm also in charge here in his absence, so I invite you again to come within to dry and warm yourself. It will be night before long."

"I am Litholt Stonebreaker," the Lady Wizard introduced herself.

"Ah, I've heard of you!" Owl cried, genuinely pleased. "Last I heard, Flarman and Douglas and the others had found you in the middle of a desert."

"Correct, friend Owl. And I am on my way . . ."

"Come in, please, ma'am! No need to stand in the drips from the thatching," interrupted Owl. He led the Lady Wizard past the empty front parlor, down the center hall past the sweeping curved staircase into the big, brightly lighted kitchen.

"Ah, just as I heard!" cried Litholt, striding at once to the Dwarf's Fireplace. "A marvelous stone construction, this! Made of lovely stones and powerful and everlasting magic as only a Dwarf Prince could do. I adore it!"

"Yes, I remember now," said Bronze Owl, perching on a handy chair back. "You're a Geomancer. A lover of fine stone and stonemasonry."

"The wonderful, marvelous stones here will help restore to me the powers I must have to continue my journey to assist the Apprentice Myrn Manstar!" explained the Geomancer, running her hands lovingly over the craftily cut and closely fitted stones. "Stones like these are as life's blood to an Earth Adept, you must realize."

"Make yourself right at home," Owl invited politely. "And when you've imbibed what you need from the stones, come and have supper as only Blue Teakettle can prepare, before you go flying off again. Mistress Myrn would be the first to recommend it, I know well."

He fully understood what the Lady Wizard's mission must be.

"Have you the proper warming spells?" Owl asked Litholt a bit later, after she was seated at the table before a hearty supper of golden waffles with maple syrup and butter, spicy sausages, strawberry jam and peach butter (always a great favorite with Geomancers, because of the stones), with strong black coffee—just as Geomancers like it. Somehow Blue always knew.

"My spells were rather rusty, just now," she replied to the Owl's question. "Both from long disuse, you understand, and because of the buffeting I suffered at the hands of the great storm at Sea. Fair stripped my repertoire of everything useful, I'm afraid, which is why I unwillingly landed so short of Stony Gorge."

"Better stay here tonight, then," Owl urged. "Plenty of room here at the High, Mistress Wizard. Rest and a couple of Blue's good meals will do wonders for recouping your magic, as well. You'll need all your wit and craft to break the Stone Warriors free, if what Douglas tells me is true."

Said Litholt, "Yes, I *am* weary and a good night's sleep is certainly what I need. Thank you for your kind offer,

Bronze Owl! In the morning I'll ask you to speak precisely of the location of this Gorge where Douglas's fiancée is being held hostage."

"I'll draft you a map showing all I know of it," promised Owl, "while you bathe and get some sleep."

Black Flame, ever protective of Wizards no matter their gender or specialty, showed the weary Geomancer to a comfortable guest room above stairs.

Owl summoned Deka the Wraith, who came after a short wait.

"Hail Bronze Owl of great beauty and wisdom!" she said in greeting when she'd materialized into the soft candle-light. "How may I serve?"

"We're certainly overtaxing your willingness to serve these days, poor Deka," commented Owl, waving her to a seat near the fire.

"No more than I'm pleased to serve," she answered with a curtsy.

"You appear a bit ruffled, if I may say so," observed the bird.

"I've just been battling a monstrous atmospheric dis-turbance," the Wraith explained. "It delayed my arrival by almost a minute!"

"Not so much as to be noticed, however," soothed Owl. "Rest a few minutes here. When you're prepared to go on again, I must send messages to Mistress Myrn and Master Augurian, this night."

"The storm is to the south of here," Deka reassured him. "I can leave at once, of course."

"Have some lemonade," Owl offered. Pitcher, filled with tart-sweet *misctywine* just as the Wraith loved it, appeared right on cue. "And listen carefully to my messages."

Deka popped through from some unknown Otherworld to the Stones' Column in time to hear Detritus shouting from his door yard.

"Miserable, useless, indolent, procrastinating woman Wizard! How long will you delay and betray us? We

will be freed of the curse of Obsydion, or we will bring
dire havoc on Men everywhere we find them!"

Deka cocked her head to one side and decided Detritus
was performing a ritual of some sort, of obscure signifi-
cance. Certainly his feeling didn't match the furor of his
words.

"You make a great deal more noise than you do sense,
Rocky," said Myrn in a conversational tone. "Oh, hello,
Deka! Don't pay any attention to the Chief of Stones there.
He's doing it all for political show."

"Me? Show!" howled Detritus, coming across the square,
curious despite himself to hear the Wraith's message.

"Well, you were," said Myrn firmly. She and all the
Stones had heard his tirade a hundred times in the past
three days. "And I understand it, too. But a few more hours
or days will not harm you or your people."

The Stone giant opened his mouth to hurl a stinging retort
but Deka, with consummate timing and tact, announced that
she brought word from Bronze Owl of Wizards' High. The
Stone Chief swallowed in his *pro forma* ire to listen.

"So this Geomancer will be here tomorrow, sometime?"
asked Myrn when she had heard the words Owl had sent.
"Good news, Detritus, old rockhead!"

"I'll believe it when I see this rock Wizard of yours.
Another woman! What sort of trick is that, I ask you?"

"I am a *woman* Wizard, too, I'll remind you," said Myrn,
near the edge of her great patience. "And as good as any
you'll ever find, I do assure you."

The giant retired hastily to his hut muttering to himself.

"What do they need huts for?" Myrn whispered to the
Wraith. "They never sleep or eat, and the cold and snow
don't bother them at all."

"I suppose like all creatures they need to be alone at
times," replied Deka with a wan smile.

"Oh, poor Deka! We've been keeping you shooting back
and forth like a shuttlecock! Please stay awhile and talk to
me. I'm nearly starved for news and companionship."

"You don't happen to have any lemonade, do you?" asked Deka with a brighter look. "Yes, I'll stay as long as you like, unless I'm summoned."

The two old friends, Apprentice Wizard and Wraith, chatted of anything at all that came to mind, as long as it wasn't stones or rocks or dead Wizard's enchantments.

Mostly they talked of weddings.

Chapter Sixteen

The Disspelling

STONY Gorge at that time of year hardly ever saw direct sunshine. The days were getting shorter and shorter, the sun rising only part way toward the zenith before sinking back under the horizon again. The skies were overcast, promising more snow at any moment and frequently delivering.

The dimness and drab colors got on Myrn's nerves more than anything about her voluntary captivity. She had the choice of flitting off to the nearest friendly habitation of real people—in this case, New Land and Serenit's house—or doing something to make her surroundings more bearable.

Two days before Deka's evening visit the Apprentice Aquamancer experimented with superheated steam jetting from one of the largest geysers in the valley. She enclosed a great cloud of the almost invisible gas in a globe of cooler mist, and sent it floating over the village square like a second moon, aglow brightly blue with its own heat.

Detritus and a number of other Stones, including several of the Stone women who seldom were seen out of doors, rushed out of their huts and stood gawking at the strange sight, wondering at the sharp shadows it cast on the village walls.

After a quarter hour the steam cooled enough to lose its incandescent glow, the surrounding globe warmed enough to turn to mist itself, and the whole thing collapsed in a torrential shower of warm water that rinsed all the dirty ice and snow from the village roofs and streets, making them gleam in the wan light filtering through the low clouds.

It reminded Myrn of her laundering of Pfantas some months before, but the final result was not gratitude from the citizens, but flinty looks from the populace as a whole and snarls from Detritus.

"I know you did that, Wizard!" he cried. "Where is our soft and fragrant rock dust?"

"I was not about to deny it," said Myrn, primly. "I think your gritty, grimy streets and rooftops are much more presentable, now they are clear of that ratty old snow. Why, some of it must have been there for hundreds of seasons!"

"Exactly!" snarled the Chief with a terrible scowl. "It was *our* ice and *our* decoration and you had no right . . ."

"Oh, Rockhead!" laughed the Apprentice. "You are an absolute pill!"

Detritus went storming off—mostly for show, she had long since figured out—and missed the scene, a few minutes later, when the ladies of Stony Gorge emerged quietly from their huts armed with stiff heather-twig brooms. They swept the last remaining ice and snow from their flagstone walkways, and scrubbed their stone stoops, studiously avoiding direct glances at the Wizard on the Column.

"Huh!" snorted Myrn. "That's interesting. Stone housewives are just like housewives anywhere!"

The experiment with the steam geyser prompted her to more creative hydro-engineering. Most of the very hot water spewed forth by the geysers—there were, she counted, 120 that erupted at least once an hour, or even more often—seeped back into the ground almost immediately or ran off down the vale and under the great iron gates.

Carefully maneuvering loose boulders that had long ago rolled down the Gorge hillsides, she constructed a large, shallow basin below the village and into it channeled a portion of the steaming water.

In a few hours she had created a circular pond fifty feet across, and five feet deep in the center. From its surface rose lazy tendrils of steam, which, when they hit the cold rocks all about, froze into splendid, lacy ice-crystal flowers.

The pure white flowers were very pretty, with no two quite alike, and Myrn was justly proud of her inspiration. Detritus angrily ran to the poolside and began stomping the blooms into icy dust, roaring his frustration all the while.

He gave it up when he noted a group of Stone wives standing nearby, shaking their heads in regret and their fingers in disapproval. He retreated hastily to his hut, throwing hard glances at the Apprentice, who was now busy introducing subtle pastel colors to the newer crystal flowers, lending a festive atmosphere to the shore garden about the pond's margin.

The Stone wives quietly nodded their approval. It had been a very long time since they had seen anything as beautiful. Later, when Detritus did not reappear, a number of Stone Warriors came gravely to admire the new garden with their ladies.

Later in the evening Myrn noticed a number of Stone children—the first she had seen since arriving—wading and splashing in the cooling waters of the pond, getting much quiet pleasure out of falling flat on their backs in the shallow water to see who could make the biggest splash.

Detritus ignored their play.

Their mothers watched from their hut doors and gossiped back and forth across the stone fences between their tiny yards. The village took on a much more neighborly feel with that—and the pond and the ice flowers stayed.

Some of the children walked casually past the column the next morning, looking with frank childhood curiosity at the pretty Wizard and the tented pavilion Douglas's magic had provided to keep the snow off the column top. They smiled shyly when the Water Adept caught their admiring glances at the sumptuous furs that kept her warm and cozy despite the wintry wind and heavy overnight snowfall.

"You know," she called to the youngsters, "I bet I can guess something. I guess, even though they are made of stone, Stone Warriors don't really like being cold all the time!"

The children clattered away at once, trying very hard not to giggle. Later the older ones returned and asked her politely if she would tell them a story from History, such as their parents had heard retold by their Chief.

She invited them to sit around the column—on the side away from the Chief's hut—and quietly described to them Wizards' High and Valley of Dukedom, then distant Waterand Isle and Warm Sea. Closer to home, she explained what Serenit was doing in New Land now that Eternal Ice was withdrawing northward.

They were fascinated by the splendors of Bryarmote's rock-hewn, underground Dwelmland. By the following evening, as Myrn waited for the Geomancer to arrive, virtually every child and young person in Stony Gorge came to listen to her tales of the unknown outside World. . . . Beyond the Ice, as they termed it.

Their mothers and fathers watched and listened from their front stoops. Detritus, who loved stories as much as any of them, leaned over his front wall, taking it all in while pretending to ignore everything, especially Myrn.

When she had sent the children off to their play, Myrn prepared to study for a while from several of the big, old books Augurian had forwarded to her from Waterand. Only then did a quiet and subdued Detritus approach the chair.

"Mistress," he began, "I have had enough! No more tantrums! No more cursing and ranting. This curse can no longer be endured. If your Geomancer isn't here by noon, tomorrow, I must put you on ice in a place from which you'll never find your way home, and I will lead my warriors against First Citizen Serenit, capture or slay his followers, and destroy all the things they are so proud of doing!"

He said no more, shouted no longer, appearing sad rather than angry, and went into the Meeting Hall, where he was joined after a while by the tribal Elders.

"Oh, dear, I'm afraid he really means it this time!" sighed Myrn.

She thought of calling Augurian, but decided against it. If the Lady Geomancer came in time, things would shortly sort themselves out. If not, she had some ideas on how to stop Detritus and distract his Warriors.

In preparation she spent the evening scooping fist-sized balls of hot water from the pond and whirling them about her head until they froze into balls of slush.

These she accurately hurled—assisted by a Levitation Spell Douglas had taught her—to the lower end of the Gorge, where they splashed against the inside of the iron gate.

Before she quit and crawled into her fur-lined nest to sleep, the gate was frozen tight shut by the freezing slush. As the nighttime temperature in the Gorge dropped well below zero, the ice hardened like the iron itself. Only heat would unlock the Gorge Gate after that.

Earlier that evening Litholt had stopped to speak with Serenit at his lodge. The former Ice King greeted her shyly but as a long-lost friend—he now remembered her from the days before Last Battle in Old Kay—and insisted she spend the fast-approaching arctic night at his pleasant rustic home.

Litholt was happy to rest for a while. She was fascinated with the glacial valley, carved from hard, blue granite over tens of thousands of years, forming the wide, perfectly flat bottom and perpendicular sides.

A heavy overnight snowfall slowed them down when they set out to walk to the Face the next morning. Litholt wanted to conserve her Wizardly power as much as possible, knowing she would need every bit when it came to addressing Obsydion's spell. She couldn't afford to expend even a small part on flying or teleporting.

Bundled warmly against the intense cold, she followed Serenit up the twisted and uneven pathway to the Face, said good-bye and thank you, and levitated herself up and over the river of ice, then followed its gently curving northward course until she came to its end at Gorge Gate.

"Aha!" she snorted, recognizing the ancient Geomancer's handiwork in the iron gate as clearly as if he'd signed

his name to it. When she attempted to swing the heavy
leaves open, however, she discovered Myrn's frozen slush
barricade.

"Clever Water Adept!" she chuckled.

She left the icy barrier in place, and sailed gracefully over
the gate by her own magic.

She glided swiftly up the narrow Gorge, admiring the
geothermal fountains and pools and naming the rock for-
mations on either hand as if they were old friends. When
she came to Myrn's pond, now with a thick layer of clear
blue ice over most of its surface, she recognized it as
Aquamancer's work, too.

Myrn and the Stones saw her coming almost as soon
as she had appeared over the gate, and by the time she'd
skimmed over the pond, where a few Stone children were
already experimenting with ice skating, a large crowd of
older Stones stood in silence in front of the Meeting Hall,
watching her approach and looking both fearful and hope-
ful.

The stranger could only be the long-promised Stone Wizard.

"Good morrow!" Litholt called politely.

They murmured solemn greetings and bowed in return.

"Good morrow, Earth Adept!" came Myrn's softly carrying voice. She floated down from the Column and ran to
meet the new arrival. "Welcome to Stony Gorge, although
it should be the Chief to say it, not I."

The Stones nodded agreement and turned to stare stoni-
ly at the Chief's door. He was nowhere to be seen or
heard.

"I suspect he's rather ashamed of himself and the
way he's doubted us," Myrn explained, giving the older woman a warm hug. "It's so good to meet you,
Mistress Stonebreaker! Douglas sent word of you and
how surprised he was to find another Lady Wizard in
World."

"I hope you aren't jealous of me," said Litholt seriously.

"No need, I sincerely assure you. You are a famous Wizard

even before your Journeying, my dear."

"Nonsense! There can't be too many female Wizards for my money. We've all got a lot to do, and the Wizard menfolk, however hard they try, need a woman's touch and viewpoint. Don't you agree?"

"Yes, indeed I do!" cried Litholt, and the two hugged each other again, laughing together like old friends.

"Nor would I ever do without them," added Litholt. "I like them very much, even Serenit, now that he's come to his good senses. He was always rather somber, intense, and withdrawn in the bad old days. Flarman was my very favorite magic maker. Your own Master Augurian himself came courting me once. He was so very serious. So solid and dependable!"

"Augurian?" cried Myrn. "I would never have believed it! About his courting a Lady, I mean."

"Oh, yes! And a most handsome suitor, too, although much too shy. Those were our halcyon days! The descent of Darkness began just then and all such pleasant pastimes ceased, I'm sorry to say. We were much younger then, and fighting a supremely deadly foe seemed more important than love and marriage. Which is one reason I am so pleased to learn that you and young Douglas are pledged to be married."

"You approve? I'm quite relieved, to tell you the truth. Some might say that a Water Adept wife would dampen a Fire Wizard's way."

"No, you won't stand in his way," replied Litholt, seriously. "We found out the hard way, way back then. Love is more important than any kind of power! Remember that, Mistress Myrn."

"I remember it every day," the Water Adept assured her new friend with a grave nod.

"Now, to begin with," said Litholt Stonebreaker to Myrn and the assembled company of Stones, "I'll need answers to a few basic questions from someone who was present when this wicked spell was cast. How about your Chief?"

"I'll call him out, if you wish," said Dolomit the Hardy. "However, a number of us here were present that night."

He pointed out Storyteller in the back of the crowd. Of all the Stones, he had been the first to speak to Myrn kindly and had listened to her stories and histories most closely, committing them to his remarkable memory.

"Storyteller, you were there when the Wizard named Obsydion wove his Petrification Spell, were you not?" Myrn asked him.

He was surprisingly shy before the Lady Wizards.

"Aye, Mistress! I recall it perfectly well, every word and gesture. As is my job, of course," answered the tribal historian modestly.

"Then maybe you can tell me some things I need to know to speed the disspelling," said Litholt, levitating to the top of the Stone Column and drawing Myrn with her so they could see eye to eye with the giants.

"Willingly, Mistress!" said he, coming to the foot of the Column. "Ask away! If anyone remembers that dire day, it's me—Storyteller."

Litholt asked but three questions:

First: With which hand did Obsydion actually cast his Petrification Spell?

His left, Storyteller said confidently.

Second: What was the color of the sky when he cast the spell?

Black, recalled the Stone.

" 'Twere midnight and raining hard and no stars or moon shone through that night."

Third: Did Obsydion wear a robe when he cast the spell, or was he clad in metal armor?

Storyteller thought about this question for a long while before he answered.

"I can't be sure of that, as it was quite dark, but I think, Mistress, that he wore both a black robe *and* silvery armor. I distinctly recall the bright glint of metal up his sleeve when he reached high up to hurl the spell onto us like a thunderbolt."

"Excellent, Storyteller! Exactly what I needed to know. Silvery armor, you say? Well! Now all of you—Chief Detritus, also—come sit before me where I can see you all while I do my work. Yes, the young ones, too, and the babes."

The sullen, stubborn Chief had almost to be hauled by force from the Meeting Hall where he had been hiding . . . and listening. He was made to sit on the paving stones in the middle of their half circle before the Geomancer.

"Now, dear children," she said, with a wink over her shoulder at Myrn, "it will help if you will remain quite silent throughout. Try to recall what exactly you were doing, what you wore, how you stood the moment the wicked Wizard Obsydion enchanted you and imprisoned you here in Stony Gorge under Eternal Ice."

The entire village, even the smallest children—who had remained children for a thousand years—sat in stony silence, frowning in concentration.

Litholt pushed up her sleeves, took a great breath, and began.

It was midmorning when she spoke the first chantment. Nobody moved or made a sound for hours and hours, waiting for the first signs of disspelling to begin to show.

Myrn was somehow expecting spectacular fireworks, flying sparks, or, at the least, exotic rituals, but none were forthcoming. She could, however, feel the climax of the breaking enchantment in her fingertips and tingling toes, as the sun slid toward the barren southwestern hills.

Litholt stood before them, looking calmly from one to the next as if memorizing their faces, ending with Detritus, without saying another word.

Yet, and yet . . . Myrn saw changes come over them.

Their flint-hard visages gently softened. Their faces, deeply engraved by time and sadness or chiseled fine by ten slow centuries, seemed suddenly more mobile, more infused with warmth.

Detritus stirred first, raised his right hand and watched his blunt, strong fingers move in fits and jerks. He examined his newly pink fingernails and rubbed the stiff hair on the backs of his wrists against his square chin.

He struck his thigh hard with the palm of his right hand. It made a loud, fleshly smack. In dawning wonder, he watched the muscles ripple under the tanned skin of his right forearm, as if he had just discovered muscles and tendons and skin for the very first time ever.

Great, crystalline tears rolled down his cheeks.

Sobs of purest joy escaped his heaving breast. He buried his now-ruddy face in hands of real Mortal flesh.

They all were shrinking. In a few moments, when Myrn jumped down from the pillar top and ran forward to greet them and mingle her own tears with theirs in her immense relief and delight, they were all once more of normal size for ordinary Men. Tall and muscular, surely, but no stronger or taller than they should have been.

No longer obdurate, everlasting blue gabro.

Obsydion's blackest magic was completely disspelled.

Marbleheart trotted in his rather comic gait up the last slope to the cave mouth, beaming broadly and shouting that the storm had passed. He'd made a trip alone to the shore before dawn. Pelicans, petrels, and a few frigatebirds confirmed his forecast. Fair, cooler, and light, dry winds.

"The sky at Sea is the most beautiful blue I've ever seen. There are still huge combers breaking on the beach, but the wind has shifted to the northeast and is moderating quickly," he reported.

"Damages?" asked Foggery fearfully.

"Few houses have their roofs on, still," replied the Sea Otter, accepting a cup of tea from one of Foggery's orange-clad maidens. "Not many were actually destroyed, however. They are more sturdily built than I thought, I guess."

"Typhoons are common on this coast, of course," said Wong. "Roofs are easy to replace. Walls, less so. We Choin learned long ago to build like that. The important thing is, we seem to have lost few lives."

"I saw a number of corpses washed up where streams had flooded," admitted Marbleheart somberly. "Most wore that hard leather armor the soldiers had on when your house was attacked, Captain."

"Their officers were not quick enough or humane enough to lead them to high ground," guessed Flarman. "Well, Douglas, m'lad, it's a long, long trip to the Far Northland. Shall we depart at once?"

"If we can do nothing further to help the Choinese, I am ready," said Douglas.

"We're capable of picking up, burying the dead, and carrying on," said Foggery. "Besides, this storm had one good effect. It has given us a respite of at least a few days from the Bureaucrats and their soldiers. The Bureaucrats have all fled from their country houses to the capital, taking their soldiery with them, I'm told. They'll leave us alone for a good while and when they come back, our new militia will be ready for them, with any luck."

"Marbleheart, Douglas and I will go as soon as we've had some breakfast," decided the older Fire Wizard. "Will you come or stay, Master Wong?"

"I have a date four days hence at Wizards' High," the Magician reminded him gravely. "I understand that it cannot be postponed."

"Yes, yes, the Examination!" cried Douglas. He'd forgotten it completely until that moment.

"It must be taken the night of an Equinox," Flarman said. "The next won't be for another six months, if we miss this one."

"I'll stay here and help Foggery, if I can be of use," said Bryarmote, to no one's surprise. He liked to be where the action was. "Just send a note to my sweet bride and say I'll be a little late getting home, won't you?"

With just the four of them, and Flarman's intimate knowledge of the workings of the Feather Pin, the return trip was much faster than any previous flight.

"Wrap your faces in your cloaks," instructed Flarman as they shot into the clear sky over the Choin littoral. "That way you will breathe easily and we can go twice as fast."

"Why didn't I think of that!" cried the Otter, burrowing into Douglas's coat tail, as he had none of his own.

Where it had taken them three full days to cross Sea between Choin and Dukedom before, now they were circling over Valley by noon of the second day.

"Need to check things at home," explained Flarman, as Douglas sent them into a shallow dive to land at the kitchen door. "And a couple of hours of sleep if you want it."

"I'm ready to go on immediately," said Douglas.

"So be it," said the Fire Wizard. "You, Wong?"

"I will remain here," the Choinese decided. "There are still a few Examination questions to be prepared, you'll remember."

"Give me a half hour in my study," said Flarman to the Journeyman, "and we can go by Teleport Spell, my boy, and be there in minutes, rather than hours."

"Time enough for lunch," declared Marbleheart, who had been napping with his lithe body draped like a fur boa about Douglas's shoulders all morning. He slid to the ground, cuffed playfully at Black Flame when the cat came to greet them, and added, "Wonder what old Blue Teakettle has cooked up for us?"

"Your favorites!" cried Flarman, waving to Bronze Owl, who had flown around the cottage from the front door at the sound of their arrival. "Tuna salad! Anchovy pizza!"

When they entered the warm and savory kitchen, all the utensils—Plates, Goblets, Knives, Forks and Spoons, Platters, Slicers, Choppers, Graters, Griddles, Pots, Pans, Trivets, Pot Holders, Shakers, and Spatulas—cheered lustily from every corner, shelf and cupboard.

The Otter reared to his hind feet to examine the broad, crowded tabletop and said, in awe, "She's done it again! How does she know?"

"Who's done what?" asked Douglas, seating himself at his accustomed place and reaching for a pot of fresh mayonnaise to spread on his new-baked white bread.

"Blue Teakettle! She's fixed lunch, and just what I was craving, ready when we walked in unannounced, and for just the right number, too. Amazing!"

Blue Teakettle puffed in steamy pride at his sincere compliments and made sure the Sea Otter had enough tuna salad for a second and a third helping while Flarman went off to recharge his teleporting batteries—as he put it—in his study.

Bronze Owl was telling Douglas and Wong of the visit from Litholt Stonebreaker.

"Obviously a great, remarkable Lady," was Owl's opinion. "I admit to you that the idea of a female Wizard would have seemed . . . well, *unusual*, to say the least, if it weren't for Myrn."

"I understand that there were several other Lady Wizards very long ago," the Journeyman told them. He stooped to add a log to the fire in Bryarmote's great fireplace.

"Most of them are gone now," said Flarman, returning just then, beaming with the pleasure that only returning to his beloved house after a long absence could bring. "My own mother, bless her heart, was one of them, you know."

"You never mentioned that!" exclaimed his former Apprentice. "There is a lot I don't know about you even now, Magister!"

"Gives you something to think ahead about, if you pass your Exam," teased Flarman. "Yes, Mama was an old-fashioned General Practitioner. In those days, not many specialized as Augurian, Litholt, and I chose to do."

Chatting of Flarman's mother prompted Douglas to ask him, privately, just before they started off again, "About Mistress Litholt, Magister?"

"Yes, a lovely, wonderful woman! Great lady and highly accomplished Wizard, too. I'm immeasurably pleased she's gotten over her grief at the loss of her poor Cockerel. What of her, lad?"

"I sense a . . . uh, well . . . an untold relationship between you and Litholt," stammered Douglas.

"Maybe. Maybe not," said Flarman with a low chuckle. "I mustn't tell you my whole history today, must I?"

And he would say no more, but drew a circle around them in the dust of the path beyond the courtyard gate and made a lifting, shooing sort of gesture.

There was a rush of air, a flash of bright light, and a snap of displaced air.

"Here they are!" cried Myrn excitedly, and she threw herself into Douglas's outstretched arms and kissed him eagerly and joyfully. "We were just wondering when you'd be dropping in."

Litholt stood nearby with Storyteller and a much-subdued Detritus, all beaming warmly.

"You've been restored, then!" exclaimed Douglas, rushing to shake the Chief's hand. "I can't tell you how delighted I am it's so!"

"And I," said the Stone Chief, his eyes still downcast, "can't apologize long or hard enough to you for the way I mistrusted you and your bride-to-be. I just *couldn't* believe anyone would help us unless I forced them to it. You must . . ."

" . . . do nothing at all except congratulate you," Douglas finished for him. "Come and meet my Master! Hello, Storyteller! Litholt Stonebreaker, ma'am, everyone looks just great!"

The Geomancer gave him an auntlike kiss and a broad smile when he thanked her for coming to Myrn's assistance.

"I imagine you'll find occasions to regret not being giants of enduring stone," Marbleheart said to the tribesmen and their women.

"Never!" they cried. "We've been stoned far too long for regrets!"

"There are, however, a few problems yet to be ironed out," put in the Geomancer after the new arrivals had shaken hands with the entire village and patted the lively, excited thousand-year-old children on their tousled heads.

"Let me see," said Marbleheart quickly. "Food, I suppose. Not much of it here, is there?"

"When we were stone," sighed Storyteller, "hunger and cold never bothered us. But it's been a thousand years since I had my last lunch and the cold of arctic wind is already biting my fingers and toes severely, sirs."

"I can make it cozy as toast here in Stony Gorge," Flarman said. "And I think we can get some vittles sent up, at once. Do I sense you don't wish to remain here in this interesting Gorge, now that you are Men again?"

"Too cold! Too isolated!" agreed Detritus, and the villages chorused their agreement. "And too barren. Nothing but Mistress Myrn's beautiful ice flowers grow here, as you can see, and they'd make poor eating, I fear."

With Douglas's help Flarman threw a blanket of clear, warm air, imported from Warm Sea, over the whole Gorge—somehow excepting the ice-flower garden—and a minute or two later they conjured up a great pile of foodstuffs in the center of the square, boxes, bales, bushel baskets, bundles, and casks all neatly marked as to contents.

"Now, if you good Stone Ladies remember how to cook," Douglas said, "we can have a feast and be warm and cozy while we discuss our next move."

"I've dreamed of cooking meals again for nine hundred years," gasped one of the older women, clapping her hands like a child. "I see beef and pork, turkeys and chickens, flour and butter and splendid eggs! Eggs! Come, Ladies! Let's show our gratitude to our wonderful Geomancer, to the patient Mistress Myrn, and their Wizard gentlemen by preparing a Stone Warrior victory feast!"

As they went to work, Flarman spoke of professional matters with Litholt, while Douglas told Myrn of their adventures in Choin, the typhoon, and how they'd discovered a Darkness Outrider in the storm.

Marbleheart enthusiastically supervised the cooking until he was good-naturedly shooed away by the village wives for sampling the berry pies, marble cakes, and cookies too liberally before dinner.

"Where shall we go, I wonder," asked Detritus of Myrn and Douglas. He had apologized again and again for his vile temper, impatience, and unsuitable language. They smilingly forgave him, again and again.

"I doubt my people will want me to remain as Chief," Detritus said glumly.

"Why would they change?" wondered Myrn. "You brought them successful relief from the spell, didn't you? They must be very grateful for that."

"Well, perhaps you're right, although I did it rather poorly, I think," said the Chief of Stones.

"Cross that bridge when you come to it," advised Douglas. "For now, they seem quite content to follow your lead."

"Which brings us back to your question," said Myrn. "I have an idea."

"The same one I have in mind?" asked the bridegroom. They knew each other very, very well.

Chapter Seventeen

Master's Examination

"WELL, I don't know . . . ," temporized Serenit. "I'd do it for you, Master Flarman, and for Douglas, who has been my mentor and adviser since I became . . . what I now am. But these Stones are neither farmers nor lumberjacks, but savage warriors. . . ."

They had stopped at Serenit's lodge on their way home, to offer him the Stones as settlers in New Land.

"Oh, come now, First Citizen!" exclaimed Myrn rather impatiently. "A new nation needs a few trained fighters handy, just in case."

"And they'd come to you not just as warriors," Flarman pointed out. He took a bite of Clangeon's freshly made bread, thickly spread with wild raspberry jam. "They're experts in quarrying and stonemasonry, as you might guess. And they'll be very hard workers. They'll need some polishing, of course. Some sophistication that a trusted leader could give them."

"He means you, Serenit," said Douglas, clapping the First Citizen on the back. "Beside, New Land needs hardy settlers—tough, resourceful, and experienced in the wilderness. The Stones are ideal for you!"

"And we're loyal and rock-solid honest," added Detritus. "I personally guarantee it."

Before the tribesmen had marched out of Stony Gorge, they'd unanimously reelected Detritus as their Chief. He was beaming with pride and brimming with confidence once more.

"Well . . ." Serenit still hesitated. "Your work will be quite arduous. Very little glory in it for warriors."

"We learned patience well, while under Eternal Ice," insisted the Chief.

"For example, I need tons and tons of clean pea gravel carried from the Face of Eternal Ice to build a breakwater at Flarmanport. Ships must have a sheltered place to tie up close inshore to take on cargoes of ice and timber. Lightering in small boats is slow, dangerous, and very expensive."

"We can build your breakwater before the first of spring shipping arrives," Detritus promised. "We already know where the very best pea gravel is. We'll tote it in baskets if necessary! We'll even weave the baskets ourselves. And cut great interlocking blocks of gabro for the mole's facade."

"As a trial, then," agreed Serenit. "My older settlers have worked for a year just to begin to make this empty, barren land ready to bloom. They've put up with disappointments and earned frustrations as their wages. I must be sure, you understand, that new arrivals pull their weight."

The Stones' Chief agreed to a probationary period, after which the hundred-odd citizens of New Land would vote whether or not to accept them as naturalized citizens.

"A very good solution, I think," said Myrn with satisfaction.

"Now, what about our other problems?" asked Litholt.

"As I mentioned, I have a plan to settle things with the Bureaucrats in Choin—enough to allow the sane and sensible selection of a new Emperor," promised Flarman. "Trust an old Firebreather! When we return to Choin, it will take but a day or three to implement the Flowerstalk-Litholt plan!"

"I trust you absolutely, my dear," laughed Litholt. "But I was speaking rather of the Master's Examination, not of Choin's empty Dragon Throne."

"The day after tomorrow is Equinox, isn't it?" Myrn anxiously asked the Journeyman. "Are you ready?"

Douglas shook his head and said, "I guess I'm as ready as I'll ever be."

Flarman rose from the table in Serenit's rambling stone-and-log lodge, preparing to leave at once for home.

"I've taught you all I can," he sighed. "It's up to you and your brain and your heart to finish the task, foster son."

"Will Augurian come to the High, do you think?" Litholt asked Myrn. "I haven't seen him in over three and a half centuries."

"He'll be there when we return," Myrn assured her. "He wonders if three centuries in a desert have changed you much."

"A great deal . . . for the better, I hope," said the Geomancer. "How shall we travel this time, Flarman? Feather or spells?"

"Spelling, it must be," said the Pyromancer. "The Feather Pin is too slow for the short time we've remaining before the Examination must begin."

They said good-bye to Serenit, Clangeon, and their New Landers, and went to take leave of the Stones. The tribesfolk were busy building rounded stone huts near the bank of the rushing, milk-colored stream, which carried the glacial meltwater with its burden of rock dust down to Sea. Serenit had proposed to name it Brightglade River, and the sunken valley into which it flowed Flarman Fjord.

"I'm flattered, of course," Douglas told Storyteller, "but I gather the first settlers already call it New River, and the long bay, Frigeon's Fjord. They do agree to Flarmanport, however. I suspect their choices will stick, especially as they're more appropriate."

"Time alone will tell," philosophized the tribal historian. He proudly exhibited blisters and calluses on his hands from his work.

"Been a mighty, mighty long time since I had a callus!" he cried. "And for them, I thank you, Wizards!"

"Let's go home, shall we?" asked Myrn, eager to be off.

And they hastened to join the others standing in Flarman's magic circle in the gravel beside New River, ready to take them home to Wizards' High.

The day of the Autumnal Equinox dawned bright, cool, and clear. The hint of fall in the air the Choin Magician had enjoyed just two weeks before on his morning walks had come to full realization.

The spring that gushed from under the High giggled happily down its stone-lined channel past the byre, steaming like Soup Pot in the chilly air. There was a smell of burning leaves carried up from Trunkety on the brisk breezes.

On the cottage's east-facing windowglass fantastic scenes had been etched in hoarfrost overnight. Almost as Wong studied those on his bedroom windowpanes, they began to melt away under the first level rays of the sun striking over distant Far Ridges.

"Most remarkable!" he exclaimed to Party. She had come to waken him. "I must meet this Jack Frost elf one of these days. He has a wonderful touch in a very difficult medium! I wish he would work his designs in the most delicate Choin porcelain, too!"

The little Magician finished dressing in his most magnificent gold brocade robe, slipping dainty gold sandals on his tiny feet. He regarded himself in the mirror for a moment, then carefully put his flat, broad-brimmed black Hat of Magicianship on his snow-white hair. The last thing he did was carefully to comb his thin white beard and arrange his long-drooping moustache.

From below stairs came a musical chiming. Blue Teakettle was calling everyone to break their fast.

As he and Party gracefully descended the wide stair to the center hall, the Choin Magician sniffed appreciatively the messages carried up to him by the warm air rising from the kitchen.

"Hot coffee!" he said to Bronze Owl, who came along just then. "Fragrant breakfast tea, too! And your marvelous idea of toasted bread! I must introduce toast to my people."

"What do you do with leftover bread, then?" asked Myrn, who was waiting at the foot of the stair for them.

"Soak it in chicken broth, perhaps, for lunch. Or sauces of soy and chopped peanuts for breakfast," replied the Magician, smacking his lips at the memory. "Good morning, Master Candidate! I trust you feel alert and well rested?"

Douglas bowed to him and gave Myrn a morning buss and hug. He shook his head.

"I lay awake half the night," he moaned. "I kept thinking of things I didn't know."

"How can you think of something you don't know?" asked Flarman reasonably, already seated at table with a big, starched linen napkin tied about his neck. He spooned steaming oatmeal into his bowl and crooked his forefinger for Creamer, who slid nimbly into his outstretched hand.

"That's what kept me awake," admitted the Journeyman, seating Myrn and dropping into the chair next to her. "If I knew I didn't know it, then I could not have not known it, I said to myself."

"I understand quite perfectly! But too late for regrets!" said Flarman cheerily. "You'll do quite well, my lad! I passed my Master's with flying colors, you know."

"Yes, on the third try," said a new voice, and Lady Wizard Litholt, looking particularly beautiful after a good night's sleep and a long, hot bath, swept into the kitchen. The gentlemen rose to greet her but she waved them back into their seats.

"I'll have a three-egg omelet with onions, cheese, and ham," the Lady Wizard told Sugar Caster, who was taking orders for breakfast. "Brown bread toast and strawberry preserves with sweet butter. Oh, and a cup of the delicious tea that I smell steeping in yon magnificent stoneware teapot."

Douglas toyed with his breakfast steak, his eyes unfocused and distant.

"Are you all right?" whispered Myrn, concerned, for he was usually a wide-awake early-riser and a devotee of hearty breakfasts.

"Just reciting the *Gozintus* to myself one more time," Douglas replied with a wry smile. "I couldn't be more nervous if this were our wedding day!"

"Oh, yes, you could," she teased. "And will be, I guarantee!"

Marbleheart was banished from the Examination Room, Flarman's comfortably cluttered, book-lined study. Familiars are much too easily tempted to assist their Principals on tough questions, Augurian ruled.

"But a Wizard is *never* separated from his Familiar! He could be argued to be a part of the Wizard's self," the Sea Otter complained.

"By just being near, the rule makers felt, a Familiar might project clues and hints to the Candidate, even without intending to," countered Flarman firmly.

"But I've only been a Familiar for three months!" the Otter protested.

"Out!" growled Augurian sternly. It was his task to enforce the rules.

Flarman's task was to interpret them. He'd written most of them in the first place, anyway.

"Break a leg!" Marbleheart called to Douglas as he scampered out.

"A strange wish for his Candidate," whispered Wong to Litholt.

"I believe it's an old superstition among strolling players," the Lady Wizard explained absently, flipping through the pages of a thick, old book in front of her. "Something to do with reverse charming. Time to begin, gentlemen!"

She would be the Examination timekeeper. The Examining Board originally was to consist of Flarman, Augurian, and Wong Tscha San, but the addition of Litholt allowed Flarman to act solely as Chairman. As the Candidate's Master, he wouldn't participate in the examining, other than to rule on disputed points.

He felt both the better and the worse for it. He knew he would be too emotionally involved in the Examination of his own Journeyman, which was bad, but he also felt he should have a larger part in the actual questioning.

"This is, after all," Augurian said to him gravely, but with an understanding twinkle in his eye, "a test of *your* Mastery as well. You *were* his primary instructor in our Craft."

"Well, yes, I suppose so," said the Fire Wizard with a wistful sigh. "You're absolutely right, of course. What am I worried about? The Candidate was the most remarkable Apprentice and is the most resourceful Journeyman I've ever known or heard about, present company not excepted. He can't miss!"

"We shall begin, then," said Litholt, nodding to Flarman.

"Candidate is to present himself," announced Flarman in a loud voice, rapping on the table with an old wooden mallet he'd brought from his Workshop.

The door opened and Myrn ushered Douglas in. She touched his hand for a brief moment, then slipped quietly out to take a long walk down Crooked Brook toward Trunkety. Staying in the house would be too worrisome. She would call on Priceless and Lilac at their house across the rickety plank bridge, and perhaps go shopping in the town. It was Trunkety Market Day.

Marbleheart walked with her as far as the bridge, then turned off to take a bracing swim, hoping that his cousins the River Otters would come along and invite him to lunch on freshly caught brook trout.

The Wizards' High cottage fell absolutely silent. Even the usually hilarious washing up of the breakfast dishes was accomplished very quietly. If anything made an accidental noise, Blue Teakettle hissed sharply, *Shhhhh!*

■   ■   ■

"Candidate, state your true name, rank, and birthplace," intoned Flarman.

Douglas stood easily at attention and identified himself. Bronze Owl scribbled rapidly on the first page of a bound book of blank pages, prepared specially for just this purpose. Black Flame looked in at the door, but padded softly away, followed by Pert. Party was nowhere to be seen.

Overhead in the roof, the Thatchmouse Family settled down to being very, very still, so as not to disturb the Candidate or seem to be coaching him. Living in the roof of Wizards' High for all these years, they'd picked up a surprising amount of magical lore. Most of it they used to avoid capture by one of Pert's or Party's kittens when the kits were first learning to hunt.

The Board Chairman solemnly explained the Rules to the Candidate, and invited him to take the straight-backed chair facing them across the narrow library table.

He was allowed a clean slate, a sponge, and a supply of white chalk with which to make notes and do calculations, if need be, but otherwise he was without notes or books, papers, or devices of any kind.

Douglas was dressed in a traditional Journeyman's white shirt under a soft grey linen vest, blue buckram britches with silver buckles, and a deep blue Wizard's gown without the usual embroidered stars, comets, moons, and other mystic symbols.

He doffed a flat, blue velvet cap with a silver tassel hanging down the middle of his back. On the breast of his shirt was embroidered in gold and red threads the ancient Pyromancy oriflamme.

"Now, Candidate," began Augurian, leaning forward in his chair, "please tell us in a hundred words or less why you seek to become a Master of the Craft of Wizardry known as Pyromancy . . ."

Examination began at ten o'clock sharp, Owl noted in his book with a flourish. *It must be completed by 8:46* P.M., *the moment of the Autumnal Equinox at the latitude and longitude of Valley in Dukedom. The first question was posed by the Master of Aquamancy, Augurian of Waterand. . . .*

The questions at first were not all that hard. Perhaps the hardest was the first, asked by the Water Adept: *Why did he want to be a Master Wizard?*

How forthright should he be?

Certainly he found the Craft deeply absorbing, highly interesting, filled with potential for personal satisfaction. It gave him the tools to be useful, to accomplish things for himself and for others, too.

Flarman Flowerstalk taught that Wizardry must always be practiced for the sake of others. There were the folk of Valley and Dukedom, the Sea Creatures who had befriended him. The good folk of Flowring Isle. The Realm of Faerie . . .

Even Frigeon, once he had been compelled to take back his conscience, hidden for years in the Great Grey Pearl at the bottom of Sea, eagerly embraced this principle.

The townsmen of Pfantas and the helpless, ensorceled Undead servants of the Witch's Coven. And, of course, the Stones, most recently.

Caspar Marlinspike. Bryarmote. Chief Tet of Highlandorm. Crimeye, Tet's adopted son and heir. Oval the Great Sea Tortoise. The Waiters of Summer Palace in Old Kay. His shipwright father and his lovely mother Gloriana. The good fisherfolk of Fairstrand.

Even sweetly sad, faithful little Jenny Greenteeth, keeping vigil beside her husband's watery grave in the marshes along Bloody Brook.

But . . . he had to admit, didn't he? He wanted to become full Master Wizard because he just plain enjoyed Wizardry? It was fun! It had already brought him fame and even some fortune. And a beautiful, talented, loving bride! People everywhere recognized his name and respected his skills and powers. He was a friend to the Golden Dragons and of the Queen of Faerie herself.

After considering the question for a full minute in this way, he answered exactly and completely, just as he had formed it in his mind.

The Examiners nodded with satisfaction.

Litholt next asked, "What is the recommended formula for a Spell of Invisibility and what are its limitations and dangers, Master Candidate?"

This was familiar ground. Douglas had several times practiced Invisibility. His answer was quick and crisply professional.

The Board Members nodded again.

Wong smiled gently at the Journeyman.

"A green, a blue, a red, and a brown?" he asked; no more.

"Ah, oh," said Douglas, puzzled. "Um?"

"Take your time," said Litholt, glancing at the wall clock pointedly. "You may defer the question, if you wish, but you'll be docked five points, if you do so, even if you eventually answer correctly."

The Journeyman pondered the Magician's cryptic question. Ah! Yes! The colors referred to types of winds that can be conjured at will by a Wizard. Very handy thing to know.

Douglas explained in some detail.

"Excellent!" cried Wong.

Bronze Owl had no trouble keeping up with the questions and answers. The Board's pace was leisurely, although Douglas thought the minute hand on the wall clock spun much too fast about its ornate dial.

He explained how Flarman's Cold Boxes worked, in detail, including the properties of balsa wood or cork as insulators. He added that his researches suggested it would be even better to line the cold chamber within the box with thick glass.

"I've found glass to be a much better barrier against both cold and heat," he said, warming to his subject. Part of a Candidate's problem was to answer not in too much detail. The clock was against him.

Control.

Concision.

Care.

■　　■　　■

Blue Teakettle bustled merrily in at one o'clock, riding Tea Cart piled high with sandwiches, dill pickles ("Good for the concentration and the constitution, too"), hot cocoa or coffee, and ginger cookies ("To make the Candidate smart as a snap!"), the kind with walnuts and bits of chocolate that Douglas especially loved.

Flarman rapped the table sharply with his mallet and declared an hour recess for lunch.

Owl noted the time and the menu in his record and laid down Ostrich Plume Pen.

"May I ask how I'm doing thus far?" asked the Master Candidate, reaching for a second ham-and-cheese sandwich on rye bread with mustard. He recalled eating practically nothing for breakfast.

"I guess it would not be an infringement of the Rules to say you have scored almost a hundred percent so far," conceded the Water Adept, pouring tea for Litholt and Flarman. He glanced at Flarman for a ruling.

"The Rule is not specific about lunchtime conversation," the Pyromancer said around a drumstick of cold fried chicken. "So, I'm inclined to suggest that such questions be ignored. Talk about the weather, if you want a safer subject."

"It's going to be a nice afternoon," observed Douglas. "Wish I were with Myrn at Market."

"As do we all," grumped Flarman, but he softened his words with a grin. "When you've finished that third sandwich, my b——Candidate, we shall resume."

"We have twelve minutes left, Douglas, before lunchtime is officially elapsed," said the official timekeeper, consulting Wall Clock. "Now, you stop that!" she scolded the timepiece. "You'll spoil the Examination, cheating in Douglas's favor like that!"

Case Clock shrugged apologetically and rearranged its hands from 1:18 to 1:28 again.

"I may need those minutes later," Douglas said, shaking his finger at Clock. "I'm ready to resume."

"The thirteen types of induced ignition?" asked Litholt at once.

Bronze Owl snatched up Pen and dipped it hurriedly in Inkwell.

"And the two most useful uses of each? And how can a Wizard proceed to combine which three to intensify all the others? With examples from past experience, if you can."

Douglas blew a puff of breath at the thatch overhead and began to recite.

"Woosney!" whispered Mrs. Thatchmouse to her youngest and wriggliest child. "What *is* the matter with you?"

"I gotta *go,* Mama!" squeaked the mousling, squirming all the more.

"Then for heaven's sake, go!" said his father. "But be quiet as a mouse!"

"Remember what he says and tell me it all when I get back," pleaded Woosney of his next-youngest sister. He disappeared down a tunnel in the thatch reeds.

"Boys!" snipped one of his older sisters.

"Mind yourself, missy," her father warned. "You'll wish that your youngest is as housebroken as Woosney is, one day soon enough, mark my words!"

The mice settled back to listen to Douglas recite, explain, expound, suggest, describe, demonstrate, refute, correct, edit, elaborate, and elucidate. Most of what he said went right over their tiny heads. Much of it was beyond even Owl's vast knowledge, although he was pleased that the things he had personally taught the young Wizard had been well learned and well remembered.

Flarman listened with his eyes half-closed, nodding from time to time.

Both Litholt and Wong sat erect, hands folded, leaning forward to listen carefully to each answer.

Augurian was erect, also, but relaxed, calm, and counting off salient points on his long, slim fingers. Occasionally he made scribbled notes on a sheet of foolscap before him.

■ ■ ■

Myrn wandered aimlessly through busy, boisterous Trunkety Market.

On every hand she was greeted with warm admiration and respect by the Trunkety housewives and the Valley farmwives. On Market Day the latter were all in town to sell their eggs, cheeses, dressed chickens, apple butter, fancy breads and meats, butter in carved wooden molds, whole and shelled nuts, fudge, divinity, sticky toffee wrapped in colored wax papers, rolled soft, rich caramels, peanut and walnut brittles, pecan pralines and sumptuous penuche, fat fruit pies and artistically sugar-and-butter-frosted cakes . . . as well as knitted woolen winter wear and sturdy wicker baskets in an amazing variety of styles, sizes, and purposes.

At first they all asked how the Examination was progressing, but when it became evident that the Water Adept knew as little about it as they did, the subject changed to the Wedding.

"Lilac has done fantastically good work on your bridal gown, Mistress," exclaimed one. "Dicksey must be making a fortune on silk thread alone!"

"Nonsense!" cried another. "Good old Dicksey is donating all the materials, so good has business been since Dead Winter and Dry Summer."

"I do hope you're wrong about that!" cried Myrn. "There would be no reason in World why the storekeeper should give us so much! We intend to pay for every yard and every spool!"

"We'll all be repaid for our trouble ten times over just to have you living at the High permanent, my dear Wizardling," insisted the eldest grandmother.

"Tell us about this new Wizard who came back with you," another pleaded. "A Lady Wizard! Who ever heard of such—save for you, Mistress Myrn, of course."

She took lunch with several of them at the Oak 'n' Bucket, sitting in the Ladies' Parlor beside a cheery fire of Sea coal and pine logs. The men in the bar next door talked and laughed as they always did, although, as it was market day, their language was toned down somewhat, all the women knew. They were bragging now about their crops, which had been excellent that year, and why it was so many travelers were being seen on the Brook Road these days, now that the roads were safe again.

The women mostly talked of their children and grandchildren.

"You dint the waiting most well, Mistress Myrn," Innkeeper complimented her in kindly fashion as he cleared away the luncheon dishes.

"Not as hard as it would be without so many friends to help me through it," replied Myrn, graciously and sincerely. "I'll have a piece of the crumbly yellow cheese, if I may, and a red-cheeked Valley apple, please."

The Sea Otter swam and floated miles and miles down Crooked Brook, looking, but not too hard, for his smaller, shyer cousins, enjoying being off by himself with his thoughts for a change. The role of Familiar was still new to him, but he had to admit it was quite wonderful. Exciting. Fulfilling. Adventurous. Well fed.

And brought a measure of respect and admiration most Otters never knew, he realized. Otters were expected to be more or less clowns. And, of course, for good reason!

He found a place where a tiny joining streamlet bounded down a grassy embankment into the Brook, and spent an hour sliding down it and plunging into the tea-colored water.

A number of Blue Jays watched his antics and chortled with raucous glee every time he hit the water with a satisfying splash.

But as he shook himself damp, spelled himself dry, and turned back toward the High, a drab female Jay hopped down to him with a shy request.

"My littlest one—we calls him Azure—he's not quite right," she whispered shyly.

"Not right? You mean in the head or in his body, ma'am?" asked Marbleheart, instantly sympathetic.

"No, in his wings!" said the worried young mother. She began to weep softly. "He . . . he . . . won't or can't fly, and all his brothers and sisters are long out and about the nest already. Some of them fly miles each day!"

"Well, well, and well!" said the Otter, seriously, but with an encouraging smile, "I knew a litter-runt Otter once who refused to learn to swim, which is much the same to Otters, you see, as flying is to Jays."

"What did his poor, distracted mother do?" sniffed the Jay lady, sounding not so sure that being an Otter was the same.

"His father convinced him he could be as good a swimmer as any of his sibs. It seems he felt he couldn't do well in competition with his bigger, older sisters. It isn't easy being the smallest in the litter—or the clutch, for that matter."

"Yes, well, I suppose we haven't really encouraged him as much as we should, put that way," admitted the mother. "But his father's worried sick, and so am I."

"I remember my own mother saying, about this runt Otter I spoke of, that he learned to swim eventually because it is in the very nature of Otters to swim, and he couldn't really refuse forever."

"Oh, so you think . . . ," the Jay mother said, hopefully.

"I say, if young Azure is still not flying by Hallowed Even, you must bring him up to Wizards' High. There are those there under yonder roof who know more than I ever will about such things. I recommend you bespeak the Water Adept's Apprentice, Mistress Myrn. She is particularly good with young animals, I've noticed."

The Blue Jay and her more resplendent mate, who had been hanging back but listening carefully to all they said, thanked Marbleheart profusely and promised to try building Azure's self-confidence—and to bring him to Myrn, if things didn't get better.

"Fortunate that Jays don't migrate," said the male with a

quick shake of his head. "But what you say is so very true. It isn't easy to be the smallest hatchling in the nest."

By design or accident, the Apprentice and the Familiar met on the road up from Trunkety, just after she'd crossed Trunkety Bridge to the south bank.

"Had a nice day so far?" Marbleheart asked, not knowing what else to say.

"Not especially," admitted the young lady. "I didn't even *buy* anything, and I really wanted some marjoram and some of Frenstil's saddle soap. We're all but out of it at home, at the High."

They walked together in silence for a mile, passing Augurian's Fountain and then passing under the edge of Priceless's orchard before they set foot at last on the plank bridge. The sun was below the horizon and the sky was afterglowing with wonderfully rich fall colors, too.

Myrn stopped in the middle of the plank bridge to survey Wizards' High in the purple twilight.

"It's still going on," Marbleheart observed. He pointed to the glowing windows of Flarman's study.

"Everything's going to be just fine," Myrn reassured herself as much as the Otter.

"Of course it is!" cried Marbleheart.

He remembered to tell her about the little Blue Jay who refused to fly.

"Oh, the poor little bird! Perhaps I should look his folks up. He just needs some Wizardly encouragement, I think."

"It's too late to go back now," said Marbleheart. "But if you want, tomorrow I'll take you to them. They'd come to you, but as the young 'un won't fly . . ."

"No, it'll have to wait. We return to Choin tomorrow," said Myrn.

They crossed the bridge and as they approached the double front doors, they felt and saw the first lacy flakes of snow of the coming winter.

"Oh, I love it when it snows!" Myrn sang.

"Hmph!" snorted the Otter. "I'd have thought you'd had enough of it, up there in the Gorge."

"Never!" she said, trying to catch a flake on her gloved hand. The one she caught was surpassingly beautiful. She murmured a tiny spell to prevent it from melting.

"I'll show this one to Douglas," she explained. "I wonder how much longer they will be."

Full darkness fell by half past six, thanks to the lowering snow clouds. They saw Blue Teakettle escorting a fresh pot of tea and another of hot cocoa into the Wizard's study.

By seven-thirty, when Marbleheart stepped out the kitchen door into the courtyard, two inches of snow had already fallen. The temperature was not low, but he could, for the first time that year, see his breath.

"Want to practice blowing rings?" he asked, but there was nobody there to answer. Myrn was curled up snugly in soft, cozy Easy Chair by the front parlor grate—she could just see the head of the stair from there, in case anyone left the study and came down the steps with news—reading one of her interminable Aquamancy textbooks.

"Oh, well," sighed Marbleheart. "What's for supper, anyway?"

Douglas came down to the front door for a breath of cold air. It had become rather stuffy in the Examining Room toward the last, what with Flarman's and Augurian's pipes and the many beeswax candles burning. He was drenched with perspiration.

He almost passed the front parlor but Easy Chair waved an overstuffed arm to attract his attention. Myrn was sound asleep in its embrace, her book fallen to the floor.

The young man went softly to his betrothed, stood looking at her for a bit, then reached out to touch her cheek.

"I'm so sorry!" she murmured, hurling herself into his arms. "I wanted to be near when you finished."

"Well, and you are, and most prettily, here by the fire," soothed Douglas. "I want you to know I love you, no matter what the outcome of the Examination."

"I love you, too! So much! What *was* the outcome?" she demanded.

He settled on the arm of the chair when she slid over to make room for him. Easy Chair sighed contentedly for them both.

"We'll know in a couple of minutes," he told her. "They're still up there, toting up my score. Come outside and let me catch my breath and not think of anything except you for a while. It's snowing hard, I see!"

The snow covered the front stoop to a depth of four inches and still fell, slowly and very, very softly. There was no wind.

Bronze Owl found them standing very close together, blowing their steamy breath into rings that would have made Bryarmote very proud. Owl clanged himself onto his nail, attracting their attention.

"You are now . . . a Master Pyromancer!" the metal bird shouted. "Congratulations! One of the highest scores ever achieved by a Journeyman, Augurian claims. Personally, I never doubted the issue."

"Well, neither did I!" cried Myrn, hugging Douglas anew.

"*I* did," admitted the brand-new Master Pyromancer, heaving a tremendous sigh of relief. "Whew! Let's go inside before we freeze to the ground!"

Marbleheart was on the stairs, jumping up and down from step to step in highly pleased excitement. Flarman and Litholt, followed by Augurian and Wong more slowly, came down, beaming broadly at everyone.

For the center hall was suddenly crowded wall to wall with the whole Wizards' High household, from Blue Tea-kettle, blowing hot, pink steam to the ceiling, to Sugar Caster, shaking with excitement, and all the Plates, Spoons, Knives, Forks, Tongs, Griddles, Grills, Slicers, Mashers—well, it was a madhouse.

"He made it with twenty minutes to spare," announced Litholt over the din. "You could have taken the twelve more minutes for lunch, Wizard Douglas Brightglade!"

"There were no infringements or infractions," claimed the Water Adept, heartily. "Nothing to argue about at all."

"My task was the easiest," said Flarman, coming down to embrace his former Apprentice and Journeyman. "But then, I knew all the answers."

"Because you wrote the questions," cried Marbleheart.

Everyone roared again, this time with laughter.

Chapter Eighteen

Unfinished Business

THERE were several legal and logical candidates for Emperor, including several completely useless Princes of the Imperial Family, each of whom had long since gathered his own force of armed bullies and spies.

None of these logical candidates was ever considered seriously by the various Ministers of the Imperium, including the Ministers of Finance, Treasury and War, or even by the Minister of the Imperial Household, perhaps the most capable of all the hereditary Ministers of State by virtue of his closeness to the dead Emperor.

These gentlemen, instead, each sought a different, more pliable puppet they could control, someone with absolutely no power base, who would depend on his sponsoring Minister for survival during and after the coronation—a nice, quiet, dunderheaded fool with an easily inflated sense of self-importance, preferably but not necessarily with some slight claim to the Dragon Throne.

Bee-Wing, the Choin capital, was abuzz with ambition and uncertainty, filled from outer wall to inner palace with furtive Bureaucrats, their private soldiers and sly secret agents.

Each Minister huddled in his luxurious palace in the fashionable precincts of the beautiful, sprawling city, conferring, gathering information, stealing adherents from each other, and waiting for a chance to strike.

The main roads in a large part of the central province had suffered greatly from the floods following the torrential typhoon rains. Bridges had been swept away and whole sections of Imperial Highways were still underwater. The feverish jockeying for influence and power had slid to a halt until the typhoon passed. Communications were impossible; armed men were unable to move. Assassins and spies were hampered by the disappearance of escape routes.

The aggressive Minister of Finance had been getting the upper hand before the storm, but he'd fled his fortified stronghold on the coast and his red-lacquered private troops were scattered across the soggy littoral. Some of them had been caught and drowned in flash floods. The remainder were isolated by still-raging rivers and smashed bridges between them and their employer in the capital.

Finance talked to Agriculture. Agriculture sent for Mining. Mining brought powerful Fisheries to a meeting at Roads' villa just within the walls of the city. A day-long debate among them settled nothing but bought Finance some time.

Meanwhile Finance opened his private coffers to hire a free-lance regiment from beyond the eastern Imperial border, and sent his most trusted ally, the Minister of Trade, to Choin Harbor in a river barge to meet and move them as quickly as possible to Bee-Wing.

Trade thus found himself at the head of his own private army.

He began to move the mercenary troopers toward Bee-Wing as soon as the rivers returned to their normal beds. He was sorely tempted by the realization that he was now a force to be reckoned with himself.

From his bunker under a bank of oleander north of Imperial House, a self-styled Prince named Too Wang Sung announced that *he* was the most direct heir to the Dragon Throne. He planned to move his ragtag army of woodcutters and paper-millers into Imperial House the following morning.

It appeared a desperate outside bid for power—except that Too had gathered nearly ten thousand discontented, out-of-work mill workers, farmers, and woodsmen armed with double-bitted axes, hay knives, chain flails and wicked pruning hooks—and five ancient ballistae they had unearthed somewhere—to back his move.

He'd found them in the poorest of the provinces, enticed them with promises of unrestricted looting in revenge for real and imagined wrongs. As they faced certain starvation if they stayed at home, the countrymen flocked to Too's banner.

They were by far the best-motivated if worst-organized army in the capital. They also, purely by accident, stood between Trade's approaching mercenary troops and the capital.

Having made his announcement, Too settled back under his oleander hedge, smoked his pipe, smiled enigmatically in answer to all questions, and waited for allies to present themselves.

Within an hour delegations from several minor Imperial functionaries promised their departmental treasuries to support Too's Peasant Army. The Minister of Police, relatively powerless due to the practice of stronger Ministers of maintaining private police and military units, arrived just at dusk, bringing with him several hundred police spies and a shorthanded company of ceremonial Mounted Imperial Bodyguards whose duty was largely crowd control at rare public Imperial functions.

The Pretender and the Minister of Police met by lantern light among the oleanders and struck a bargain. Police was to have overall military command of the peasant rabble. His new command would surround Imperial House, flood its network of dry moats, and stand off any attempt to interfere with Too's occupation of the palace long enough to form a revolutionary government.

Police sealed his bargain with Too by striking his forehead on the ground before him three times—the traditional submission to an Emperor—and as soon as he could get away on pretext of preparing for the morrow, sent a message to the Minister of Finance, offering to betray the Pretender as he approached Imperial House, in exchange for the highest police post in the new Imperium, when Finance had selected the new Emperor.

Privately, Police thought he himself would be the ideal candidate for the Dragon Throne. He sent his police spies out to put the suggestion in important ears about the town.

Finance, when he received the offer from Police, almost choked himself laughing. He sent back word that he wanted time to think about it.

"No time to *think*!" shouted Police when he heard the reply. "Time only to *act*. Finance will regret his decision not to decide."

This situation met Flarman, Douglas, Myrn, Litholt, Marbleheart, and Wong Tscha San the morning they returned to Choin.

"How can we contact Foggery and Bryarmote?" wondered Flarman.

They had chosen Wong's own house near Choin Harbor as their starting point. Wong was delighted to extend them hospitality, although his low, pleasant house had been badly damaged by the typhoon and by vindictive Constables of the murdered Imperial Governor of Harbor. They'd torn everything to pieces searching for mystic secrets left behind by the Magician when he'd escaped to Caspar Marlin's ship earlier that year. It seemed much longer ago than that, as Myrn said to Douglas.

"I'll summon an old retainer of Captain Foggery's," Wong decided. "He has a farm a half day's journey to the west. He'll certainly know where his master is."

He asked one of his neighbors—all of his own servants had long since fled—to fetch Foggery's retired gardener and, meanwhile, he, Douglas, and Myrn, helped by the Otter, restored some order to the Magician's house.

Flarman and Litholt excused themselves, went outside, and stood facing southwest for an hour, seemingly con-

juring a slow but hot wind that brought more than a hint
of Serecomba, drying the deeply rutted roads and flooded
fields left by the awesome typhoon.

Augurian went in the other direction to a delightful little lake surrounded by weeping willows and inhabited by
graceful blue herons with bright orange beaks and legs.

"He's gathering an overall picture of the situation,"
guessed Myrn, wielding a puff of damp breeze like a
broom to sweep debris from the floor of Wong's parlor.
Douglas was resetting paper panes in the sliding windows
that opened on Wong's badly neglected garden.

"I think Flarman and Litholt are enlisting an ally," he
said.

"Do you know their intent?" asked his fiancée. "If it were
my own Magister, I'd expect him to conjure up a tidal wave
or reroute a few rivers. But I'm not sure what that pair
would do."

"I've a good idea—with which I'll let them surprise
everybody," grinned Douglas. "There, those windows will
keep out the chill night air, or as chill as it gets here. What
shall I do next, do you think? You're the experienced home-
maker here."

"Fill the roof reservoir with fresh water, if you can
handle an Aquamancer's task," teased Myrn. "No, let me
do it. That table needs a new leg. The wicked Constables
expected Master Wong to hide his secrets in table legs and
down-filled cushions, it seems. *Woof!* It's good to be rid of
all those feathers."

They had arrived in early evening, and by noon the
following day the house was fairly well refurbished and
ready for occupancy once again.

Wong stood in the middle of his sitting room and spun
slowly on his heel, taking it all in, tears in his aged grey
eyes.

"What would a man do without good friends?" he wondered aloud.

Litholt bowed deeply and respectfully to their host and
said, "It is a privilege to serve a good friend. It will take

us a while to set your perennials and peach trees to rights,
I'm afraid. Those wicked, thoughtless men were certainly
destructive!"

"It's a result of serving a master like our late Governor,"
sighed the Magician. "My people are not usually destructive
or violent. Only fear could drive men to such vandalism."

"How about some lunch?" demanded the Otter, who
had been exploring the house, the grounds, and the
neighborhood. Housework was not his forte, he'd decided.
Dust balls gave him fits of sneezing.

"I'll take care of it," said the Water Adept's Apprentice.
She began the spells that would import a hearty hot lunch
from distant Wizards' High. Lunch was soon laid out on
the repaired table.

"First order of business," declared Flarman. "Find out
what the political and military situations are before we go
any further."

"We can rely on Foggery to supply us with that information," observed Wong.

A very old, gnarled Choinman, in rusty brown robes and
wearing straw sandals and a broad-brimmed straw hat, rang
the bell at the front gate.

"Here's Lee!" Wong interrupted himself, and Douglas
hastened to admit the old man, who grinned happily at the
Magician and bowed rapidly to each in the company as he
was introduced.

"I am Lee Liung Lee," he said several times. "Until I
became too decrepit to hoe and plant, prune and graft, I
was honored, sirs and ladies, to care for the garden of the
revered Seacaptain Foggery."

"If Captain Foggery's beautiful garden is your handiwork," said Litholt, making the newcomer comfortable at
the table, "you do splendid work, Master Lee. Such grace
and poetry!"

"You must teach me the names of the flowers and the
trees of Choin. So many of them are unknown to us across
Sea," added Myrn.

The retired gardener beamed ecstatically and offered to begin teaching botany and horticulture to the Water Adept right then and there.

"First," Augurian reminded them, "we must attend to the sad business at hand. A garden needs a dedicated gardener, and an Empire needs a good Emperor, do you not agree?"

"No doubt at all about it!" cried Lee. "How may I serve you in that cause, Masters? Lee Liung Lee is at your service!"

"You can put us in touch with your former Master, Captain Foggery," said Flarman.

"Of course! By last word—it came yesterday evening by messenger—he is in a village in the hills above Bee-Wing."

"What said he then?" asked Wong eagerly.

"Well, sirs and ladies, it made mention of his present location in case you came, not a detailed account of what he did. I understand from other sources that he gathers information and organizes his farmers' granges and artisans' guilds, and contacts trustworthy noblemen who can be relied upon to assist us. I would also suspect they're busy trying to discover the good gardener we spoke about."

"Perhaps it's best if we go to him, then, rather than ask him to come here," suggested Augurian to Flarman.

"I intend to go to him," said the older Pyromancer. "It's important to Litholt's plan that we be close to Bee-Wing, once Foggery's people agree on their candidate."

"They're such a diverse group! I fear they'll never agree on a single candidate, sirs, except through force of arms," Lee sighed.

"We'll see about that," was all Flarman would say, and he suggested that they depart at once for Foggery's headquarters.

"We'll all go with you," said Myrn. "We can each contribute at least some common sense to the outcome."

"A commodity all too scarce in rebellious times," observed Wong. "I dislike leaving my beloved home so soon again, but it's necessary, so I must be content."

"What is it Flarman plans to do, I wonder?" Myrn asked Douglas again as they prepared to leave.

"I'm not entirely sure, and even if I were, I would rather have him tell about it," Douglas said most seriously.

"Oh!" she said. "I can't wait!"

"Nor can I, but we must. Tomorrow will probably bring it all into the open."

"Tomorrow," she murmured, lifting her face for his kiss.

They found the retired Seacaptain and the Dwarf Prince in a large, airy workshop in the middle of a small village set just under the brow of a hill overlooking the lush, landscaped splendor of the Imperial Capital.

Foggery sat surrounded by large, flat tables covered with tall stacks of blank paper and amid various mysterious pieces of ink-blackened machinery. Beyond they saw Bryarmote, spattered with greasy ink, working furiously on one of the machines with a long hand-lever and a confusing welter of rollers, pivots, plates, pedals, cranks, and gears.

"This is the Imperial Print Shop," Foggery explained after he greeted them. "It was damaged by a mob sent by the Minister of Finance a few days before the typhoon, but not destroyed. Bryarmote hopes to get it up and running shortly. Very useful."

"Not many knew it even existed," explained Bryarmote. "The Bureaucrats printed paper money and Imperial edicts here and thereby controlled the economy and all official news from the Throne."

"A print shop!" exclaimed Douglas. "I've never been in one before."

"How does one *print* money?" wondered Marbleheart, who was just getting used to the notion of paying for materials and services with metal coins. "I thought money had to be silver or copper or gold and things like that."

"I'll explain it to you later, Sea Otter," said Litholt. "If done properly, it is a convenience greater than carrying heavy metal coins, of course."

"Thornwood has spoken of introducing the practice to

Dukedom," observed Flarman. "It was used long ago in Old Kingdom, until King Grummist got greedy and printed far too much and its value fell to almost nothing."

"Sounds complicated to me," sniffed Marbleheart. "Well, I learn something new almost every hour of the day."

"And we are here to learn the political and military situation," reminded Augurian, getting back to business.

"I'll answer all your questions that I can, then," said the Seacaptain, seating them all at one of the tables.

He described the confusion of cross purposes that had been wracking the country since even before the typhoon. Minister against Minister against demagogue against parties and factions.

"It all appears to be on the verge of exploding, I fear," he said. "Given a tithe of a chance, by tomorrow the conflict may shake out as between the two major factions—that of the Minister of Finance and Too's Peasant Army. Everyone else will be forced to take sides."

"Tell us of them," suggested Flarman.

"One is led by the very ambitious and ruthless Minister of Finance. You remember, he sent the soldiers to attack my house on the coast? He's managed to draw to himself a majority of the important Bureaucrats, including most of the top Ministers. At least on paper. What strength he actually has, no one can guess—least of all old Finance himself.

"He faces this unknown Too Wang Sung and his so-called Peasant Army. Do you know this Too, Magician?"

"I never heard of him," replied Wong, shaking his head. "Yet he has gathered an army?"

"An army of ten thousand hungry rebels, mostly from Doonchong, which has been sorely depressed for years, the scene of unrest and violence, ever since the Bureaucracy ordered a stop to papermaking."

He gestured to the piles of paper on the counters around him.

"They announced that, as no more books needed to be published, no more paper was required," Wong remembered. "Doonchong is a most sore spot, I know. The poor woodsmen and paper-millers were cut off without a trade or craft, almost overnight, when they were forbidden to cut trees."

"Right, Magician! Well, these men have flocked to Too Wang Sung, who'd been a rascally itinerant gambler, as far as I can find out. He purchased a minor position as Inspector of Forests from the Minister of Manufacture with his winnings, they tell me, and milked it for all it was worth."

"How does he come to lead an army, then?" asked Marbleheart before anyone else could ask.

"When the Bureaucrats decided to cease papermaking and woodcutting, Too took advantage of the unrest—it took no great vision—and began making speeches in the idle logging and mill towns of Doonchong. He claimed he was related to the late Emperor's fourteenth son. No one in the Bureaucracy bothered to dispute his claim so it's probably true, as far as that goes. It became a common belief among his followers. Then it was too late to dispute his claims.

"When it became obvious that the Bureaucrats would start a civil war, contending among themselves to appoint the next Emperor, Too told his followers that if they would set him on the Dragon Throne, he would pension them all, resume logging and papermaking—and in the meantime provide plenty of loot, rape, revenge, and bloodshed. It proved an irresistible combination. Thousands flocked to follow him."

"And now?" asked Augurian.

"Now his rabble is armed and camped on the northern edge of the city, just within the walls. Too has announced he will march on Imperial House tomorrow. Once in the palace, he will proclaim himself Emperor and form a new government. I think he reasons the people of the Empire will gladly accept him rather than submit to the confusion and bloodshed of the Bureaucrats and Princes. He must think he has men enough to withstand attacks from the Minister of Finance and his allies. He may very well pull it off."

"Is that your estimate of the outcome?" asked Myrn.

"It's a toss-up!" exclaimed Foggery, waving his hands

wildly. "Too has a large number of men willing to risk death in his cause, but they are ill organized and ill equipped, even if you count the few professionals the Minister of Police has provided.

"On the other hand, Finance has hired highly trained and well-armed mercenary soldiers, professionally led, but they are few. His officers are said to be bidding against each other for power, prestige, and higher pay."

"Seems to me history will favor the trained, disciplined force," put in Douglas.

"Except that Finance's mercenaries were until last evening isolated from the capital by the aftereffects of the storm," explained the Seacaptain, "and are just now moving this way."

"Finance took a terrible risk hiring foreign mercenaries," declared Wong.

"Yes," agreed Foggery, "Finance's own officers are on the verge of mutiny! They all want to be the one in command, it seems."

"Well, then, what *will* happen?" demanded the Otter.

"What we've said all along," Foggery replied, suddenly quite angry. "Chaos! Bloodshed! Anarchy! Looting and rapine! Disruption of food supplies, hence widespread hardship and starvation far beyond the battlefield. You can write your own log on this, can't you, Sea Otter?"

"I've read of such times in World history," Marbleheart said, shaking his head. "Such things never happen among us beasts. I guess that's what keeps us from being civilized."

They went out to the hilltop, which provided a splendid view of the whole capital, with its sparkling, pagoda-towered palaces, shining lakes and wide canals, public buildings with manicured lawns, gardens and groves.

In between stood the neatly aligned houses of merchants, lesser Imperial servants, and minor court officials.

Around it all looped a fifty-foot-wide boulevard lined with graceful, ancient weeping willows. To this came roads from all points of the compass.

Every half-mile along this road stood a tall, round tower

looking out over a countryside cleared of trees and brush for at least a mile beyond the boulevard. No huts or farmhouses were allowed to stand here, nor was anyone allowed to plant crops or trees.

In normal times the lawns were kept close-cropped by flocks of black sheep that Wong explained belonged to the Emperor himself. This day, no sheep were in sight.

"Probably herded in by the country folk against food shortages," guessed Marbleheart gruffly. "Well, can we blame them?"

A dusty messenger arrived on foot, laboring up the steep hill from the capital. He thrust a sheaf of papers into the Seacaptain's hand, saluted, and fell panting on the grassy verge without a word.

"You've managed quite well, getting information and setting up your organizations," Augurian complimented Foggery. "What news?"

Foggery read quickly through the dispatches, nodded his head, and gave them a brief summary.

"Too is on the move. He'll be at the palace before dawn tomorrow, unless he's stopped by Finance's mercenary force. Too's people are singing and marching and looting private houses in the north suburbs. Too, who is calling himself Prince Too now, has been joined by the Imperial Police, as we suspected. Too rides surrounded by these mounted policemen! That sounds foolish to me. He shouldn't trust the Minister of Police."

Other messages were also fraught with perils.

"Finance's mercenary troopers under the Minister of Trade hasten to cut off Too's Peasant Army from Imperial House. They may try to drive the rabble away and install Finance, or some unknown candidate of his picking, in the palace, although they are vastly outnumbered.

"Finance's own soldiers are moving swiftly toward the capital after crossing the largest of the swollen rivers by an ingenious bridge of boats. Whether they'll attack the mercenaries or help them beat off Too's army, no one will hazard a guess."

"Chaos!" exclaimed Augurian. He turned to Flarman. "It would seem time for your plan to be put in motion, Firemaster, if we are to save many lives!"

Flarman shook his head.

"Before we make our move, we need one thing to be decided or it will all be in vain. Who will your people choose, Foggery, to be your next Emperor? Once that's agreed, it'll be time to spring Litholt's surprise."

"You ask a tremendously difficult thing," warned Foggery.

"But we must and can come up with a suitable Candidate," insisted the Magician. "Come! Let us again urge our leaders to agree for once."

"Can they do it in time?" wondered Myrn, almost to herself.

"They *must*," Flarman insisted.

Augurian agreed. "We *could* dictate their choice—proclaim Wong himself the new Emperor."

"He'd be popular," said Marbleheart approvingly.

"But magic and politics *never* mix," Douglas said quite firmly. "It's proven historical fact, dear friends. The Choinese must decide for themselves who will rule them. After that—well, after that maybe we can give him a fair chance to succeed."

The Combined Council of the Grange, the Workingmen's Association, the Artisans' Guild, and the Patriotic Society of Choin met with Wong and Foggery at dusk on the reverse slope of the hill so as not to be seen too easily from the city.

Armed patrols from various Bureaucrats' strongholds tried to penetrate the thick forest clothing the lower slopes of the hill, but were turned away time and again—not by force of arms, but by maze confusions sewn by the four Wizards. Marbleheart, a slightly darker shadow in the night, acted as their eyes and ears.

The soldiers thrashed about, swearing in frustration and tangling time and again in wild grapevines, thickets of briar, and deadfalls that always seemed to block their way.

Myrn attended the Geomancer, listening to her mazing spells and learning something of her craft. At moonrise they stopped to rest under a spreading chestnut. Marbleheart came gallumping up the hill to report nothing moving in the woods below. The soldiers had given up and returned to their masters.

"I'm getting sleepy," said the Flowring lass, yawning mightily. "Will we watch all night?"

Flarman's voice came from nearby.

"I've got some coffee brewing here, if you want some. Augurian has gone around to the other side to see if he can get some sort of progress report from the politicians."

Litholt and Myrn found the two Pyromancers hunched over a tiny flame screened by thick holly bushes. Over it bubbled a scarred and scorched blue-spackled coffeepot, a distant kin of Blue Teakettle. The delicious aroma of fresh coffee wafted to them in the cool wind off the heights.

"Never travel without a Pyromancer," advised Myrn, accepting a cup and sipping it appreciatively.

"I'll agree to that," said Flarman. "Here comes someone. It'd better be the Water Adept or we're in deep trouble."

"It's my Master," Myrn assured him, and a moment later the tall Aquamancer sat down on the soft grass next to her before the fire.

"Well, the Otter says the last of the Bureaucrat troops, including their scouts, have given up and gone back to their beds," Flarman said in greeting.

"Coffee? Wonderful! If I may?" said Augurian. "Delightful!"

"Anything from over the hill?" Flarman asked as he poured.

"Well, yes and no. They've spent hours arguing with Wong Tscha San that he should accept the Dragon Throne. They trust him as no other, they say."

"And Wong refused," guessed Marbleheart. He, too, accepted a cup of Wizardly coffee, although he felt wide awake.

"Yes, of course! No White Wizard would let himself be placed on a throne," said Augurian.

"Aren't you ruler of Waterand, though?" asked the Otter innocently.

"Of course not!" snorted the Water Adept. "The Wateranders rule themselves through an elected all-island Council. They have the courtesy to ask me to attend their meetings, but I have no vote."

"And if they make a wrong move, or pass a bad law?" asked Marbleheart. "Do you veto their action?"

"No," said Augurian. "I feel obliged to point out pitfalls, if any. If they still insist, I give way as gracefully as possible."

"I don't recall there ever being a bad law passed, do you, Magister?" asked Myrn.

"Well, from time to time they get a wild idea. I let them have their way. People sometimes learn best by making mistakes."

The midnight passed quite pleasantly, despite the chill wind soughing among the trees. From time to time the Otter slipped away to scout the lower slopes, but he found no further expeditions coming to pester them.

"They weren't really trying very hard to find out what was going on up here," he decided when he last returned.

"The Bureaucrats find it hard to think of commoners as any sort of threat, I guess," said Litholt. "They are too caught up in their own ambitions and plots."

At length they wrapped themselves in their cloaks and tried to catch some sleep.

The moon dropped below the hilltop and plunged the east-facing slopes into velvety blackness. The wind died with the moon. With his sharp ears Marbleheart heard, from a great distance across the city, shouts and screams, drums pounding and shrill laughter, sometimes cries of anger.

He shook Douglas gently by the shoulder.

"I think I'll slide down into town. See what's going on."

"Be careful, Familiar," said the young Master Wizard sleepily.

"I'll find you when I get back," the Otter assured him, and in a moment he was gone.

Chapter Nineteen

Battle on Fair Ground

A flock of large, white Gulls circled the town on the hill. Their good-humored badinage awoke the Earth Wizard just as dawn broke in the east.

Litholt climbed the hill to the edge of the town, looking for Wong Tscha San and Captain Foggery.

"Wake up, lazy Wizards!" called the Geomancer when she returned to the fire. "What! Drunk all the coffee and left none for poor, overworked Stonebreaker?"

Myrn rolled from her blanket with a cheery greeting and set about repairing her tossled hair. Douglas reached for the coffeepot to refill it for the early-rising Earth Wizard.

Flarman waved the Lady Geomancer to a seat on the soft grass beside him.

"Are those your Gull friends?" Litholt asked him.

"I sent for them, yes. They'll give us some useful aerial reconnaissance," Flarman yawned. "Sugar?"

"One lump, please," she replied. "Can you trust Gulls?"

"Never failed me yet! Why? Do you have reason to mistrust the breed?"

"Oh, no. In fact I know very little of them. I mistrust Crows . . ."

"So do I," agreed the Pyromancer.

" . . . and these birds seem alike in size and shape, if not color."

"Gulls," said Myrn, pulling a platter heaped with hot caramel buns from empty air and passing it around to the

221

others, "are among the noblest of birds. They're dedicated guardians of Sea, harbingers of storms, rescuers of shipwrecked sailors. I could go on and on."

"Yes, yes," complained Augurian, "but on the other hand, they've never learned when to keep silent, as you can hear."

"They'll keep watch for us from above and tell us of battle movements and such," declared Flarman, nodding toward the city. "For maximum effect, Litholt and I need to time our next and final brilliant gambit just so. Too soon, and it'll be less than completely effective. Too late, and many innocent—and a lot of not-so-innocent—people may be harmed or slain."

"That's enough of a reason for me," said Litholt. "I withdraw my objection to Gulls forthwith."

"But you haven't told us yet what decision they reached up there," Douglas said to her. "How did it go?"

"Here's Wong," she answered, pointing to the tiny Magician as he moved carefully through the underbrush to their fire. "He can tell you better than I."

Wong stopped before them, declined to sit down, accepted a cup of coffee, and reported the night's momentous decision.

"We agreed—at long last, just before false dawn—to raise a certain bright, personable, well-liked young physician named Phong Foo Chong to the Dragon Throne," he told them.

The assembled Wizards, Dwarf, and Otter applauded sincerely.

"Phong's of good family, yet not ennobled," Wong went on, bowing to their praise. "Foggery and I recommended him highly. He's not tainted by political or regional biases. Given a fair chance, he'll think clearly, act wisely, and rule compassionately. He now enjoys the support of all Foggery's diverse groups—farmers and professional men, merchants and artisans, the backbone of an Empire."

"Long live Emperor what's-his-name!" cried Marbleheart, who'd just rejoined the group. "Got any more of those luscious sticky buns, Myrn, my sweet love?"

"If there aren't enough for your dainty appetite," said the Apprentice fondly, "I'll send to the High for more."

"When you catch your breath," Douglas said to the Otter, "tell us what's happening down below."

"Catch my breath! Me? Catch my . . . I ran at top speed up the hill just now, faster'n Black Flame could ever go, and I'm not even sweating! Catch my breath!"

"Well, then, when you've filled your tummy," amended the young Wizard, "tell us your news."

"That's more respectful-like, anyway," snorted the Otter, pretending to choke on his second sweet roll. After a generous gulp of coffee, he began.

"Too's Peasant Army, I heard, came up against the Minister of Finance's paid foreigners just at midnight. On the north side of the palace complex. There was a great deal of shouting and swearing and some arrows were shot, but no great damage done."

"Were you there?" asked Myrn, concern for the Otter in her voice.

"Oh, me? I was safely hidden under the Minister of Finance's command post. Bee-Wing has a remarkably elaborate sewer and storm drain system, fortunately. Perfect for moving about unseen and unheard."

He swallowed a bite of his third bun before he continued.

"Runners kept coming in from the fight and I just listened. *They* were breathless, I can tell you, sirrah! Anyway, the Peasants now hold fast in the fields just to the north of Imperial House—the Emperor's residence, that is. The Finance Minister ranted and raved for an hour but his vaunted Mercenaries refused to attack again until first light or later, since their ambush failed to send the Peasants running for home. The Peasants outnumber 'em something like ten to one."

"Wise of them to wait for light, I would imagine," said Augurian, "from what I hear of this Too person and his followers."

Marbleheart nodded and went on, "The idea now is to bring up Finance's personal Guards—who've just now

entered the city from the east—and combine them with
the mercenaries to fight on an open stretch of level ground
mostly used for fairs and jousts and such. From what I
hear, it should be getting started just about now. Can't you
hear it?"

Faintly from the valley rose sounds of drums and trum-
pets, the clanging of brass gongs. And the shouting of a
multitude in extreme excitement.

"Time we got our own show on the road," grunted
Flarman, jumping quickly to his feet and assisting Litholt
to rise. "Douglas, call our friend Cerfew the Great White
Gull, and get his people started observing. I'll be right along
to hear their first reports."

With the arrival of Finance's own soldiers, the odds
against the Mercenaries were reduced by an encouraging
amount. With the rising of the sun, the soldiers were able
to see that the Peasants were a disorganized rabble, badly
led and impossibly armed. Most of them carried only their
heavy, double-headed felling axes. The small company of
mounted policemen around "Prince" Too made a brave
splash of color but posed no great threat to anyone—except
perhaps to the Prince himself.

The Minister of Finance, accompanied by his allies,
the ministers of Agriculture, Mining, Transportation, and
Imperial Household, most of whom contributed moral support but very little military strength to the joint cause,
climbed to the pagoda roof of Imperial House to watch
the fighting.

A constant stream of couriers dashed importantly back
and forth from the palace to Fair Ground. Unfortunately,
both the Mercenary Captain and the former Minister of
Trade, who now commanded Finance's personal soldiers,
insisted *he* was in overall command. Each dispatched his
own message to Finance for confirmation of command.

Mercenary's was terse and factual, usefully realistic.
Trade's was over-long, filled with meaningless, flowery
flattery, and wildly optimistic.

A dozen Great White Gulls circling overhead had a much better idea of what was going on than either military leader on the ground.

"They're mostly shouting insults at each other, in splendid parade-ground voices," Cerfew reported to Flarman and Douglas, trying to keep a straight beak. "The Peasant rabble has brought up its throwing machines, whatever they're called . . ."

"Ballistae," Douglas supplied.

"Yes, whatever you said. Throwing machines. Quite heavy and cumbersome. I imagine they take forever to load and shoot, if they're like those Thornwood had at Battle of Sea. Completely useless in an infantry battle."

Flarman nodded, listening with his ears to the Gull's report but searching the southern skyline with his eyes. Douglas could just make out the figure of the Lady Geomancer standing on a rocky promontory against the morning sky. She seemed to be casting a spell of some sort, but the distance was too great to be sure.

"Maybe I should return to the battle skies with Cerfew," suggested the new Master Wizard. "You may need a more experienced eye."

Flarman nodded. Cerfew was fierce and faithful to a fault, but not terribly bright, his grasp of military matters limited to being at the Battle of Sea. "You guess what's about to happen—if I'm not entirely wrong?"

"Yes, Magister, I have it figured out, all but the timing."

"Timing is the hard and uncertain part, relying on Gulls as we are. You may have to use some spell of your own to keep the whole thing from getting really serious. I leave it to you, Douglas my son."

With no further word, Douglas selected a spell magically reducing himself to about four inches tall and hopped nimbly onto the Great White's back, shouting, "Let's go to war, Cerfew!"

Myrn watched him leave, biting her lip to keep from insisting she go along. Flarman put an arm about her shoulder and gave her a hug.

"There'll be times you'll go and he'll stay behind," he soothed. "As I'm sure you must realize."

"Oh, I'm not worried about Douglas," Myrn stoutly insisted. "I just want to fly over there and help keep things under control."

"Do you guess Flarman's mysterious plans?" inquired Wong, nervously flicking his ornate ivory and peacock-feather fan open and closed. "He has not confided yet in me."

"Nor in me," said Myrn. "But . . . well, that's Flarman's way."

"See?" called the Otter. "Flarman keeps watching Mistress Litholt to the south."

"Tongs, the Fire Dog, perhaps?" guessed Wong.

"Hardly," scoffed Marbleheart. "Look out, something's going on down there!"

Douglas had a perfect view of the beginning battle.

The combined Mercenary Force and Finance Guards line formed a wide arc around the north edge of Imperial House's beautiful grounds, facing the empty Fair Ground.

They were armed with long pikes, with broad, curving swords, and with short spears. They lined up neatly in perfectly straight ranks, ready on command to stride forward.

On either flank rode cavalry mounted on the tough, shaggy ponies of Choin with long, thin lances held high, poised. Flags snapped in the light morning breeze, looking rather brave and gay.

Their opponent was by contrast a vast, dun-colored, milling crowd of men in plain, often ragged leather jerkins and filthy hose. The Peasant Army wasn't organized into discernible companies or troops. It stood about in groups of various sizes, shouted, laughed, and cursed at each other and at the enemy across the open ground.

They shook their gleaming, sharp axes on high and dared the enemy—or their own fellows—to make the first move. They showed no inclination to attack.

Yet, Douglas saw, their position was not entirely without logic or purpose. The ground north of the Fair Ground was roughly furrowed by a great number of intersecting, steep-sided ditches half-filled with slowly flowing muddy water, hidden below tall grasses and clumps of bamboo.

Heavily armed soldiers and, certainly, heavy and short-legged ponies, would be at a grave disadvantage, Douglas realized, if the Peasant Army could hold its ground and draw the enemy to them.

That was their main advantage—that and their great superiority in numbers.

"If they stick close together and take their lumps," observed Cerfew, glancing sideways at his passenger, "they have more a chance than I would have thought."

"Where is the man, Too Wang Sung?" wondered the Wizard. "Ah, there he is!"

"Yes, the tall, lanky man with the metal cap and the much-too-long sword," agreed the Gull. "He's found a mound to stand upon, to see and be seen. Brave sight!"

"Now . . ." Douglas started to say something, but movement below caught his eye. "The Finance center moves out!"

Mercenary foot soldiers heard their officer's shrill orders, walked slowly forward, slanting their pikes and spears at a slight angle, poised to thrust and jab or slash.

The Doonshong axmen stood their ground.

Sudden silence. Then renewed shouts from both sides.

As the professional soldiers came within a few yards of the Peasant line—it wasn't really a line, but an edge of the crowd—they slowed, expecting the inexperienced countrymen to break ranks and flee in panic.

Without orders, the Peasants in the forefront suddenly dashed at them, swinging their heavy, double-bitted axes over their heads and screaming like madmen.

The lines collided, producing sounds of axes on armor, of blades on flesh—terrible sounds—combined with screams of the first wounded on both sides.

Companies of mercenary archers rushed on foot to either side until they were within bowshot of the close-packed Peasant Army. Most of the ragged woodsmen never saw the bowmen until the first cloud of black arrows wacked into their ranks, some fired directly at them, some launched in high-arching trajectories to fall straight down from above.

Men cried out in surprise, pain, and fear. For a breath the Peasant front shivered and quaked.

Into that quiet came a shouted command even Douglas could hear. A crowd of Too supporters suddenly dashed from flanking ditches on either hand, where they had hidden, flinging themselves straight at the bowmen as they reached for a second flight of arrows.

The archers were preoccupied with the massed target before them. Before they could change their aim, the lightly armed farmers bowled into them, dashing their bows to the ground and slashing and stabbing at the fallen bowmen with skinning knives and hayforks.

Another loud, clear shout and a blast of trumpet call. The bowmen retreated in good order, defending their backs with their own light swords and knives, pursued by the flankers.

Still another cry over the din of battle caused the Peasant flankers to swerve suddenly to the right and left, converging from both sides on the Guards infantry in the middle of the line.

The Finance soldiers were, for just a moment, confused by the attack from the sides. Many turned to meet the new threat, easing their deadly pressure to the front.

The massed horde of axmen surged suddenly forward again, sensing the soldiery's uncertainty in the face of the flank attacks. Hand-to-hand fighting flowed back onto the level grass lawn of Fair Ground.

Here the Peasants were at a disadvantage, Douglas saw, for the soldiers managed to shift themselves into a solid wall defending both sides and the front. Just before a renewed archery attack came flying over the soldiers' heads, the attacking Peasants fell back to their original defensive positions between, among and in the deep ditches.

Rather than mounting a counterattack at once, the Mercenary troop beat a hasty but orderly retreat to the south edge of Fair Ground, to regroup and fill in the ragged gaps in their lines.

The suddenly empty field was littered with swords, spears, lances, axes, scythes, hayforks, spent arrows, discarded red-lacquered armor—and a hundred dead or dying bodies. As the sounds of the attack and counterattack died away, the screams of the wounded became terribly clear.

"Back to Flarman!" ordered Douglas, shaken by the sights below. "Hurry!"

He found the older Pyromancer studying the southern horizon with a pair of binoculars he had taken from his right sleeve. He lowered them when Cerfew landed beside him.

"There has been an attack, and the Peasants rolled it back. A draw at the moment," piped the temporarily tiny Douglas. "Why Finance's officers didn't order a cavalry attack, I can't imagine, unless it was fear of the uneven ground north of the Fair Ground. Both sides have drawn back. In a minute or two . . ."

"Listen," said Flarman sharply. "When the next attack comes, right at the climax of the effort, with both sides fully occupied, then . . ."

"I understand," said Douglas. "Where are Myrn and Litholt?"

"They went down with Wong and Augurian to help tend the wounded," explained Flarman, impatiently. "Do your own job, young Master Wizard! They can take care of themselves!"

Douglas sent the Gull into the air again. In two minutes they were circling low over the bloodied Fair Ground.

"What will they do next?" wondered Cerfew, caught up in the intense excitement of the battle.

"If I were Too, I'd order an all-out attack," decided the Wizard. "Casualties would be high, but at the moment the soldiers are shaken and surprised that they couldn't win it all in one frontal attack."

"You still want to keep an eye on that Too person?" asked another Gull flying close by.

"Yes! When the climax comes, I'll need to know exactly where he is."

The tableau seemed at rest for a moment.

Douglas searched for Myrn and the Lady Geomancer. At last he located Myrn on the edge of the Fair Ground, right where the worst of the fighting had taken place moments before. She was directing volunteers to carry the wounded away, far to the side, where they wouldn't be trampled in the next attack.

Litholt was not with her, but he saw her a moment later bending over a line of fallen men laid under a pergola at the edge of the formal garden. Wong, Marbleheart, and Augurian were nowhere to be seen.

"My boy," he heard Flarman's excited voice ring in his ear, although he knew him to be several miles away, "I'm all set here! Just need the right moment to move in and scare the leather shirts off these gents. It's up to you! Give me the word but allow a minute or two for us to get into position."

"Right!" Douglas cried aloud. Cerfew took it as a word of encouragement and spurted forward, heading back to the center of the field. Douglas snatched a glance to the south, but saw nothing unusual.

Except perhaps a coarse grey cloud shot with silver lightning, a great distance away.

Having failed to move the Peasant Army back with a direct attack, Manufacture argued, they should send the Mercenary cavalry around to both sides. The thunder of tough little war ponies had always struck fear into farmer's hearts, he insisted. They'd flee at once!

"Pony soldiers be damned!" yelled the Mercenary Captain. "We need something more fearsome than a few little horses prancing about! Order an advance of the entire line, I say! Cavalry to fight on foot once they get inside the defenders' front. I'll send my best company straight after Prince Too. He's still posturing about on that hillock, making a clear, fine target."

Manufacture shrugged, "Well, give the orders yourself. My men will follow yours. It's your responsibility if they fail!"

With such sudden, cowardly abdication of command, he turned his own pony and trotted back to where Finance and the other notables were watching the action and being served iced drinks.

The morning sun was quite warm and the air filled with acrid dust. Despite their close view of the first encounter—perhaps because of it—the Ministers had no idea of what had happened in the field right in front of them.

"We should keep riding straight on through the city and out the other side," suggested one of Manufacture's officers, shakily. "Let those boorish hirelings do the bloody work. He intends pure slaughter for both sides, I can see."

"No, not yet," snapped his commander. "We'll tell Finance that we are falling back to guard him, just in case the others aren't able to overrun Too's rabble this second time. That way, no blame to us if the Mercenaries fail."

"There they go!" shouted Douglas to Cerfew. "Hold steady now!"

"Steady as she goes, sir!" responded the Seabird.

The entire Bureaucrat line began to walk, to trot, then to run across the level Fair Ground. The Peasants fell silent, watching them come swiftly on.

The voice of Too could be heard urging his men to stand firm, meet the attack among the ditches. Douglas was surprised that so few of the axmen turned to flee. They were both brave and desperate!

The lines crashed together with a furious shout. Horses screamed in fear and pain. Men cried out in terror and in anger. Blade met blade and bright red blood stained the long grass.

"Now!" shouted Douglas in a far-carrying Wizard's voice. *"Now!"*

■   ■   ■

The sky, a moment before bright with sunlight, turned grey, and darker grey yet, then almost black. A deep bass vibration filled the air, and a swirling wind shook the trees and rippled through the grass.

Fighting men on both sides froze in the sudden twilight. They glanced up . . . and almost to a man threw down their weapons and fled or flung themselves to the ground, covering their heads with their arms, whimpering in abject terror.

The cloud that blocked the sun resolved into hundreds of individual bodies, great black-winged, red, gold, and green Dragons!

They came on in all sizes, from foot-long Fire-Drakes snorting shafts of red flame before them, to ten-ton, fifty-foot-long Great Goldens, singing their ancient battle song, charring the Fair Ground lawn, sending up roiling clouds of steam from the watery ditches.

Men who were present later often tried to tell what it was like, looked like, sounded like, smelled like. Few found the words, ever. For while the Dragons carefully avoided serious injury to men of both sides, panic spread faster than their flames.

The few warriors who, for whatever reason, held their ground found their weapons smoking and glowing red in their hands, until they threw them to the ground and howled in pain.

Tough lacquered-leather body armor began to fume and stink from Dragon's-breath fire. Soldiers stripped off their breastplates, greaves, and cherry red iron helmets in panic. When they tried to run, low-circling smaller Fire-Drakes herded them back toward the center of the field.

Among the Peasants, it was the same story. The dragons forced them to the ground. Some tried to hide in wet ditches but the water steamed and bubbled about them, forcing them to scramble out and throw themselves on the smoking ground, hands over their heads, calling for mercy, offering their bits of stolen treasures for escape.

The entire Battle of Fair Ground was over in less than four minutes.

Douglas flung himself from the Gull's back as Cerfew dropped to the ground in a heart-stopping dive. Before his feet hit the grassy verge of a canal, he suddenly shot back to full size.

Leaping over the narrowest part of a boiling ditch, he sprinted up the hillock to confront the tall, lanky Pretender. Too Wang Sung stood frozen in dumb shock.

"Too Wang Sung, order your followers to throw down their arms and lie flat on their faces," the Wizard cried in a tremendously amplified voice that carried over even the screams and clamor, the crack and the whirr of dragon's wings, the roar of fires. "Do it *now*! Or I can't guarantee your safety!"

"He's right!" said Myrn, coming up the other side of the mound. "Enough—too many—have already been hurt here. Only instant obedience will stay these terrible Dragons!"

The two magickers stood on either side of the shattered former petty gambler, looking like avenging Fairies on the torn and bloody field.

"But . . . but . . . ," stammered Too. "We *must* defeat the Imperial Bureaucrats or die trying! We must seat our own Emperor! Can't you see that?"

"No need," said Douglas, calmly. "The Bureaucrats are already beaten—and so are your wild woodcutters. The matter of the succession has been settled in the best interests of all—including you. Long live the Emperor Phong!"

"*Emperor* Phong!" screeched Too. "Who in World is he? *I* am a grandson of the old Emperor's Honored Fourteenth Son. The Dragon Throne is mine by right!"

"If you'd care to argue the point with a few angry Dragons," said Myrn, with a grim smile, "I think I can arrange it in no time at all!"

"When your men are headed back to their camp," added Douglas, "we'll escort you to Imperial House to offer your allegiance to the new Emperor. You'll find your enemies are there, too, for the same purpose."

The dazed Pretender gave the proper orders in a shaky voice. Most of his officers were already prostrate in the grass, cursing or weeping in frustration and fear, by turns. They rose and stumbled northward, back to the oleander hedges.

"Come along, Master Too!" the younger Fire Wizard said, more gently now. "Your army is to remain in camp until ordered home by the new Emperor. Food and medicines will be brought to them there. For the moment, you're all prisoners of the new Imperium, but good behavior may earn them parole."

"And as for me?" asked Too somberly.

"I don't know what Emperor Phong will decide about you, but as far as I'm concerned . . . in your shoes I'd probably have done the same thing. Perhaps not for the same motives—who knows? You did what you thought was right, and you might have succeeded in the end—if that's any consolation. I'd forget about being a great-grandson of the old Emperor, however. There're a dozen or more other Princes with closer ties and better claims, if it comes to that."

Heartened by assurances from the two young Wizards, Too Wang Sung walked between them passively across smoldering Fair Grounds. Above them the Horde of Dragons circled, watching and calling excitedly to each other, but no longer raining down fire and fear.

By the time they had walked their prisoner across Fair Ground and through the badly trampled formal garden to Imperial House, things had settled down to a low roar.

The lawns, gardens, and avenues about Imperial House were filled with Dragons of all sizes, shapes, and colors, mostly green, red and gold predominating. The beasts were in a jubilant mood.

"We don't all get together so very often," explained one, recognizing Douglas from the muster on Waterand before Battle of Sea against Frigeon.

He escorted them through the throng of scaled fliers admiring a life-size bronze statue of a quite fantastic Dragon at the palace's main entrance.

"You're the Pyromancer Douglas Brightglade, aren't you?" one of the medium-sized dragons asked politely.

"Yes, and this is Water Adept Myrn Manstar, my fiancée," replied Douglas.

"A great pleasure to meet you! My great-great-great-great-grand-uncle, the Grand Golden Dragon, said I should look you up."

"My old friend!" cried Myrn. "We spent many a happy afternoon talking and telling stories on Highest Point of Waterand Island, you know."

"He's told me," said the young Golden with a delighted laugh.

"Is your great-grand-uncle here in Choin?" asked Douglas.

"He insisted on coming, although Wizard Flarman told him not to stir from home if he didn't feel like it. Great-grand-uncle says reports of his advanced age are greatly exaggerated. He's within the palace right now, taking charge of everything, as usual."

They parted from the Dragon, promising to spend some time with him later—and extending an invitation to attend their wedding in December, which pleased him even more—and led their utterly amazed and thoroughly frightened prisoner into Imperial House.

Self-appointed ushers showed them to the Grand Audience Hall in the center of the huge palace complex. They were members of Foggery's Patriotic Society of Choin. If they'd grinned any more broadly, Myrn whispered to Douglas, they'd probably dislocate their jaws.

The scene inside the enormous, ornate Audience Hall was close to pandemonium. Around the wall of the circular room crouched a solid phalanx of fierce-looking Dragons, the biggest ever, glaring at the Choinese with fiercely glowing eyes.

Douglas, who knew the breed better than most, could see that their fierce looks were just part of an act. The Dragons were intensely excited—as witnessed by the occasional bright bursts of fire when they sighed, laughed, or coughed—and even a little awed by the majestic palace.

A densely packed crowd of jubilant Patriots, Guilders, and Grangers milled about, looking for vantage points from which to view the events about to begin before the solid jade Dragon Throne, set in the middle of the floor on a high platform.

To one side, watched intently by the Dragons, were the ministers of Finance, Commerce, Transportation, Roads, and so on and so on, pulled from their rooftop perch and looking sick with apprehension.

Their faces were smudged with smoke and tears, and their clothes, once splendidly elaborate, embroidered, and bejeweled, were dirtied and rumbled. They had been rounded up by a platoon of medium-size dragons led by Wong, assisted by Bryarmote, waving his gleaming Elvensword and giving orders in a loud, rough voice.

A smaller group was held on the other side of the room. These were dressed only in the underclothing warriors wore beneath full body armor. Their rumpled doublets and jerkins of wool and linen were marked with black scorches and burns. They were completely disarmed, looking rather fearful but still rather pathetically defiant.

Wong Tscha San stood as an island of calm on the second step of the Dragon Throne, his hands folded in his wide sleeves, waiting for some sort of order to be established by the shouting ushers and marshals.

Augurian, Litholt, Marbleheart, Bryarmote, and Flarman stood together just to his right on the lowest step, chatting amiably with Foggery and the leaders of his coalition.

"Here's the man Too," said Flarman in a cheery, loud voice. "We can begin, if it pleases Your Imperial Majesty!"

He turned, as did everyone else, to face the throne of green jade and the new Emperor of Choin seated upon it.

He was a youngish man, taller than usual for his race. He had a pleasant, kindly face, honestly open, broad, and round. He was dressed in the sober robes of a physician, unadorned except for Wong's ivory-and-peacock-feather fan, which he waved self-consciously as he waited for silence to fall.

"What do you suggest we do first, revered Wong Tscha San?" the new Emperor of Choin asked in a carrying but pleasantly modulated voice. "May we have silence, please, so that all may hear?"

"And obey," added the elderly Magician. "I think I shall begin by introducing everyone to Your Majesty. I know things have happened very quickly, and you are probably confused by so many new faces and names."

"Please!" said the Emperor. He sat back gingerly into the throne's cushions, ready to listen.

The Magician began with the Wizards' party, not excluding himself, saying who each was and how each had helped in the crisis following the death of the late Emperor.

"I—or should I say 'we'—will shortly attempt to express my gratitude for your powerful and timely assistance," said Phong, smiling at them broadly.

"Not at all necessary, Majesty," said Flarman with a low, sweeping bow. "It was both our pleasure and our duty."

"Nevertheless . . . ," replied the Emperor. He nodded to Wong to continue.

The Magician of Choin introduced by name and title, with no further comment, the Ministers, Clerks, Officials, and other Functionaries of the imperial court and government.

There were thirty in all. All but a handful, Douglas knew, had had greedy hands in the civil unrest of the past months. Some had bloody hands as well.

Wong introduced the Mercenary Captain and his officers. Phong nodded to them calmly. They returned his nod with respectful bows.

"You need no longer tarry here," said the Emperor to their Captain. "Recross our borders, sir, and never return. Choin is henceforth closed to you."

The Captain bowed even more deeply, muttered his gratitude in formal words, and the Mercenary officers left quickly, looking neither left nor right. The former Ministers carefully averted their eyes as well.

Foggery introduced the elected leaders of the various organizations that had contributed to the swift end to the civil war, and who had, meeting peacefully together, selected the new ruler in the name of the people of Choin.

All of this, stripped of almost all ceremony other than common courtesy, took well over two hours, with everyone standing except the Emperor on the Dragon Throne and the silently watching dragons.

"Wizard Flarman Flowerstalk," said Wong, "please introduce our fiery friends from the south of Serecomba."

The Grand Golden Dragon himself stood forth, bowed haughtily to the Emperor, and said in a booming voice, "Majesty, Magician Wong, Flarman Dragonfriend, Water Adept Augurian, Master Douglas, and Mistress Myrn, my good friends and war companions! I move we dispense with the naming of Dragons. A Dragon's name is his own private business, and he will tell it in his own time, to whomever he chooses."

"Of course, if that is what is suitable," agreed Emperor Phong. "I do not wish you Dragons to think we are ungracious or unmannered!"

"We were called to assist our friends in a matter to which, to be frank with you, Lord Emperor, we would have paid no attention whatsoever, if they hadn't asked. I mean no disrespect, Majesty! The doings and misdeeds of Men, Elves, and Fairies are generally of no concern to us. If anyone is to be thanked for our participation, it is the Wizard Flarman Flowerstalk and the Lady Geomancer Litholt Stonebreaker."

"Nevertheless," said the Emperor, leaning forward earnestly, "I offer my heartfelt gratitude, not for my humble self, but for the sake of my whole people."

"The people of Choin have been always most courteous to us," said the Great Golden Dragon with a smile—a rather fearsome sight for those unused to Dragon smiles. "And I must admit to you, Majesty, that we are not as indifferent to Choin's fate as I led you to believe. Our ancestor, the Highly Honored Primary and Primordial Dragon, was a close friend and mentor of your Founding Emperor, Chan Lee Fwong, known as the Sensible. Which is why he called his jade chair there the Dragon Throne."

"I had suspected it!" exclaimed the Emperor with great interest. "Records of those early days were long ago muddled and lost, dear sir! Could you perhaps, someday, send us someone of your clan to tell us what actually happened at our beginnings?"

"Be delighted, once you've settled the fates of these wicked culprits, here assembled under guard," rumbled Grand Golden, a bit pompously, glaring ferociously at the quaking Ministers. "We'll have a long, long talk about it, the first pleasant afternoon available, I promise you, Honored Emperor of Choin."

The Emperor rose and walked down the five steps of the Dragon Throne, surveying the assembled throng, culprits and heroes together.

"It is well past the middle hour, dear friends. If someone will direct us to the dining hall, I hope we will find enough to feed everyone adequately."

As if on cue, a gorgeously attired imperial servitor appeared to announce that luncheon was served. There was a general movement through the side doors in his wake.

Phong grinned delightedly at the Magician and the Wizards and their companions.

"I was scared out of my wits, I can tell you!" he confessed.

"The hardest part is over, I think," Flarman Flowerstalk chuckled. "We'll consult with you further, if you wish, on what's to be done with the offending Ministers and Princes."

"Let's find a quiet place to eat our own meal. I never had breakfast," said the Emperor.

"Come to think of it," cried Marbleheart in surprise, "neither did I!"

Emperor Phong listened gravely to their advice and ideas over lunch, but the decisions he announced were his own—and showed him to be a clear-minded, compassionate, yet realistic man.

"He'll do," said Wong later, with a deep sigh of satisfaction. "I suppose it is too much to expect that everything will go smoothly, however."

"I guarantee it won't," said Douglas. "Which is why there are Wizards."

"That's why one so often finds a Wizard where there is trouble," said his pretty fiancée. "So a sailor friend of mine once told me."

"Old Caspar Marlin!" Flarman laughed aloud. "Majesty, if it hadn't been for Caspar and his loyalty to Foggery, his retired Seacaptain, we might not have been around to help put down the Bureaucrats' plots."

"I think I'll have to raise some monuments," said Phong. "One to the Dragons, or at least the Primary Dragon, we already have. It should be covered with purest gold! One to Seamen like Captain Foggery and this Marlin, of whom I've never heard until now, would be appropriate, I believe. I have so much to learn!"

"As long as you're willing to learn, you'll do just fine," said Augurian.

The Mercenaries were returned what was left of their armor and arms and marched to Choin Harbor, where they took ship for their homeland, away to the west. They were allowed to keep the fees advanced to them by Finance Minister from his own treasury. No one came forth to accuse the hired soldiers of rapine or pillage. They had behaved quite professionally, all agreed, whether you favored their employer or not.

The Peasant Army from Doonchong, stripped of their loot but allowed to keep their weapons (as they were necessary tools of trade) was disbanded immediately and sent home with a generous present each from the imperial treasury—which surprisingly contained far more money than anyone ever thought, thanks to the careful collection of taxes, imposts, duties, and fees by the Minister of the Revenue. Although Revenue had given cautious lip service to his more powerful colleague Finance, he was an honest accountant. Phong decided to keep him in his post.

"Honest and capable accountants are very hard to find," he explained.

The woodsmen and paper-mill workers were promised the new Imperium would shortly lift the illegal ban on logging and papermaking. Phong announced an end to all imperial censorship of printing and publishing. The paper mills would soon be back at work, giving full employment to the mill workers in their mills and woodsmen in their forests. They in turn would patronize the farmers and merchants of the Doonchong, once they were earning their keep in the forests.

Too was truly shattered by the horrors of the Battle of Fair Ground. The Emperor was inclined to be lenient. They had a long, private talk.

"Yes, I admit that I formed and led the Peasant Army as much for my own purse and glory as for any cause," Too confessed. "I have been a gambler since my earliest youth. I saw my chance and I grasped it, eagerly and knowingly. I am now ready to take my losses like a professional."

"I don't see that your reasons were so shameful," decided the Emperor. "I allowed myself to be persuaded to take this Dragon Throne as much for my own glory and enrichment as for what I could do for my country. Well, *almost* as much. To gain great rewards, Too, we have to take great risks."

He decreed that Too could return to Doonchong and work to improve that poorest of provinces. He would be granted certain imperial mandates. One was to establish a good, honest, professional police force. Doonchong had for too long had the reputation of a rough, tough, lawless place, Phong said severely.

Master Too eagerly agreed. His good repute with the Peasant Army veterans would be his biggest asset, Douglas decided. But he advised the Emperor to keep an eye on the man just the same.

The ministers quaked in their tattered slippers when Phong started to examine their roles in the civil war.

"This will take some time," he said to them. "Meanwhile, the Dragons, specifically the Fire-Drakes, have agreed to act as your close keepers. You will be taken to a distant spot in the very center of the Serecomba and held there while we examine your actions most carefully."

The Ministers wailed, begged, and wept, but Phong was firm.

"You may not take servants or luxuries of any kind," he ruled. "You will be safely housed and adequately fed. Your families may visit you once each month for a day and a night, if you behave well for the Dragons. Some of you may be cleared of the greater crimes. Those will be restored to their lands and honest titles.

"Others of you may look forward to a number of months, perhaps years, of healthy but lonely desert life. He who complains the loudest will be longest held, I suspect. Meanwhile, your departments will be reorganized, modernized, and assigned dependable new Ministers chosen on the basis of competitive examinations—with the advice and approval of the Combined Council. There is some talk of establishing an elected parliament, but that is a way off, yet. In the meantime, the Combined Council will serve without pay in its place."

Complaining and wailing ceased as though someone had closed a valve, and the Fire-Drakes herded the thirty mournful miscreants off to where the largest Golden Dragons waited to carry them off into the bleak, broiling hot, almost endless Serecomba.

"Rather harsh, wasn't it?" asked Myrn. "Not all of them did great wrong, surely?"

"Ah, but you miss the point, my dear," explained the Emperor. "While not all of them *caused* the crisis, not a one of them did a single thing to *prevent* it. That in itself is abdication of responsibility."

"I'm inclined to agree with Your Majesty," said Augurian. "Sins of omission are as serious as sins of commission."

"Or, to put it in terms of my own profession," the Emperor added, "a physician who refuses to treat a patient when he has the skill to do so is as culpable as one who knowingly mistreats him. The patient dies just as surely."

They had a picnic lunch on the broad lawn before Imperial House, on a gentle hill, where passersby on the broad, paved avenue that circled the palace could see their Emperor entertaining his friends.

A politely nodding and bowing crowd of minor civil servants and merchant's clerks on their lunch hours gathered on the far side of the dry moat. Almost as soon as they began to gather, pushcart vendors with savory fried rice balls, egg rolls, and mounds of crisply fried noodles appeared and did a lively business.

"You really should try their egg rolls," suggested Emperor Phong, pouring tea. "I adore them myself! Better than even in the best restaurants, I swear."

"I would love to spend a much longer time in your beautiful country," said Myrn. "However, I have a few other things that must come first."

"Ah, yes, your approaching wedding!" The Emperor smiled brightly. "I would not ever presume to suggest you delay that."

"A lot of events have tried to delay it already," said Flarman, chewing lustily on a rib of spicy barbecued pork. "Luckily, nothing can stand before a woman's determination to be married, it seems."

"There is also the matter of Journeying in your Craft," cautioned the Aquamancer, waving his finger. "You are still but an Apprentice, Myrn Manstar."

"I'm well aware of it, Magister," said she with a loving smile for the Water Wizard. "It's not at all forgotten."

"Time for that after the Winter Solstice," he relented. "We Wizards have a great deal to do yet to untangle Frigeon's evil enchantments. With Witches' Covens and enchanted Stonemen and Choinese rebellions, we've neglected the poor ice-enthralled, I fear."

After they'd eaten and were seated in a semicircle on the lawn before the Emperor, Phong signaled for their attention.

"You are eager to return to your homes, I know. I said before that I could never adequately thank you each for your help in a dire and dangerous hour. There is still much to do here, of course, but to continue that work I will have the inestimable assistance and wise council of Wong Tscha San, my very own Imperial Magician."

The picnickers applauded and the modest Magician blushed crimson and bowed to them all several times.

"Master Wong has agreed to act as my chief adviser and mentor," continued the Emperor. "I am most grateful for that! I couldn't do it as well or as quickly, if at all, without him and other trusted advisers like Captain Foggery."

"Speech! Speech!" called Marbleheart. He reached for the last piece of banana cream pie.

Wong stood, tiny and delicate as a child yet somehow strong and forceful, in the brilliant, warm subtropical sunlight. A vagrant breeze from distant Sea stirred his silken robe and ruffled his thin white beard.

"My friend and Emperor will be laboring for some time to bring this huge land back to calm, justice, and good government. There are bandits in the forests, pirates on the coast, thieves in the cities, wicked magickers under our loveliest hills. I will advise him and his people, and so will my very good friend and fellow subject, the Geomancer Litholt. I hope that, if you will find time in your busy lives, you'll come back, singly or together, to lend your own skills and wit. Or to just sit and enjoy jasmine tea under the fragrant peach trees in my garden."

"Ever and for ever!" called Flarman. He was lying flat on his back, cradling his head on the Otter's soft flank. "You can depend on us, Magician and Majesty!"

They all added their agreement.

"Now, Imperial Master," said Wong, "will you be upset if I ask your leave to absent myself for a short while, a few weeks hence? I have a wedding to attend."

Everybody, especially Myrn and Douglas, shouted with delight. The Emperor beamed, saying he gave his leave, but only if he could come to the wedding, also.

"You *are* invited, Majesty!" cried Myrn. "You'll find we heartily enjoy ourselves at such celebrations at Wizards' High in Valley."

"Come and welcome!" chimed in Flarman, rolling over on his stomach.

Across the moats an old man in ragged trousers peddled sweetmeats from a wheeled cart, smiling broadly at his customers, most of them children.

"Hear that, boys and girls?" he chuckled. "An Empire that has an Emperor who can laugh with friends on the grass has a *very special* ruler, I can tell you!"

All around him the children, grown-ups, and even poor old women and men peddling dried fish and green spun-sugar floss joined in the laughter.

"Oh! Look!" cried a pretty ten-year-old girl dressed in yellow. "They're gone! All expect for the Magician and the Emperor."

And so they were.

Chapter Twenty

Home to the High

"YOU *what!*" screeched Bronze Owl. "You invited *who?*"

"Not the whole Dragon clan! Just the Grand Golden Dragon and his great-great-great-great-grandnephew—a most decent sort," said Marbleheart, shrinking from Owl's sudden wrath.

"Grandy will bring *at least* twenty others, I promise," howled Owl, spinning his head three times completely around. "Where will we put them? Where, where, where? They'll blanket the whole Valley! They'll eat everything in sight! Do you have any idea how much a single Dragon eats in a day!"

"Easy! Easy, old bird!" soothed the Sea Otter. "We can handle it. Put 'em up in Parch. They'll like it there better than anywhere else, I believe. Dragons prefer barren, desolate places, I hear from Black Flame."

"I suppose you're right," the harassed bronze bird agreed reluctantly. He was perched at Flarman's study table, surrounded by bales and stacks of paper covered with Plume Pen's precise calligraphy, lists and checklists, memoranda, notes, and diagrams.

Marbleheart, deciding the matter of the Dragons was settled, scooted off to look for his friend Black Flame. It was time for his daily Familiarity lesson.

He was replaced at the door to the study a minute later by

the new Master Wizard, bearing a double armload of envelopes just brought from Trunkety by Postmaster Possumtail and three postal ponies.

"Owl, let me help you with these. I'm not at all busy at the moment."

Bronze Owl accepted his offer gratefully and set the young man to opening and sorting the day's mail into three piles: "regrets," "acceptances," and "special handling."

"Here's 'regrets' from Pargeot," Douglas said. "He'd like to come but the Town Council of Pfantas voted to send Featherstone as its official representative. Pargeot says he doesn't wish to steal the new Mayor's thunder."

"Huh!" Owl snorted. "He's still a bit smitten with your bride, I'll wager."

"I don't think good old Pargeot is that small-minded," Douglas disagreed. "We know that Featherstone will be coming, anyway. As Mayor of Pfantas, I suppose you'll put him up here at the High?"

"No chance of that!" snorted the bird. "The cottage will be crammed, packed full of really important people like your mother and your father and the Manstars of Flowring. And the Emperor of Choin, too. We can't very well put an Emperor up in a Valley farmhouse, can we?"

"Actually, I don't think he'd mind that at all. He's not that highfalutin, I assure you."

"Still, some protocol *must* be observed. Hmmmm! Bryarmote wants to use the secret room over his fireplace. That's agreeable. Few people know how to get behind the fire wall, anyway."

"I'd worry more about the Fairies," said Flarman Flowerstalk, popping his head through the door while passing by. "Aedh and Marget Brightwing are at least equal in rank to Emperor Phong. And they're bringing the infant Justin Flowerbender with them. The little Prince of Faerie must need a corps of nursemaids and launderers, I suppose."

"I've already taken care of them," Owl assured him. "Aedh has arranged to open a Fairy Gate for just this purpose, over near the First Ridge."

"They'll make a splendid sight riding down from the hills for the wedding," exclaimed Douglas. "Can't we put Featherstone up with Frenstil? They should be about equal in rank, I'd say."

"Perfect solution!" cried the Owl, directing Plume Pen to make the entry. "I was wondering with whom to saddle the former Master of Horse, anyway."

The older Wizard laughed loudly and nodded with satisfaction as he went his busy way.

"Any surprises in this batch that you can see?" asked Owl.

Douglas skimmed rapidly through the 153 "acceptances," quickly evaluating the contents of each. "Oh, dear! Who the dickens is Pride, do you remember?"

"Pride? Pride? Let me check my list," muttered Owl. "Ah ha! He's Caspar's First Mate aboard *Donation*. Will he come? I'll put him up with the delegation Thornwood will bring from Capital."

" 'Wouldn't miss it for World,' he says," Douglas quoted.

It took them better than an hour to catalog, enter, categorize, and settle the accommodations of the day's responses.

"You go on, now," said the bronze bird at last. "The rest are merely clerical and I can do them tonight while you flesh-and-blood types are asleep. Thank you for the help, Master Wizard."

Douglas waved his hand as he disappeared through the door. In a moment the Owl heard him clattering down the winding stair.

Just like old times, when the young Wizard was a mere Apprentice; small for his age and a bit gawky, at that, Owl thought. *Eager to learn and interested in everything.*

Turning back to the dwindling stack of "special handling" correspondence, Owl swooped to pluck from the floor a much-worn, brown, stained and dusty canvas packet, where it had fallen unnoticed.

"How now?" he muttered. "This one's come a long way,

I think. No superscription. Addressed to Master Pyromancer Flarman Flowerstalk. Ha! Doesn't anyone know how to address a formal invitation anymore?"

He slit the heavy green wax seal with a sharp bronze talon, opened the heavy canvas outer wrapper, took out the enclosed letter, and began to read.

"Hoy! This is something *entirely* different! Must show it to Flarman at once!"

Grasping the folded parchment tightly in his claws, he launched himself from the table, straight through the study door, and headlong down the stair.

Flarman Flowerstalk was contentedly boiling a frothy magenta liquid in a fat glass flask over a hot blue-white flame. He hummed under his breath the while, watching the rising steam make arabesques in the Workshop's cool, still air.

Black Flame and Marbleheart sat facing each other in the dimness at the back of the vast Workshop. The tom was expounding on ways to keep a Wizard under close watch, an art at which he excelled. The two conversed almost silently, with the lift of a paw or the wag of a tail, a tilt of the head and a slow wink—ways cats have spoken since the first cat first sat on a sunlit stoop.

Bronze Owl shot from the kitchen door opposite, narrowly missing the well housing, and crashed to an untidy, rattling landing on the tabletop near Flarman's experiment. The pink steam patterns fluttered and dispersed at once.

"That took me all morning to accomplish, clumsy bird!" cried the Wizard. "Well, too late to do anything about it now. What's to do?"

"Read this, Magister!" the metal bird said, sounding short of breath—which was not possible, since he didn't breathe at all. "Read and tell me I did wrong!"

Flarman wiped his hands on his stained work smock and picked up his reading glasses as the Owl handed him the battered missive.

"Just came with the rest of the mail," explained Owl

to Black Flame and the Otter. "We almost overlooked it among the wedding responses."

Flarman scanned the letter through quickly, studied the signature, and sat abruptly on his stool to read it again, more carefully.

"I feared this," he groaned. "Well, there's not much we can do at the moment. After the wedding trip . . . it may be something that Myrn could handle on her Journey. I'll speak to Augurian about it when he returns from Waterand tomorrow. Damme! I was hoping for a few quiet weeks—at least until spring."

"What is it, Magister?" inquired Marbleheart.

"Nothing that need concern us just now," replied Flarman, folding the letter and slipping it into his left sleeve. "It would just upset a lot of people and might spoil the party."

"Yes, but is it something that should be put off, I wonder?" asked Owl.

The Pyromancer scratched his bald pate, looked pensively into the distance for a moment, then shook his head, a decision made.

"No, we won't mention it, fellows, until Douglas and Myrn are off on their wedding trip. Less than a week off, now! We've had distractions and delays enough, haven't we?"

"If you say so, Magister," said the Otter.

"If it isn't six things, it's a half a dozen others," muttered the Wizard, clearing away the ruins of his experiment.

Marbleheart looked at Black Flame with grave concern, then the two of them left the Workshop to walk down to the Brook through freshly fallen December snow conjured especially by a certain Apprentice Aquamancer for her Wedding. They quietly discussed this new development until there was nothing left to say about it.

Bronze Owl went back to his letters and lists, shaking his head in doubt.

Flarman summoned Deka the Wraith to carry a message to Waterand Island.

■   ■   ■

Everywhere at Wizards' High the excitement of antici-
pation was like the aroma of a fresh-baked apple pie,
cinnamony and sugary, sweet, tart and tantalizing.

Valley wives baked, roasted, broiled, simmered and preserved, cleaned and recleaned. Farmers selected their best
fruits and vegetables and grains and sent it off to Trunkety,
where a big, new post-and-beam warehouse was storing the
foodstuffs needed for the wedding.

Children in his class almost drove usually placid Frackett
frantic with their questions and plans. In self-defense he
took them out into the Common and set them to sculpting
snow statues—of Flarman and of Douglas and Myrn, of
Augurian, and even Marbleheart, a great favorite already
with the young of Valley who didn't consider the Sea Otter
a clown at all.

Down Crooked Brook, near a tiny waterfall not yet frozen, a deliriously happy Blue Jay nestling swooped and
looped, climbed and dived, laughing and shouting to his
amused nest mates.

His drab little Jay mother swept a happy tear from her eye
and his cocky father bobbed proudly at the neighbors before
he set off to gather some pine nuts as a special present for
Mistress Brightglade-to-be.

Blue Teakettle snapped her lid sharply at a silver-
polishing Cloth that had paused too long to chat with a
Dust Rag just returned from shaking itself at the courtyard gate.

"Get back on them trays," Blue Teakettle rumbled. "Here!
You missed a spot on Butter Dish, too, right where Masters'
guests will see it, you can be sure. Where's Master Douglas's
hot cocoa? He's in the library, being fitted for his wedding
suit. Go take him and Master Tailor a platter of our best
sugar-and-oatmeal cookies, Tea Tray—the ones old Oven
let get a mite too brown. Taste just as good, but not as
pretty, I say!"

The Thatchmouse family was at work in a cool cellar,

sampling and passing on the quality of a dozen or so big wheels of robust yellow Valley cheese sent to the High from the Valley Dairy Cooperative.

"I'm beginning to get tired of cheese," sighed Mama Thatchmouse, shaking her head rapidly, as if to rid her mouth of the taste of sharp yellow Valley, a semi-soft slicing cheese, perfect for eating with soda crackers and tomato soup.

"How can you say that!" cried her youngest child, buried up to his backside in a round of pale ivory-colored church—the holey cheese just arrived by ox cart from Douglas's mother, Gloriana of Brightglade. "This is pure heaven!"

"It won't be if you make yourself sick before the Wedding," his older sisters teased. "Take a break, little Woosney! Leave some of that church cheese for the Wedding guests!"

Mama Thatchmouse shooed them all off to their beds in the thatching over Douglas's bedroom, newly enlarged and decorated with bright chintz curtains and billowy new pillow shams on the bed.

Mama excused herself and went off to the wine cellar to retrieve her husband. If he didn't leave off sampling the fifteen great casks of Oak 'n' Bucket winter amber, she said to herself, he'd be too ale-silly to climb to their own bed that evening.

Besides, it sets a bad example for the children.

At Lilac and Priceless's cozy overbrook farmhouse, a group of Valley-farm and Trunketytown wives and their daughters sipped sweet cider and nibbled coconut wafers. They circled around, watching and offering advice as Lilac basted the final hem of Myrn's flowing white, pearl-strewn Wedding gown.

Myrn stood on a footstool, straight but relaxed, ignoring the bustle about her. She was silently reciting a mnemonic poem that hid clues to tracking still waters running deep, a difficult and demanding Aquamantic skill. She was sure it would be part of her Master's Examination, when it came.

Lilac, her mouth stuffed with straight pins and her hands so busy they seemed to blur, pinned and measured, stood back to look, and pinned and measured some more, ignoring the well-meaning chatter, also.

"The most beautiful Wedding gown ever seen in Valley!" said an elderly granny, sniffing back a sentimental tear.

"In all Dukedom!" said Marletta, daughter of Dicksey, the General Store proprietor. "I've been to Capital twice, and I never saw the likes of this gown even at Thornwood Duke's court, b'lieve me!"

Marletta enjoyed bragging about her distant travels. Her father had taken her once as far as Wayness, far to the south, right on Sea. Most of the ladies had never gone farther than Farango Waters or up to the broad, grassy north slopes when the flocks were summered.

"My Joel," said another housewife, "brought me a colored picture of the Duchess, Thornwood Duke's mum. She had on a flame red velvet gown that reached from chin tip to toes! Gold piping and diamond embroidery, it had!"

The ladies exclaimed, as they always did when the Duchess's red velvet gown was mentioned . . . about thrice a week, these days.

"Speaking of embroidery," said Lilac, straightening up with some difficulty and carefully spitting the remaining pins into a glass dish so she could safely speak, "where is that border lace you were working up, Milida?"

Milida ran to fetch the thirteen yards of most finely tatted lace she had made for the gown. After everyone had exclaimed at its delicacy and frothy whiteness, Lilac held it up to the hem and bodice of Myrn's gown and expertly tacked it into position with neat rows of pins.

Myrn, aroused from her spell study, bent to glance down and exclaimed, "Oh, how exquisite! Oh, Milida! You do the most splendid tatting!"

The tatter was so overwhelmed with gratification at the Lady Apprentice's praise she had to go out onto the back porch to regain her composure. She found orchardman Priceless and Squire Frenstil standing together in the biting eventime chill, smoking their pipes.

"Lilac says she don't want the gown smelling like Hayseed's Best Latakea," Priceless chuckled. "Mistress Myrn never complained on it before, that I recall."

"No accounting for ladies fussing for a Wedding," observed the Squire. He was as close to Quality as Valley boasted, having long ago been a Master of Horse in the ducal household. "Well, must be off before it gets total dark, friends. Have you carried that aged cider up for the wedding, yet?"

"No, tomorrow I'll get Possumtail and his boys to help me haul it over the Brook," decided the orchardman. "Best year for apples and pears, too, since long before Flarman ever came to Valley."

"For beef and lambs and porkers, too, thank goodness," said Frenstil, preparing to mount his favorite chestnut mare. "We'd have trouble feeding this wedding crowd if it'd been a worse year. Might have some shortfalls, at any rate, as 'tis."

Priceless waved him off onto the Trunkety Road and excused himself to Milida to go open the byre doors for his small dairy herd, already standing patiently in the barnyard waiting to be relieved of their milk and bedded down with sweet hay from the loft.

Myrn joined the ladies in oohing and aahing a few more minutes before she pulled on her doubly furred coat and snow boots for the walk back to the High.

"If you'll come by in the morning, not tomorrow, but the next," said Lilac, kissing the Apprentice's rosy cheek and giving her a grandmotherly squeeze, "we'll make final adjustments in peace and I can look to your special night things, as you asked me to do."

"Friday morning, then," agreed Myrn. "Dear, wonderful Lilac! What would I do without you! My mother sews a fine sail, but she never learned to make such dresses as you make, so easily and beautifully."

"Oh, lots of the ladies could have done as well, I vow. I was just the logical choice, as we lives so close by," Lilac demurred—but she blushed with great pleasure.

"I'd have come to you for my gown, if you had lived in Stony Gorge in midwinter!" the Flowring lass declared with a bright laugh.

"Well, here it *is* midwinter," said the orchardman's elderly wife. She hugged herself, feeling the bite of the cold. She'd heard the tale of Myrn's captivity by the Stone Warriors, and shuddered at the thought. "Imagine how cold it is up there right now!"

"Makes me feel quite toasty to be here," exclaimed the bride. "I'll never complain of winter in Valley."

They stepped off the porch and met Priceless returning from the byre, whistling cheerfully and swinging two ten-gallon pails filled to the brim with steaming, creamy fresh milk on a yoke across his shoulders.

"How is your supply of cream up there, missy?" he asked Myrn. "We've got more than we'll ever use on our peach cobblers if Blue Teakettle needs more."

"I'll inquire, sir," said the Apprentice.

She gave him a quick peck on his whiskery cheek, smelling the air about him of winter orchard, cows, cider press, hayloft, milk shed, and Hayseed's Best Latakea, a comfortably homey odor for all its diversity.

She skipped up the path from the gate to find Douglas sitting on the front stoop in his shirtsleeves and open vest, sipping cocoa and talking to Bronze Owl.

"You'll frost your fingers out here," Myrn chided playfully, plopping down beside him. "Do you realize that my Wedding gown has fifty-two tiny pearl buttons down the back? One for each week of a year, Lilac says. You'll undo each one, one night very soon! Keep your fingers warm and supple, please! Share the Hot Spell, darling Wizardling!"

Douglas blushed bright crimson, and in a moment she was warm as toast, partly from his spell, and partly from the arm he put about her.

The three sat in contented silence for the while, the young people puffing clouds of pale breath-steam but not attempting anything as demanding as blown rings.

The Stones had been delivered from a wicked and ancient enchantment. A new Wizard had joined—and an old Wizard rejoined—the Fellowship of Wizards. Marbleheart Sea Otter proved a useful, talented, and companionable Familiar—and a good friend to them all.

Party was roundly pregnant again, and pleased as punch about her condition—as happy as Black Flame was proud and Pert was envious.

Despite the mysterious letter, everything was as perfect as it could possibly be, Owl thought. And a new adventure on the horizon wasn't the worst that could happen to them.

That's what Wizardry is all about, after all, he said, but the bride and groom didn't hear his words of wisdom for he said them to himself.